Pieces of a Murder

Pieces of a Murder

COUPLES & CRIME BOOK TWO

LYV LAMERE

Tuxtails Publishing, LLC

www.tuxtailspublishing.com

First Tuxtails Publishing Print Edition October 2024

ISBN: 978-1-957211-34-3

eBook ISBN: 978-1-957211-35-0

Cover design by Lvy Lamere and Tuxtails Publishing, LLC

Learn more about the author at www.lyvlamere.com.

*To all those we have lost. You might be gone, but
you're never forgotten.
And to those left behind. You never have to be alone.*

How the hell had it come to this? This was not supposed to happen.

Everything had been going well for weeks now. But no, somebody had to be nosy.

"I'm sorry. Really am. But it's your own damn fault. I didn't want to do this. And really, you should be glad it's me," the hunched-over figure mumbled to the large, unmoving mass – so much easier to not see it as a person – on the floor, then reached for the large blade nearby.

Don't puke. Do not puke. They can probably get your DNA from that or something. You didn't come here and set all this up just to present yourself on a silver plate for them. On the other hand... Better the cops than... While cutting off an arm, a shudder ran through the dark shape.

It was true, coming here, cutting up the poor bastard lying on the cold concrete was bad enough. But coming *here* to do it was a risk. One that would hopefully pay off and prevent the cops from making any connection.

Enough. Stop making yourself crazy. You're wearing coveralls, you have put all these damn covers everywhere; you're good.

It's gonna be fine. Just do as you're supposed to. You have a plan, stick to it. Then it's done, and after that everything is going back to normal... Yeah, sure. Keep dreaming.

The cutting continued. Then the pieces were put into bags, all the bloody garbage collected, and the blade was cleaned. That should do it. Part one of the plan had worked better than expected.

Let's hope the next part will go like this, too.

Chapter One

October in New York could be gorgeous, and the view from a high-rise office building breathtaking. Julia Stone knew she was lucky to be working as a Social Media/PR consultant for a global agency. The job came with a lot of perks, one of them being an office with a view some people would kill for. But if you had to tell your clients for the twentieth time in one day how to make their pumpkin-spice-latté post the ultimate one to stand out from the crowd, you could forget the beautiful foliage in Central Park, or that you were looking forward to Halloween in a couple of weeks. Sighing, Julia ran a hand through her mass of long, blonde curls. Her blouse strained over her breasts and restricted her movement. *Great, it's either wearing a sack, or hardly being able to move. Whoever invented the pattern for most blouses clearly didn't have boobs,* she cursed internally. She gave up and finished the email she was writing, then glanced at her ringing phone.

The caller-ID put an instant smile on her face. "Hey, girl," she answered the call and saw her friend Scarlette fill the screen. Her friend's long, dark-auburn hair was caught in the sunlight and seemed to burn. July thought it reminded her of the desktop background she had seen on Scarlette's husband's laptop: a picture he had taken a little more than a year ago when he had first met Scarlette and the two of them had fallen head over heels in love. Mentally, Julia shook her head. It was a story which could only happen to her friend: meeting a guy in a bar and enjoying a one-night stand with him, just to run into him again the next day and find out both their families had been blackmailed for generations. In the end, Scarlette and Tyler had not only solved the mystery, but Scarlette Langella had become Scarlette O'Brien, Tyler's wife.

"Hi, sweetie. You almost finished with work?" Scarlette asked with hopeful eyes.

"Ah, yes. Two more client questions, but they can wait until tomorrow. Where are you?"

"Outside your office, hoping for that answer. Come down here, we still need to do our costume shopping. Halloween this year needs to be properly celebrated again."

July kept the phone in one hand, with the other she shut down her PC, collected her things, and started out of the office. "Honey, if I remember correctly you had a wedding party around that time last year. I think that trumps Halloween."

"Like Ty and I ever needed the post-wedding wedding party. But yes, I know. And it wouldn't have felt right to celebrate Halloween last year, either, with his and Josh's parents and my biological mother dead and the case and the whole story behind it getting all that press."

"True. Don't worry, knowing your family, we'll make up for it this year."

"We will. Ty and Josh have no idea what they're getting into. It's gonna be epic."

"As always."

Julia was in the lobby by now and finished the call when she stepped out onto the sidewalk. She spotted Scarlette a few feet away and the women hugged each other tightly.

"Hey."

"Hi. How was work?"

"The usual seasonal madness. I had to tell a lawyer today that she would do better deleting the profile picture in which she had painted her tits as pumpkins. A lawyer. Shouldn't she know better? Anyway. What about you?"

Scarlette shrugged. Her pet consultation business meant she was also faced with the same topics every year, even if they were different from the problems July had to deal with. "The usual, too. Newsletters are being sent out with the warning that it isn't the best idea to feed your pet Halloween treats because you could poison them with the chocolate, and that lots of animals don't appreciate being put into stupid costumes. Shock, amazement. I wonder how the owners would feel if they were stuck into some BDSM outfit without being asked if it's okay, and then forced to sit still while somebody took a ton of pictures. It's a wonder there are so few serious injuries – on both sides."

"People."

"Oh yeah. I mean, come on, I love Halloween. But I don't have to force it onto a pet, because the pet doesn't understand it. Whatever. So, speaking of costumes, what do we need to get for you and Luke?"

"Not that much, really. We decided to do *Pulp Fiction*."

"Cool. Do some dance practice before the party, you know you'll be forced to dance dressed up like that."

"Not a problem. What about you and Ty?"

"*Nightmare Before Christmas*, Jack and Sally."

"Aww, that's cute."

"Yes, we're adorable, I know," Scarlette commented with humorous irony in her voice.

"You might not like it, but you are. What are you doing in the city?"

"Well, shopping for one. But I also had some on-site consultations today. I drove here early this morning. And Ty texted me he managed to arrange for a spontaneous interview with a guy he's considering writing about. They met this afternoon here, too. Now we'll probably just stay here, definitely have dinner at Granny's and Papa's restaurant, and tomorrow we'll enjoy the fun of a photo shoot because Vi wants the first round of cover shots done. That means she'll contact you sooner or later."

"No problem. I work well with her. Tyler got lucky with her as his agent."

"He did, yes, and I know it. She doesn't force too much publicity on me either, I appreciate that. Anyway, how's your dad? He had his last check-up yesterday, right?"

Julia nodded, and pure relief was written all over her face. She was back in the US now, but she had been staying with her father in Australia for quite some time to help him after he had been hit by a drunk driver the previous year and had needed extensive surgery. "He's doing great. His doctors say he has almost more range of motion now than before the accident. He's even jokingly thanking the idiot who ran him over. But yes, all good. It was good that I went back again for the two months last year after the whole blackmail ordeal, because he needed someone to push him to do his PT every day, or the joints might have gone stiff. But then he could start working again, and that kept pushing him. And now I can relax and know he's totally okay, even with me back in the States."

"I'm glad to hear that."

With Julia's office being close to several stores, the women were ambling down the street and found what they needed soon enough.

Loaded with bags, Scarlette bumped July with her hip. "Are you and Luke coming to dinner at the restaurant?"

"I wish we could, but we're invited to his parents because he wants to borrow one of his dad's old suits to get the bulky look for the costume."

"Too bad, but okay." Scarlette checked her watch, did a quick calculation. "Guess I'll take the subway from here, or I'll never get to the restaurant in time given the traffic. Say hi to everybody from me and all the others."

"I will. See you, the latest on Halloween."

"Yep."

With Scarlette gone after a quick hug, July got out her phone and texted her boyfriend that she'd be home soon. She slid the phone back into her pocket and wondered, not for the first time, how it had happened that her best friend had been married for over a year and she herself had found this terrific guy, too.

Admittedly, she and Luke had taken things a lot slower than Scarlette and Tyler. Except for having sex, and that was still a surprise. Usually, it took time for her to feel secure enough to sleep with a guy. But she had ended up in Luke's bed after only a couple of days.

From that point on, he had stayed true to his word. He had done what he could to get to know her, had spent time with her before she left for Australia to help her father. And when she had thought he might forget about her once she was on the other end of the world, he had phoned her, texted her, and they had had some of the most intriguing video calls she had ever dreamt of.

And when he had visited her, as he had promised, she had been sure they'd pounce at each other straight away. Instead, he had taken her to bed slowly, gently, and had made love to her until she had been drifting on a cloud of pure bliss. He had run his fingers down her cheek, had looked directly into her eyes — and had told her he loved her for the first time.

She was still a little embarrassed when she remembered she had started to cry at that, no matter that it had been happy tears.

Now they were living together, after Luke had moved into her apartment four months ago; and she suddenly, unshakingly knew what she wanted. Scanning the area around her, she smiled at a shop that should offer what she was looking for.

She was in and out of the store in twenty minutes and didn't realize that she made the way home more in a trance than with conscious steps. Dropping the shopping bags and her handbag at the door, she crossed to the living room to its comfortable couch and levered herself down on it, then took out her phone again to call Scarlette.

"Hey sweetie, that was quick, I just arrived at the restaurant. You wanna say hi to Granny?"

"Ah, no. Scarlette, I think I have done something crazy," Julia answered, breathless and paler than she had been earlier.

"Have you dumped Luke and hooked up with the weird hipster guy down your hallway?"

"No."

"Then I highly doubt you're the crazy type."

"Wanna think again?" Julia asked and held a ring up to the camera. It wasn't the most ornate ring in the world, but rather a simple, wide band in brushed titanium. It would be perfect for Luke, and it could withstand the strain of him handling a gun or getting into physical confrontations on a regular basis.

Scarlette's mouth dropped open, and July saw Ty leaning into frame, kissing his wife's cheek. "Hi, Sparks. What's u..." He stopped mid-sentence when he glanced at the screen. "Holy shit," he took the words right out of Scarlette's mouth, but after she nodded, she forced some composure into place. "You, not a word to Luke," she told her husband, "you," she addressed July, "do you have five minutes?"

"Yes, and I need them, that's why I called."

"Okay, let me find a quiet corner here."

When Julia had her friend's full attention again, she sighed. "I don't even know why I did this. I didn't plan it, we've hardly been talking about it before."

"Give me some details. What were you doing before you just bought a ring on a whim?"

Now July narrowed her eyes. "Are you the right person to tell me about acting on a whim? You married a guy you had planned to have a one-night stand with – after a week."

"Yes. Best thing I ever did. I never said the ring was a mistake, did I? I just wanna understand what made you do it."

"Okay, okay. So, you were gone, and I texted Luke, and I just thought how crazy it was that things had worked out so well for all of us, and how happy I was to get home, our home, and how he had told me loved me the first time."

"And you were crushed by a huge wave of love?"

"Yeah. It's stupid, it was an impulse, I shouldn't have done it."

July could see Scarlette roll her eyes. "It's not stupid. Maybe impulse, but a good one. You two are great together. You love each other, that's the most important thing in this whole business. You belong together. You'll figure out the rest. But sweetie, you bought a ring because you want forever with Luke. That's special. You know why I jumped into the relationship with Ty – I had tried other things; I knew myself well enough to know with him it's different. For you, it's different with Luke. You've been through messy relationships or guys who only wanted sex when you wanted more. That's not Luke."

"I know. You're right."

"Good. Ask him tonight. Ask him, before you guys leave for his parents'."

"What? Oh, no, I can't! Shouldn't I plan something special?"

"And lose the courage? Honey, you're giddy with love, there's nothing more special. Ride it."

July huffed out a heavy breath. "Ah, yeah, okay. I think you're right."

"Good. We'll think of you and raise a toast. Text me later."

"I will."

July had hardly hung up when she heard the apartment door open behind her. She turned around on the couch and over the backrest saw Luke tossing his keys on the table next to the door. His dark hair was tousled and his favorite brown leather jacket had a few new scratches, his jeans were ripped where they had been whole in the morning and his shirt was missing a button, his right hand was slightly swollen and scratched, and he smiled. Meeting her eyes, that smile widened to beam. "Hi, baby."

Everything inside her warmed, and all her nervousness evaporated with the sight of him – dirty, worse for wear, and his brown eyes shining just for her. Scarlette had been right, Julia definitely wanted forever with Luke Preston. "Hey. You look a bit roughed up there."

"Maybe a bit. It came down to tackling our suspect or shooting him in the back. I chose the first, and we arrested him, got a full confession."

"Nice job. Come here." She held out her hands for him and guided him around the couch to sit beside her.

She studied him for a moment, leaned in for a kiss, then took one of his hands, reached behind her with her other.

"I went on a very spontaneous shopping trip today. Then I thought I would need a big plan for this, tell you so many things. But the only thing I really want to say is, I love you so much. Will you marry me, Luke?"

It took him a second to process her words and the ring she held out to him now, but he needed no time to think about his answer. "Yes, of course. I love you, too, Julia."

Overjoyed, she slipped the ring onto his finger, then threw herself into his arms with such force that they tumbled to the floor, both laughing.

Kissing playfully, Julia pushed his jacket off his arms, started on the remaining buttons of his shirt. Since she had held several customer meetings earlier, she was still wearing her suit from work. When his fingers were unsteady while trying to open the buttons of her blouse, he cursed. "Fuck this," he muttered and just ripped it open, and his mouth came down on hers hard.

In baffled surprise, July gasped. They often had passionate sex for sure, but this was new. She could feel his desperate need radiate from him into her, and even though she wanted him just as badly, she gentled the kiss, laid a hand on his cheek. "What's this?"

Luke realized how rough he had been, rested his forehead against hers. "Sorry."

"Babe, I don't need or want sorry, I just wonder where this came from."

"I'd say from the fact that I finally got what I want. I've had a need to ask you for months, but I wasn't sure you'd say yes. This is one of the best days of my life, plus I was already pumped from work. I want you, I need you, and all that just swallowed me and any control with it. You're everything, July. To know you want to be mine forever only makes me want you more."

She fixed her eyes on his for a moment, then jumped him again, kissed him violently, because his words had flooded her with the same desperate desire she had felt from him. "Great point. God, I want you, too. Take me!"

They tore into each other, and hungry to taste him, July ran her mouth over his skin. She dragged his jeans down, and this time giggled, when she heard the fabric of her suit rip under Luke's greedy hands.

He knew he should cherish this moment with her – everything had changed for them.

But he couldn't stop himself from taking more and more from her, from rolling her over and plunging deep inside her. She had chosen to be his forever, to make him hers. The thought alone was intoxicating, and he could do nothing but ride the high.

His hands fisted in the mass of her blond curls, and he felt her nails dig into his back. They were both mad for each other. Slick skin slid over slick skin, their breath came in pants. Luke could hear her moans growing louder, becoming more demanding. And when he rammed himself into her even faster and harder, she begged for more, the wet heat of her clutching around him again and again. And her mindless scream pushed him further still. They raced together, until July finally arched beneath him with another orgasm and her tightened muscles left him no other choice than to climax with her.

Out of breath and weak, Luke managed to roll off her before he ended up staring at the ceiling just like Julia.

When she was sure she could take a full breath again, July rolled onto her side and brought her hand to Luke's cheek. "I'll say, wow. That was some celebration."

Her fiancé grinned at her. "Oh yes, it was."

"Guess we'll be late for dinner at your parents'."

"Baby, once we tell them we just got engaged, they'll forgive us anything."

"Good to know. Okay, I still need a quick shower, and so do you. Then you drive, I'll text Scarlette on the way and let her know your answer, and I'll have to call my mom and my dad."

"Okay."

Chapter Two

At her grandmother's and father's restaurant, Scarlette had broken her own and her family's rules and had kept her phone with her at the table. Normally, all the family valued the time together and everybody just left their phones in their bags or in the office area in the back. But when Scarlette had told the others about Julia and the ring, everybody was as curious as she was to hear Luke's answer.

They were all having dessert by the time Scarlette finally got a text, and she read it to the others.

Julia:
Luke said yes!
Sorry for the late update, we got carried away with
the celebration.
Guess you still remember how easily that happens ;)
We'll talk soon! Love you!

"About damn time," Beatrice commented with a grin and was about to get up, but Tyler beat her to it, and laid his hand on her shoulder to keep his wife's grandmother in place.

"Stay, Bea, I'll get the champagne."

"Thank you, Tyler."

Over the last year, he had come to feel as at home in the restaurant as in his own house and now wandered over to the wine fridge next to the kitchen, while Scarlette passed around the glasses she had stashed close to the family table earlier that evening.

They all raised a toast to the newly engaged couple, and Scarlette sent her friend a picture of the celebration, before snuggling close to her husband and leaning into his arm.

"You haven't told me about your meeting yet, Link," she said and ran her finger over Ty's shoulder right where his Triforce tattoo was hidden under his shirt. She had seen it the night they first had met, and had given him his nickname on the spot, enjoying the fact they were both *Legend of Zelda* fans.

It hadn't taken Tyler much longer to come up with a name for her, either. From their first night together, her eyes had captivated him and he had called her Sparks ever since. "I'd say we were all a little distracted after July called you, Sparks. And then there were lots of other family updates," Ty added with a look around the table and the various aunts, uncles, and cousins who had joined them today.

"Yeah, okay, true. Still. How did it go?"

"Well enough. Cory agreed to come to Vi's office tomorrow before our photo shoot to talk about the contract and all the rest to see if he's really up for me to write about him."

"Sounds good. I hope it works out; a deep-sea fisher studying marine biology to set up a sustainable fishing company is kind of cool."

Tyler narrowed his eyes, tugged on Scarlette's hair to tease her. "Do I have to be careful and keep you away from him?"

"Oh, yes, absolutely. Since the day I married you, I've only been waiting for you to come up with an even more interesting guy as a subject for your next book so I could dump you," she told him and poked a finger into his ribs. Ty grabbed her finger, bit into it, and made her laugh. And when he leaned closer and whispered in her ear, he made her swallow hard. "Remember, Sparks, nobody will ever make you scream like I do."

"Uh-huh, yeah, that's an important point. I'll keep it in mind."

"Good. I love you."

She rolled her eyes for effect, but smiled and stole herself a long kiss. "I love you, too. Good luck with the negotiations, then. Now, about Halloween. Has Josh told you what he and his girl-friend Bonny will be going as?"

When Scarlette's mother heard the word "Halloween," she shifted her attention from a conversation with her sister-in-law to her daughter and her son-in-law. "Excellent question, I'd love to know that, too."

Feeling the inquiring looks from both sides now, Tyler shrugged. "Sorry, Cynthia, sorry, Sparks. My dear brother didn't tell me, just like he didn't tell you. When I asked him before leaving home earlier today, I got the same answer as the last weeks. It's all a big secret, but it will be really cool, and you especially will love it, Sparks. I don't even know where they're putting everything together."

"That's not helpful. We need to know how much room they'll need at the least," Cynthia said, more to her daughter than to Tyler.

"I'll talk to Josh, I guess I can get that much information out of him."

"You do that soon, girl."

"Yes, mom."

Ty observed the women, shook his head. "Okay, I have come to understand that this family loves Halloween. But why is this important? And how much space can they need? They're two teenagers."

Scarlette sighed, faced her husband, and shook her head. "How can a writer – even a biographer – have so little imagination? I once went as Marie Antoinette. Okay, without a guillotine next to me, but even just this massive hooped skirt meant I was taking up as much space as two people, and then I had to make it look like I carried my head around. Costumes can grow very large, babe."

Ty blinked twice, then lifted his glass to have another sip of champagne. "Forget I ever said anything. But my question still stands. Why do you need to know?"

Now Cynthia patted his hand. "Oh, Tyler. Yes, this family loves Halloween, you are right about that. But I think you haven't understood yet just how *much* we love it. Some people might say we tend to overdo it a little, but it's just so much freaking fun. We decorate the whole street between our place, Bea's home, and the restaurant in the middle. Every year we get a permit to close the street and set up a big horror maze for the kids outside, and there's always a little parade riding around the block, throwing candy, visiting the closest children's hospital. And for the cart, we need to know how much room we need to plan for Bonny and Josh."

The information took a second or two to be processed, then Ty merely shrugged. "I thought I'd be surprised, but nope, that's pretty much what I expected from all of you. And it explains your daughter's love for horror novels and movies. It sounds amazing, to be honest. I'm looking forward to it. And I promise, Scarlette and I will talk to Josh and let you know, Cynthia."

"Perfect." She gave her son-in-law a quick kiss on the cheek, then returned to her other conversation.

During the rest of the evening, Tyler began to realize the full scope of the Halloween festivities when Scarlette's father Marco closed the doors of the restaurant for the public and rolled out blueprints for the maze that year and Bea assigned roles of builders, helpers, and family members who'd work as actors in the maze and do some little scares. Yes, his wife and her family were crazy about Halloween, and they put their hearts into making it special. No wonder he loved her, and all of them.

And when he and Scarlette decided to spend the night in their apartment in New York instead of driving back to their house in New Jersey, Ty made her scream on principle, then gave her a smacking kiss while she was still shuddering beneath him. "Just so you don't forget," he told her with a smug smile in place, his long hair curtaining both their faces.

She giggled, slung her arms around him. "Trust me, I never will. Now, why don't you take a shower with me?"

Standing up with his wife still clinging to him, Ty nuzzled her neck and strolled over to the bathroom. "Why don't I?"

Chapter Three

No on-site consultations and staying in the city meant Scarlette had time to decorate her office for Halloween after she had checked on the paperwork and before heading to the photo shoot. She might not be there every day now that she lived in Hope with Tyler, and even her employees spent a lot less time in the office nowadays since they could work from home, but when people *were* there, she knew they appreciated the effort. And they still had clients coming in for Saturday group consultations with their veterinarians – no need to let the office look like nobody took care of it. Her pet consulting business was Scarlette's baby, and she was proud of what she had done with it. She had started everything here in the building with only a few consultations and one tiny room at first, educating people on what to expect before they even got a pet or how to take better care of the ones they already had. Now she was renting almost an entire floor, had several employees, and often worked with the authorities, especially when it came to handling more exotic animals some people kept at home with or without permission. And just because the pandemic had reshaped work over the last years didn't mean she cared less about the appearance of her office.

She had just taped a paper bat against the glass of her office door when her phone rang. She answered the call and listened to the explanation of a veterinarian working for the authorities who sounded overwhelmed by what he had been asked to do. "I'd appreciate it if you could come by and help us out, Mrs. O'Brien. I talked to a colleague, and he mentioned you have some experience with this."

"Ah, maybe not exactly this, but I have worked on some marine projects in the past, that's true. Okay, to make sure I got you right: there's an arm stuck in one of the shark tanks in the Midtown Aquarium, you have cops there, but none of the employees are allowed to retrieve it because at the moment they're all suspects, and you don't know enough about sharks to go in there?"

"That sums it up. Plus, I've never been diving before."

"Right." Scarlette checked her watch and did the math. "With some luck, I should be there in about thirty minutes. Try to keep the sharks away from the arm, but don't feed them. I want them relaxed when I go in there, not agitated and competitive over some treats."

"Okay."

It wasn't hard to find the fish tank in question, Scarlette soon discovered. A big crowd had gathered as near to it as possible and was blocking her way, but when she saw a familiar face behind the police line, she put her fingers in her mouth and whistled before smiling at the cop. "I heard you need a shark wrangler."

Luke grinned and ducked under the barricade keeping people away from the crime scene. "Scarlette, hi."

"Hi. First of all, congrats." She hugged her friend with a smile.

"Thanks. Now, about this, I didn't know the vet would call you. But yes, please, I'm glad for your help."

"Sure thing."

He guided her through the bulk of curious onlookers, and once she was closer to the aquarium in question, she could see what had been drawing the sharks' attention. Behind the large window, one wall was covered in artificial rocks. And lodged between two rocks was a human arm with no body attached to it. Most sharks had lost interest in it by now, but one smaller fish was still lingering close and swimming in circles, once in a while poking its nose against the net that had been lowered into the water as a makeshift barrier to keep the animals away.

"Well, shit," Scarlette mumbled quietly to keep her voice from carrying over to the crowd. Luke appreciated her caution and nodded. "Yep. They tell me the pump and filter system are behind those rocks and the arm was probably caught in a current and carried there. The fish are known to avoid the area, but with the body part there they were more interested. That's how one of the caretakers spotted the arm on his morning round. He noticed the group of sharks close to the rock wall, looked up, and started yelling for his supervisor."

"Can't say I blame him."

"Me neither. I got the rough specs. The arm is stuck about eight feet above the ground, and ten feet below the surface. This isn't their biggest tank because it mostly functions as a pool for the younger sharks until they either get moved or released, if possible."

"Yeah, I can see that. They're all still relatively small."

"I would have sent one of the employees to retrieve the arm with me, but..."

"They're suspects. Yes, the vet who called me said so. It's no problem, I can get it."

Luke scratched his neck and shifted his feet. Scarlette could read his unease without a problem. "Let me guess, a cop should get it?"

"Yes. And yes, I know how to dive, but I have no real clue about sharks."

"What about this? They should have equipment for two people here, why don't we both take a swim? You get the arm, I keep the sharks away."

"Remind me to tell Ty later he married an awesome woman. Yes, let's do that."

About an hour later, they were almost getting ready to go up to the surface again when the curious shark Scarlette had seen earlier swam over. It had kept its distance so far like the others, likely due to the sharks being used to divers in their tank for cleaning and the additional electronic shark deterrent bracelets she and Luke had been handed before the dive just to be sure. But now that Luke had collected anything around the arm he deemed as possible evidence and had taken pictures with an underwater camera they had borrowed as well, he was freeing the arm. And the smell of it swirled in the water again, drawing the shark back, curiosity apparently winning out over its survival instincts, despite the magnetic fields generated by the bracelets which were supposed to irritate the sharks' senses and keep them away.

When Luke had put the arm into a net bag and was turning to Scarlette to signal her to get back up, the young shark darted forward, ignoring the net between them.

Scarlette had about two seconds to react. She gave the animal a punch on the snout, then pushed it firmly away with her gloved hands. It wasn't violent, but it was enough to stop the shark's dash forward and make it swim away again. Luke goggled at her through his mask; Scarlette shrugged, pointed a finger at the surface.

Out of the water and with evidence handed over to the Crime Scene team, Luke walked beside Scarlette to get out of the wetsuits. "You punched a shark."

"Yeah. I'm not entirely proud of it, but I figured it was worth a try."

"You punched a freaking shark. You're my new official hero."

And now she giggled. "Good to know. Question: did I see it correctly, was there a tattoo on the wrist?"

"Yes, an octopus wrapping its arms around the wrist. Why?"

"Call me crazy, and I know many people have tattoos, but I've got a hunch Ty will see his agent alone later. He told me the guy he was planning to write about, Cory something, has an octopus tattoo around his wrist. He saw it at their meeting yesterday. And an aquarium fits his line of work."

"Oh fuck this."

"If it helps, Link was with me all night."

Luke huffed out a humorless laugh. "Yeah, don't worry, I highly doubt Ty would end up on any suspect list. And that's good info because I think identification via fingerprints might take longer than usual – if it works at all – if the ME has to prepare the skin after being in the water for some time. You didn't sound like you knew the full name of the guy."

They were standing in front of the doors to the dressing rooms, and Scarlette shook her head. "No, sorry. But you can call Ty, he was at our apartment and had planned to do some writing before a meeting with his agent. You should reach him."

"Okay. Thanks. Maybe it's somebody else."

"Let's just hope so. I'll meet you back here, then we can check if you need me for anything else."

"All right."

Luke was talking on the phone when he stepped back out in his regular clothes. "No, you don't have to bail her out, Ty. I think she could charm her way out in any case. And no, you don't have to worry, she's fine. She's my new hero, by the way. She punched a shark for me today."

After a moment of listening, Luke chuckled. "Yeah, that's what I thought, too. Anyway, she was called in by the authorities to help out, and it's related to my new case. We found an arm, only an arm. When she recognized a tattoo on it she told me you might know the guy. Somebody named Cory?"

Taking notes, with his phone tucked between his shoulder and ear, Luke came over to Scarlette. "Thanks, Ty. I'll check on him and will let you know. I might have to talk to you if that's really the guy. Scarlette told me you had a meeting with him yesterday. I'll call you again if it turns out to be him. For now, thanks. Bye."

After ending the call, Luke first called his boss, Lieutenant Leroy Porter, to have colleagues check on Cory's apartment in case the man was in there and possibly alive. Then he grinned at Scarlette. "Ty says 'Holy shit' and can't wait to hear the full story when you get home. Feel free to tell him, it's not exactly confidential in regards to the case – and knowing people, somebody probably shot a video and posted it already anyway."

"People suck sometimes."

Thinking of the arm he had just carried to the surface, Luke agreed. "They do. Okay, look, I don't think there's anything left to do for you here. But I really appreciate your help."

"No problem. I'll catch up with the vet who called me in

and then I'll be on my way back to the office before heading over to meet with Tyler and Vi. Just call me if anything comes up."

"I will."

Luke stayed behind to ask the first questions and couldn't say he was surprised when he found the name Cory Gilbert – listed as part-time help – on a list of employees handed to him by the owner of the Aquarium. Going by the schedule, Cory wasn't supposed to work today. *And I don't think he'll show up tomorrow either,* Luke thought grimly, because his gut told him Scarlette could very well be right with her hunch.

When he had finished his first round of interviews and checked on the alibis of several employees, he allowed the facility's vet and some caretakers to go to work; what had happened wasn't the animals' fault, neither in the tank in question nor in the other pools, and they needed to be fed, their enclosures had to be cleaned.

Luke was on his way back to his car when Leroy called him back to let him know Gilbert wasn't at home, and the apartment had looked undisturbed. "Okay. I'll run him, find out where he goes to university, see if he showed up there."

"Already did," Leroy said on the other end of the line. "I sent everything over, and I'll meet up with you at some point. I got a call from the captain already asking why the NYPD punches sharks. You gotta love the internet. Now the upper levels want to be informed about every step. Might be a good idea to hook Julia into the PR part of this. Mind if I call her?"

"No, go ahead. Ah..." Luke tapped his fingers on the car roof. Aside from being his boss, Leroy was a good friend of both him and Julia. "I wanted to tell you in person later, but well. She might be expecting some congratulations. She proposed to me yesterday, we're getting married."

"Damn, that's great. Congrats to you, too. I'll tell her. And you'll have to get her to the station soon for some celebration."

"Will do."

"Good. Okay, you go on with this, I'll call your gorgeous fiancée. See you later."

Several hours later, Luke found himself ringing the doorbell to Scarlette's and Ty's apartment. They had agreed to wait for him there instead of driving home when his day so far had only strengthened his suspicion of whom the arm likely belonged to.

When he walked from the elevator to the apartment door, he heard somebody squeal from the inside and was hardly surprised to see Scarlette thrown over Tyler's shoulder after the door was opened.

"Things never change around here," Luke said simply.

"It's entirely her own fault. She practically begged for a spanking." Ty said and playfully slapped his wife's butt. "She has given Lorraine a week off in early December."

"She deserves it, Link. She's an amazing cook and does an outstanding job making sure our household keeps running smoothly even with us being as busy as we are. But she needs time to do her Christmas shopping and everything. Did you ever starve, when she was off and I was cooking?"

"No, but that's the week of the Winter Charity Ball, we'll be extra busy."

Ty took a step to the side, gestured Luke inside, but kept carrying Scarlette over his shoulder.

"Then I don't see the problem. We'll be here half the time anyway, and Josh will probably be at Bonny's. Her parents adore him, you know that. Lorraine wouldn't have a lot to do for us that week. Plus, she helped with mom's and dad's anniversary party-slash-vow renewal in June instead of taking her holidays. She really deserves the time off, especially in December. Thinking about it, let's get her and her husband a suite in a nice hotel for a few days, spoil them a bit."

"Okay, okay, fair point. You have escaped further spanking," Ty told her and set her down. She grinned at him.

"I don't think I complained about it, did I?"

Luke took a deep breath, shook his head and tried to change the topic. "Too much information, guys. But about that anniversary-slash-vowel renewal. I still have one question I didn't get to ask back then. How come your parents celebrated their 25th anniversary..."

"When I'm thirty and they adopted me as a baby?" Scarlette finished his question.

"Yeah."

"They were high school sweethearts and had been together forever and always wanted to get married. They just never found the right time. There was school, then my mom studied medicine, and she had two miscarriages."

"I'm sorry," Luke said.

"Thanks. She's still sad about it, but at the same time she says it put her on the path to help other couples. And it made her and dad decide to adopt a baby. From what I know it wasn't easy with them not being married, but they knew some people at the agency, and lots of friends and family vouched for them being a stable couple with wedding plans. So, they managed to adopt me. And after that, they wanted to wait until I was old enough to be the ring bearer."

"That's very sweet."

"It is. But as much as I like that story, that's not why you're here."

"No, it's not."

Scarlette sobered, nodded. "You two sit down and get started, I'll get us all some coffee."

Chapter Four

Carrying steaming mugs, Scarlette walked over to the living area a few minutes later and sat beside Ty on the couch. Luke had taken one of the armchairs and was already writing in his notebook.

"Scarlette said you met Cory Gilbert yesterday and were supposed to have another meeting with him today."

"Yeah. We met yesterday early afternoon at the café at the Aquarium. It was the most convenient location for him, and for me it had the side-benefit that I could have a look at their new mermaid act in the show pool built around the café. I wanted to see if it was any good and would be worth taking Scarlette there sometime."

"Nice idea, I'd like it, yeah," she said with a smile.

"I thought so. Regarding Cory, I only know that he was supposed to come to Vi's office today to discuss a contract in case he decided he would agree to have me write about him. Have you already confirmed it's his arm?"

With anybody else, Luke wouldn't have said anything, but he knew he could trust his friends. "We're still waiting for the prints to confirm it a hundred percent. We tried to reach him all day without any luck, he wasn't at home or at the university and his boss at the fishing company he works for hadn't heard from him, but he wasn't expected to work there this week, so no surprise there. The woman he's been seeing for the last few weeks didn't know where he was either, but she also said things had slowly been fizzling out between them, so she wasn't surprised not to hear from him for the last few days. We checked the hospitals, but nobody's come in fitting his description. Though, when we talked to his mother, she recognized the tattoo. The way it's wrapping around the wrist, it's fairly unique."

"So it's likely he has not only lost his arm, but his life, too," Ty concluded.

"We're not giving up on finding him alive yet, and Leroy is currently looking at other angles. But after a quick first glance, the ME let us know the arm showed signs that it might have been cut off after he was dead. It's hard to tell, though, due to the time in the water. I take it he didn't contact you either, then."

"No, neither me nor Vi. We tried to call him, since you weren't sure when you first called me, and I didn't want to divulge any information to Vi without talking to you first. But we didn't get an answer. So you'll see our numbers, if you find his phone and check the call log."

"Okay, that's good to know. And thanks for the discretion."

"Sure," Ty said with a shrug, and Luke knew for his friend it was just as much a given to keep quiet as it had been for Luke when Tyler had taken him into confidence the year before when the O'Brien family had been blackmailed and Tyler hadn't known whom to trust, even in the police force, not to leak everything to the media.

"Can you tell me more about Cory?"

"Not that much, sorry, Luke. I met him personally for the

first time yesterday. Before that, we connected on social media on a basic level, and even that was with a large break in-between, as he had been at sea for long stretches some months ago. I'm pretty sure at this point you know more about him than I do."

"How did you find him?"

"You better ask your fiancée that, she can explain it better I'm sure," Ty said, and Luke shot him a puzzled look.

Scarlette chuckled and took over the explanation. "It's my fault, really. Ty and I had been talking one evening. I liked the flowers on the balcony here the first time I came here with him, and he told me he kept them because some bees were coming by like this. And with the whole blackmail drama going on last year, we used the family plane way too much during that time. You know his family had it customized to transport the race-horses they breed personally, so usually it's not used that extensively."

Luke nodded in acknowledgment, and Scarlette smiled at him thoughtfully when she kept talking. "We both felt bad and were talking about ways to optimize it, maybe not completely change it to electrical, especially as the technology isn't perfected yet, and you might never be able to make long-distance flights completely without fuel, and it's a lot of work to restructure the plane. Anyway, we discussed some options to at least improve it, and naturally we googled a lot of things. Keywords like 'sustainability' for example. And here's where July comes in for the explanation, because I know enough, but she can explain the algorithm behind search engines, social media, and so on much better than I can. Long story short, at some point this guy came up in Ty's social feed, looking for ways to reform deep-sea fishing, make it greener, more sustain-able. I was sitting next to Ty, and we both thought that might be an interesting person for Ty's next book."

"Okay, yeah, I can see that. When was that?"

Scarlette looked at her husband, thought about it for a moment. "About ten months ago, right, Link?"

Ty nodded. "Yeah, sounds about right. Like I said, Luke, I contacted Cory, we stayed in contact on and off, depending on his schedule. He had to plan his job with the fishing company around his projects and exams at college, and vice versa, to get the most insight into both worlds. He had had a little bit more breathing room lately because his employer had to adhere to some new fishing restrictions and couldn't send out his whole fleet as usual. Meaning Cory could focus on college and his job at the Aquarium here. That's when we started talking more seriously about the contract for the book, about getting together for some meetings and interviews. That would have been a month or two ago."

"Did you get the feeling anything was off during the last two months?"

"No, not at all. He rescheduled our original first meeting to a few weeks later because he had started seeing a woman lately. He told me she's a single mother and he tried to make dates work between both their jobs and her taking care of her kid. But when we actually met, he told me the same she told you, things didn't seem to be working out between them. They were both too busy to make it work. Being thirty-four, he was one of the older attendees of his college courses as he had decided to start studying only two years ago, but he was comfortable with it. He studied because he was interested in the field, not in the social aspects of college, at least that's what's come across so far. That's the extent of his social life I know, though. We would have talked about that in person, not in emails. I want to know the people I write about are comfortable. And yes, I also want to see them and get a feeling if they tell the truth or tell some bullshit to sound good in the book. So far, Cory always had seemed sincere in our video calls, and any mails or texts were always consistent."

Luke chuckled. "It's strange to know you look for the same things in people a cop would, but I suppose you have to. In any case, I'm glad about it, and I know I can trust your take, you're good at recognizing people, you always have been."

They kept talking a little longer, but Ty had been right, he couldn't tell Luke any more details he hadn't known already. After he finished his coffee, Luke got up and was accompanied to the door by the couple.

"Oh, Luke, I usually love to help you out, but should anything come up again tomorrow I'll have to send one of our vets because I have some important appointments scheduled. But Michelle has been cleared by authorities in the past like the rest of my team, and he's knowledgeable when it comes to sharks and everything."

"Okay, no problem. Thanks for your help, both of you. Good night."

"Sure thing. Good night," Scarlette said with a hug.

"Night," Tyler said as well, and gave his friend a one-armed hug, too.

Chapter Five

Back at home, Luke moaned at the smell of dinner floating through the whole apartment after he opened the door. "Oh god, that smells so good."

July looked out of the kitchen, grinned. "It should. Bea brought it over personally, since we couldn't be at the restaurant with everybody to celebrate our engagement. But her real engagement present to us was an envelope with the secret recipe to her pasta and her Bolognese."

Luke was sincerely touched. He had come to know Scarlette's grandmother over the past year. July had always been family to the old woman, but even within her family she didn't give out the recipe to everybody. "That's..."

"Huge. I know. I almost cried when I had a look at the paper and saw what it was."

"I get why. We'll bring some flowers with us next time we go to the restaurant."

"Sounds good to me. Now get ready for dinner and tell me about your day. You coming home this late usually means you caught a case. And Scarlette texting me you're on your way home from their place just makes me more curious how she's involved in this."

Luke cocked his head and grinned. "Ah, that's how you knew to heat everything up. Guess word travels fast."

"Yep. But she didn't say anything else, so I hope you'll fill me in."

"I can do that. Give me five minutes to freshen up."

"Sure."

When he was sitting with July at the table a few minutes later, he made her laugh as soon as he came to the shark punching incident. "Oh god, that was Scarlette? I saw the video come up all over the place the whole time. I really shouldn't be surprised."

"You didn't know? I thought Leroy or his boss wanted to call you."

"They did, but only asked for help with PR, they didn't tell me who the person doing the punching was. So I gave them some cursory advice, but to do it properly, they first have to set up a proper contract with my company, so that's what they have been up to. Their PR department hasn't done the worst job so far, and I think I will be able to step in tomorrow."

Grinning, Luke reached over the table to take her hand. "So we'll kind of be working together?"

"The last time turned out pretty great, don't you think?" she asked with a smirk and brushed his knuckles with her thumb.

"It most certainly did."

In the spirit of working together again, he told her about the rest of his day, and Tyler's connection to the victim.

Over the last year, they had both found out how helpful it could be to have somebody to talk to about your cases or clients, even just to say some of your thoughts out loud to put them in the right order. Strictly speaking, it wasn't something either of them was allowed to do, but they both knew the other was a vault, and neither of them would have it seeing the other irritated or like there was some nagging thought they couldn't get out of their mind if they could offer an open ear to each other.

When he had finished, Julia studied the glass of wine she had poured for dinner. "Hmm, so I'll mainly be hired to make the department look good even with the shark punching, and I'll have to check if they will disclose Scarlette's name. And I might have to talk to Ty's agent in case that connection becomes public. But I could also check the victim's social media, too, if you want me to. Maybe his coworkers' accounts as well. I might save you some time combing through them."

Luke chuckled and gave his fiancée a quick kiss. "Be careful, baby, you do that, and Leroy will want to hire you to do that for the whole department full time. Most of us hate sifting through all the fake stuff people post to look good online and then try to align it with all the things we get from interviewing witnesses and suspects. And you love your job now. Plus, trust me, the department wouldn't be able to pay you as well as you're paid now."

"Okay, good points, even though you actually like the tech stuff, in your case it would just be a time saver. But you're right, I love my current job no matter how often I complain about some clients. So maybe I can do it more secretly here at home for you for this case; you have all your tech here, it would be safe security-wise."

"True, and I won't stop you. Because, yeah, I like the tech side, I like finding the end of a long trail of servers being used to hide the original location of a post, but the posts themselves, most of the time I share my colleagues' view that it just creates even more layers before you finally find the real person, victim or suspect."

"I completely understand your point, believe me. So let me help you with this one. That could be my engagement present to you, since I never really took the time to think about things like that before I just bought that ring," she offered with a shy smile.

Luke felt a jolt of panic race along his nerves when he saw her smiling in that slightly insecure way. "I don't need a present, July. All I need to know is that you won't change your mind."

"I would never do that. You are… I don't even know how to tell you what you are to me…. All I can say is, since the moment you've kissed me the first time, everything has felt right, like coming home. You're home to me, Luke."

He felt like his heart would burst. "I think you just said it perfectly. You're home to me, too, July. Things with you have been so different from the start, so good."

She nodded, because he was right. Neither of them had been quick to act when it came to flirting usually, but when they had bumped into each other for the first time at Ty's and Scarlette's place the year before when they were helping their friends solve the mystery of who had been blackmailing them, it had felt incredibly right to follow the pull of attraction.

It had felt right ever since.

"Yeah, you're right, things have been different for both of us, but good. I'm still glad we took more time with the engagement than Scarlette and Ty, though. I love you so much, Luke, but we needed to see if we work in the long run first. We know now, so don't ever be afraid I'd change my mind, okay?"

"Okay." He happily pulled her onto his lap, nuzzled her neck and made her giggle. "But speaking of presents, what would you like, baby?"

Glad that they had finished talking about the case before changing topics, July got up and enthusiastically dragged Luke from the chair and toward the bedroom. "Oh, not much. Just promise me that you'll never stop doing that thing you do with your tongue when you go down on me."

"I can do that." Her eagerness sparked a fire in Luke and he undressed them both quickly.

July hit the mattress with the back of her knees, then fell onto it with a giggle when Luke gently pushed her. Her eyes never left his while she crawled further onto the bed, her smile inviting him to follow.

So he did. He hovered over her for a second, studying the face of the love of his life, a face he knew better than his own. The pure happiness he saw there tempered his raw need to have her right that second. Instead, he lowered down gently, her soft body melting against him, her lips meeting his in a kiss that reached the deepest parts of his soul and warmed every cold corner. He never could put into words what she truly meant to him, how she had become his beacon of light against the darkness he faced every day on the job. But what he couldn't say, he could show her.

His lips left hers and slowly wandered along her neck. Featherlight kisses until he reached that spot right below her ear. Then the tip of his tongue drew a lazy circle on her skin in a preview of what he was going to do to her soon. July's sigh told him how much she enjoyed the caress.

He took his time, but when she began to move beneath him looking for more, he wouldn't deny her. Usually, he would let his hands roam over her body to find all the places that made her gasp and moan. But when she had joked about his tongue earlier, he had come up with a different idea for the night.

Luke's hands found July's on the covers and he linked their fingers together, holding her still. She looked at him in surprise but Luke winked at her. Then he let his mouth travel over her. Down her neck to her collarbones, placing kisses everywhere. Back to her throat, oh so carefully nipping there so he wouldn't leave a mark. That drew another sigh from her lips.

Luke shifted a little, his hands still holding hers, and he

could see July's eyelids flutter closed when his lips roamed toward her breasts. Not wanting to rush, he began to kiss a slow circle, first around one then the other, never touching her nipples. His hot breath on her skin left her with goosebumps and her slow movements became more pronounced.

"Luke, please."

Smiling, he gave in and licked across one nipple before sucking it into his mouth.

July moaned. She didn't know why Luke wasn't touching her with his hands that night, but she wouldn't complain about what he was doing instead. His lips and tongue on her skin were like a drug and she had been addicted to them for a long time.

His mouth let go of her hard nipple just to find the other. A jolt went through her when his teeth gently nipped at it. Her nerve endings were humming and she felt herself climbing closer to a first small climax already. He could tip her over the edge like this, make her beg for more. And when he switched from nipping to sucking hard he did just that.

Groaning, July writhed underneath her lover. "More, more, please!"

Luke placed a soft kiss between her breasts. "Okay, baby."

But he went slow, mapping her ribs and her stomach with his lips first, running his tongue around her bellybutton. And even when he was between her legs, July swore he wanted to torture her. His lips kissed up and down the insides of her thighs. He nipped at the sensitive skin, then sucked there leaving her with a mark only he would know about.

Then, finally, she felt his breath ghost over her center. Luke pressed one more kiss against her skin, right onto the trimmed curls of her pubic hair, before his tongue dragged slowly across her clitoris. Her head fell back on a moan, anticipation making her quiver because she knew this was only the beginning.

He used the tip of his tongue to trace all along her entrance, then dipped it inside her, tasting her, playing with her. July thought she heard him groan but a moment later all her senses blacked out. She could only feel now. Feel his mouth covering her clitoris again, forming a seal around it and gently sucking. It was a feeling like no other and it always drove July crazy.

Between her legs, Luke only focused on July's pleasure. If he thought about her smell, about how wet she was for him, about how much he wanted to be inside her, he wouldn't be able to stop his own orgasm. So he sucked rhythmically, every so often changing the pace and intensity until she was a sweaty, quivering mess. Only then he did with his tongue what he knew she loved: he sucked her hard and kept her inside his mouth, then circled her clitoris with his tongue before pressing down on it with the flat of his tongue.

July exploded with a load moan. The orgasm left her panting, but she tugged on his hands, dragging him back on top of her. "Inside me. I want to feel all of you."

Luke didn't need to be asked twice. He was painfully hard and panting himself from holding back. Sliding his length into her always felt both new and exciting and like coming home. It didn't take long for them to find a rhythm, their hips meeting, their breaths catching. And when he was close Luke fisted his hands in July's curls, while her nails now dug into his back. He climaxed when he felt her constricting around him and swallowed her cry with his lips covering hers.

And later, when he drew July close against him for the night, he grinned to himself and thought back to one of her comments from earlier. *Yeah, the last time working together had turned out pretty great, indeed.*

Chapter Six

L uke wasn't surprised to find a text from Leroy the next morning:

Leroy:
We managed to work things out with Julia's boss,
she's ours for now.
Bring her to the precinct with you or hook her up with the
contacts to our media people for a video conference, whatever
works best.
We'll split the work today; I'll check with the ME for more
details, do some interviews, you check if you can trace the
victim's last whereabouts through his phone.
I don't care where you both work, but if I have to call you, you
better be dressed ;)

"I'm lucky he likes you," Luke said with an eye roll at Julia and showed her the message.

"Yep. But he's also in a better mood because you guys gain, while we apparently make a loss by contracting me to the NYPD, but we don't want the bad press of a refusal. I just got this," she said and held her own phone for Luke to read the message from her boss.

Kenneth:

Do your job, but make it quick and don't make it a habit, this is one expensive favor we're doing for your boyfriend.

"Tell your boss it's our engagement present maybe?"

"That would imply I had the desire to share personal information with him. Your boss likes you and you like him. We all tolerate Kenneth because he's brilliant at his job. But he doesn't like New York and hates that he was transferred here two months ago. The fact that his wife dumped him just before that doesn't help, trust me. We get along, that's good enough. He's in a sour mood most of the time."

Luke grinned. "I know what Scarlette would say to that."

"So do I. But if I get him a masturbator or a hooker, I'd be fired for sexual harassment," July answered with a laugh.

"Fair point. Okay, do we work from here then, if your offer to also help with the social media angle still stands?"

"It still stands, and I can easily work from here and coordinate with your PR department, so no problem."

After breakfast and some quick introductions from Luke, July moved to her smaller office to work on the media strategy while Luke kept working in their larger home office.

When he had moved in, she had happily given over the office space because she rarely worked from home, and Luke's setup took up more space than her laptop and camera. She wasn't bad when it came to tech, but her job meant she got along fine with a basic computer, sometimes a graphic tablet and a second screen, while Luke often required more than one PC, several screens, several external hard drives and, in most cases, room for a case board.

They both had been working for about an hour and Luke was just setting a fresh mug of coffee next to July and stealing himself a kiss as payment when his phone rang with a video call. "Leroy, hey."

His boss answered with a raised eyebrow but there was humor in his dark blue eyes. "I can see July's hair behind you."

"I'm dressed, I just had my coffee slave bring me a cup," she chimed in from the background.

"Good excuse. Anyway, Luke, I just was at the morgue. The ME had some time to take a closer look at the arm. Not only does it look like it was removed after death, but it also seems like a precise removal. While it's not a clean cut and the edges of the wound point to the use of a serrated blade, possibly an electrical knife or a bone saw, the location where the cut was made indicates somebody knew precisely where best to start cutting."

"Meaning we might be looking at a medical professional."

"It's at least a possibility," Leroy agreed with a nod on the screen, and Luke could see him run a hand through his short, bright red hair, his angular face serious. "And I got a call from the Aquarium that another shark is showing signs of distress. They apparently did an ultrasound and found something that looks strangely like part of a leg. But given the possibility of a killer working in the medical field, I don't want the Aquarium's vet cutting open the shark. I was planning on contacting Scarlette."

"Do that. She already told me she doesn't have time personally today, and I wouldn't know if she knows how to operate on
a shark, but she said in case anything came up her vet would be
up to the task."

"Okay. You two keep working."

"Sure. Keep me updated."

"I will."

Chapter Seven

With the wind howling, Leroy was glad for his well-worn black leather jacket while he waited at the entrance of the Aquarium's medical bay for Scarlette's vet to arrive.

When a tall man with dark golden skin and deep green eyes came around the corner, Leroy cocked his head. If that was Michelle Jenkins, he wasn't exactly what he had been expecting, but he surely wouldn't complain. Scarlette hadn't had time to talk much about it over their video call because she had been right at her next clients' front steps, and she had just smiled at Leroy. "No problem, I'll send my vet over. Don't worry, you'll be fine, Michelle does a great job."

The man extended his hand in greeting. "Lieutenant Porter? Hello, I'm Michelle Jenkins."

"Dr. Jenkins, hello. Nice to meet you."

"Likewise. So, the boss said you have a shark that might need something extracted."

Leroy nodded, scratched his neck. "Yes. And it would be best if I could be there as well when you open the fish, because we suspect it has swallowed the leg of our victim, or part of it, and I have to collect it for our ME."

"Well, that's something new for a change. Let's get to work then, before the shark suffers longer than necessary and the leg gets digested even more."

Both men turned to the doors of the medical unit and entered after a sharp knock.

They saw that the team still had the shark in question isolated in a large, portable tank with a raisable platform, and the frozen ultrasound picture still on screen. But they had followed Leroy's orders to stay away from the animal otherwise. For security, he had had a uniform placed here already, but it seemed unnecessary. Everybody stared in a horrified trance at the leg with the attached foot on the screen, clearly visible even for a layman.

The Aquarium's vet took a step over to Leroy and Michelle, greeted them with a nod. "Morning. The shark is currently lightly sedated so it will stay calm during the scan. We can increase the sedation if you need to do another check, or we can adjust the medication to induce full anesthesia, help you turn the shark on her back, and then leave you to operate. We have developed the raisable platform ourselves. You can adjust the angle, so the shark's head stays submerged, and the gills will get a constant flow of water and anesthetic. It's a little less than ideal as it displaces the internal organs a little, but we found for most things we have to do, like treating larger external wounds, it works well. All the equipment you might need has been sterilized and is set out for you."

The Aquarium's vet shot a disapproving look at Leroy. "To make this clear, I'm not happy with this, but I want our animal treated quickly, so I won't stop you. It's not that I don't trust a colleague, I would just prefer to operate on our animals myself, given that I know them better. Should anything happen during surgery, I will hold the NYPD – and you personally – responsible for it."

Leroy kept his expression blank. "Understood."

Michelle and the Aquarium's vet prepared the shark for the surgery. The vet gave Michelle some final information on their self-made equipment, then left with the others. It wasn't exactly a small operation, but Michelle was confident he would be able to handle it alone.

He guided Leroy through scrubbing and properly donning the sterile surgery scrubs. "I probably won't need any help for the surgery itself, but if you want to attend and get the leg out, you need to follow procedure."

"I have no problem with that. It's hardly the shark's fault, I wouldn't want to risk any infection or anything for it."

Michelle looked at him with appreciation in his eyes. "Thank you, that's very thoughtful. Let's get to work."

Leroy quickly learned that operating meant being very close to the person next to you sometimes, even when the animal you were operating on was a ten-foot-long shark. And he also realized he didn't mind being close to Michelle. The man radiated calm whether he was studying a colleague's DIY surgery equipment or cutting into a shark's stomach and stopping a small bleed with his skilled hands. *And I really shouldn't wonder if his hands are that skilled doing other things, too,* Leroy scolded himself.

Focusing on the job he was there to do, Leroy was strangely glad about the fact that he had seen his fair share of gruesome scenes over the years so he could easily stomach it when Michelle asked him to lend a hand and carefully pull out the leg.

Once Leroy had the limb, Michelle checked the stomach for any other content that might irritate the shark, and pulled out a silver flake about the size of a fingernail.

"What's that?" Leroy wanted to know.

"I don't know, but it looks artificial and might cause some issues; the edges are pretty sharp. It looks like there's some blood on it. See those dark patches on it? That's usually how blood looks after contact with the stomach acid. It could be that this piece got into the shark together with the leg because I don't see any visible injuries in the stomach lining that would make me think it's been in there long on its own. Here." Michelle dropped the flake next to the leg on a table close to them so Leroy could bag everything after the surgery.

"I can't see anything else in here. I'll close the stomach now, do a lavage, then close the abdominal cavity again."

"Do a what now?"

"Ah, I'll use some sterile liquid to clean everything in there in case something dripped and could cause inflammation after closing."

"Okay. Thank you, really."

"No problem, it's my job after all. And I'm happy to help the shark," Michelle answered, and Leroy was sure – or maybe he just hoped – under the surgical mask he was smiling a little shyly.

They finished the surgery and once Leroy was sure he had all the evidence he might need, he handed the shark back to the Aquarium's vet. Michelle gave his colleague a report and by the nod he gave to the post-surgery treatment plan, he apparently was confident the shark would be in capable hands from here on out.

Back outside, Leroy knew he was pressed for time, but he thanked Michelle again.

"It was my pleasure, really. It wasn't my first time operating on a shark, but it's always exciting and not something I get to do every day. I feel like I should rather thank *you* for calling me in to help. I just hope it was all worth it and this helps you with your case."

"I'm sure it will. Tell Scarlette thanks again for sharing her resources with us. Ah, I gotta go. See you around."

"Yeah, sure. See you."

Leroy climbed into his car but sensed some of the same reluctance to leave from Michelle that he felt himself. Then he remembered Scarlette's invitation to her family's Halloween party. Maybe he should thank her personally for everything again, and try to inconspicuously find out if Michelle was invited as well.

Chapter Eight

In their apartment, July knocked on the doorframe of Luke's office. He had updated her about the successful operation almost two hours before and they had gone back to working on their separate tasks. But now she held out a fresh coffee to him with a bright smile. "Here you go. Have you got time for a little gossip?"

Luke raised an eyebrow. "Thanks. Case related gossip?"

"Not entirely."

"Then shoot. I could use a few moments to clear my mind."

"Let's see what we can do about that," July said and walked over to him, and after setting her own mug on the desk started to gently massage Luke's temples. She was rewarded with a content groan. With a smile, she picked up the gossip again. "So, Scarlette just called me. She let me know about the surgery, too, and that Leroy asked Michelle to thank her again."

"Not unusual so far, is it?"

"Nope. But apparently Leroy called her a little later himself to do the same. And ask about Michelle."

"What, if he can be trusted or something? I wouldn't know why. We know Scarlette's business, and with it her whole team, is cleared to work with authorities. Otherwise we wouldn't have worked with her earlier. Did anything happen during the surgery that made Leroy doubt that?"

"Oh, no, absolutely not. And I don't mean Michelle's work or performance; I mean he asked about *Michelle*," July said with a pregnant stress on the vet's name.

"Oh... Really?"

"Seems so."

"Well, I thought you both knew Leroy's bi."

"We do, we've run into him making out with guys or girls at parties more than once by now. That's not the reason why I'm bringing it up."

"Then what is?"

"Scarlette wants to know how Leroy normally goes about dating. Like, real dating, as opposed to having fun at parties. We've never heard Leroy talking about dating somebody for a stretch of time, and Scarlette is just a little worried about Michelle. He had a bad break-up a while back. You remember how I said I had to leave here one night about six months ago to cheer up a friend?"

"Yes."

"That was the night Scarlette and I picked up a desperate Michelle to bitch about his ex right after the break-up. Michelle is sweet, and he just recently started to even be open to the idea of dating again. And while I love Leroy, if he's more the type for a casual hook-up, that's totally fine, but I don't think that's what Michelle is looking for. So that's why Scarlette asked me about Leroy. You know she's not judging him either..."

"July, baby, don't worry. I know neither of you is judging him. And I understand that you care about Michelle. I've known Leroy for quite some time now, and I know he is a little like Scarlette was before Ty – up for a one-night stand or more if it feels right, but always honest and upfront about it. Depending on what Scarlette thinks is best, she can talk to Leroy first, let him know about Michelle's break-up. I can tell you, Leroy won't want to hurt Michelle, so if he wants only some fun he'll either back off, or he'll at the very least be honest about it with Michelle."

"And Michelle can make the decision himself."

"Exactly."

July nodded. "Yeah, okay, that sounds good, thanks. I'll talk to her later. Now back to your case: we're back in control of most of the media depiction, which leaves me more time to look at social media aspects. Do you want to know more about your likely victim, or should I take a look at the coworkers first?"

"You could check Cory first and see if his accounts are public and with whom he's connected online from not just the Aquarium, but also college and the fishing company he works for, and his college friends, while I'm working on his movements of the last few days and locating all his connected devices."

"Sure, no problem."

When Julia walked back into Luke's office another ninety minutes later, she smiled at him. "I just sent you a spreadsheet with his social media contacts, and their real names for those I could access easily. For the others, you might need a warrant or something. I cross-referenced contacts that are also connected with each other, not only Cory, and I also gave you the last time of contact and highlighted people he had more contact with – as opposed to people he mainly talked to for birthday greetings and stuff. Fair warning, there are a lot of contacts. Seems like he was one of those people who accepts pretty much every friend request. And this is of course only what I could access by looking at his profile, checking his likes and stuff, no DMs or anything, since I couldn't log into his account, obviously."

Luke grinned at her. "I'd say marry me, but we've already agreed on that. That's amazing, thank you, baby."

"You're very welcome. I'm gonna take a short break from this; I have a meeting with Kenneth in a few minutes. It shouldn't take long."

"Don't worry about it. You've already helped me a lot. And I have enough to do; I finally got the surveillance footage from the Aquarium, so I'll go over that, too. Again, thank you," Luke said and drew July in for a quick kiss.

With his program still running in the background, Luke had a look at the spreadsheet and was impressed right away. He picked the few users without an identifiable username and marked them to take a more detailed look at them later, then opened the surveillance videos. He didn't really expect to see the killer throwing body parts into the fish tanks, but you never knew.

Unfortunately, Luke was right about the surveillance footage. It had been tampered with and was showing a loop of nothing but empty hallways. He sent a text to Leroy to question the security guard on duty the night of the murder in detail, and was himself deep into the paperwork for the warrants he needed to get access to the Aquarium's network to find how and when the footage was altered and the user data he had highlighted when his phone rang.

"Detective Preston."

"Hello, Luke. It's Rose. Leroy told me to call you since it's actually your case," the friendly voice of a middle-aged woman greeted him.

"Hi, Rose. Yeah, he's just helping out on this case after all the media play to placate the brass. Do you have any news for me?"

"Would I call you if I didn't? Have some faith in your favorite pathologist."

Luke chuckled, before he apologized. "I'm sorry, I don't know what came over me to expect anything else, oh grand Dr. Miller."

"That's better. Now, the arm you brought us didn't make it easy for us, but I managed to confirm that it was cut off post-mortem, and I also managed to get some prints off the hand."

"Seriously? How did you get the prints?"

"Do you really want to know in detail how I removed the macerated epidermis, carefully treated it to reduce the wrinkles, basically wore it as a glove, and then took the prints?"

"You know what, no, I'm good. I always think we have a shitty job looking at the crime scenes, and then I hear what you have to do so we can get the information we need from our victims. Suddenly a crime scene sounds only half bad."

"That's very sweet of you to say. But it all comes down to perspective. Let me tell you, sitting in a wheelchair comes in handy sometimes. I couldn't get to most crime scenes, and I'm happy I only have to work with the bodies here. I get to know them closely enough like that; I don't think I could stand it to look at their homes, see how they lived, see how they fought for their lives or maybe just tried to get a last look at a picture of a loved one. That would break my heart even more.

"But as I'm sure you have enough to do, as unfortunately so do I because people love to kill each other, I called to let you know I was able to get the prints and compare them to some of the prints Leroy sent me from the apartment of your potential victim. They match – if the print from the apartment indeed belonged to Cory Gilbert, then the arm is his."

"Damn. But thank you, Rose. Can you already tell me something about the leg Leroy brought in today as well?"

"Yes and no. No, because, at this point, I cannot guarantee

you it's from the same person without a DNA test. The test is running, but it takes a while. But yes, from what I have seen, the DNA will probably be a match. Skin tone and hair color match, at least as far as I could see on some patches less affected by stomach acid. And it appears that the leg was cut off with a serrated blade, too. With the leg it was the same as with the arm: the exposure to water and, in this case the digestive enzymes in the shark's stomach, make it hard to determine with a hundred percent accuracy, but – lucky for Cory – it seems that the leg was removed post-mortem as well. Like with the arm, I should be able to confirm if that's the case with certainty soon after having a more detailed look."

"Small mercies. Anything else I should know?"

"Not much more I can tell you at the moment. But as for the limited toxicology we could run with what we have, results have been negative so far."

"This is all good information, thank you."

"Sure. Bring me the rest of the body, and I'll see what else I can find out for you."

"I'll do my best. Bye, Rose."

"Bye, Luke."

Luke sent another text to Leroy with an update on everything and let him know he had created a shared folder for the case with access for them both on their secured police servers. He was sincerely grateful for the fact that Leroy was only a few years older and belonged to the part of the police force who believed not all tech was there to torture people and technological advancement was actually a good thing.

Trusting his boss would keep him updated as well, Luke returned to his paperwork with a sigh, because some things like bureaucracy never changed.

Chapter Nine

Leroy got Luke's text when he stepped back onto the street after his interview with the security guard. He sighed deeply. After talking to the pathetic excuse for a security guard – seriously, who spent *hours* jerking off to a porn magazine he had found by chance simply because, *"You know, it's just fish, what are they supposed to do? Crawl out of their tanks? So I thought, the security office doesn't have cameras, why not have some fun?"* – he now would have to confirm to a mother that her son was truly gone forever. It was the hardest part of the job for him. Seeing the hatred and brutality people could inflict upon each other was bad enough. But even after years on the force, notifications never got any easier.

And while Mrs. Gilbert had already been confronted with the idea that something had happened to her son when they had had to ask her about the tattoo, Leroy knew there was always a thread of hope the people left behind clung to. *Maybe it was a tattoo his colleagues on the fishing boat had also gotten? Maybe the tattoo artist had photographed the design and somebody else had liked it so much he had tattooed it on their wrist, too?* Leroy had seen the hope in her eyes. Now he had to crush that hope, had to tell her that her son would never come visit her again, never finish the degree she was so proud of him for getting.

Knowing they could have been looking for the killer hours earlier if the guard had just taken his job more seriously and had made the rounds instead of just checking the monitors every once in a while didn't help to curb Leroy's frustration in the least.

But he knew dwelling on it would only distract him. He made a conscious effort to focus on the next necessary steps after the notification, and was just opening his car door when his phone rang. He was surprised by the name showing up on his display, but answered the call in a friendly voice. "Lieutenant Porter. Hello, Doctor."

"Ah... hi. I didn't expect you'd save my contact details right away," Michelle replied with surprise in his voice.

"Habit. My phone storage hates me for it, but it helps to keep things organized during investigations and after, and you never know when you might need to reach people again or could use their help in the future. I usually add either a note with a case reference or something characteristic about the person to the contact, so I can recall details quicker after a longer time," Leroy said and leaned against his car, all the while wondering why he was explaining this to basically a stranger.

Oh, there's no wondering, you know exactly why you're babbling, his subconsciousness provided unhelpfully.

And even through the phone he could hear Michelle's grin when he asked, "Do I want to know what you added to my contact?"

Leroy bit his tongue, or he would have told him the truth, that the added information read: *"Kind and smart veterinarian, cute, gorgeous green eyes. Hopefully single."*

Instead, he cleared his throat and went with a more innocuous statement. "Great vet, works for Scarlette."

"Oh. Really?"

"You sound disappointed. I do call you a great vet, you know," Leroy teased.

"I know. I... You know what, this was a stupid idea. I shouldn't have called."

Leroy straightened and got more serious. "No, wait, don't hang up. Why did you call?" On the other end of the line, Michelle was breathing shakily but didn't answer. When he was quiet for almost half a minute, Leroy gently nudged him with his voice. "Doc? Tell me."

"I, uh, I heard Scarlette talk to her friend about you. She was coming down the stairs from the office after a meeting, and I was in our storage area in the basement, and voices carry in that building. Don't get me wrong, I usually don't eavesdrop! And she wouldn't talk about confidential stuff in the hallway!"

Okay, Michelle was just plain adorable, and Leroy couldn't stop the smile spreading across his face. The confident professional he had met before had completely vanished. "It's okay, I can see how you could've overheard her."

"Yeah, okay. So, I heard her, and she said, um, that you, ah..."

"Yes?" Leroy drew out the question, still smiling.

Michelle took a few seconds to analyze Leroy's voice, then huffed. "You're teasing me. You know exactly what she was talking about."

"Humor me, Michelle," Leroy said with a chuckle and decided it should be fine to use the vet's first name seeing the direction this conversation seemed to be going in.

"She seemed to have gotten the impression that you might want to know more about me, and not in a professional sense."

"She has, hasn't she? And what if she has the right impression?"

"Well, I'm pretty sure she'll give you a call at some point. I don't know how well you know her, but she is great. A fair boss, and a good friend of mine, too."

"She's a friend of mine, too. I like her a lot. One of my detectives, a close friend, just got engaged to her best friend."

"Wait, what? Julia got engaged? Good to know, I'll have to get her something. Anyway, it sounded like she might want to talk to you about me. She wants to protect me, and I love her for it. And to be frank, she's got a right to. I went through a pretty bad break-up a while back, and I even had to take off a few days at work because of it."

Leroy's ears pricked up at that statement. "What happened, Michelle? Were you hurt?"

"No. At least not physically. But when I confronted my ex about cheating on me, he stole some of my money before I could let the bank know to block his authorization to my account."

"Tell me you reported him."

"Hell yes, I did. But aside from being emotionally exhausted, I had to talk to the cops, the bank, and a lawyer. You know how it is. So I had to take a few days off, and Scarlette supported me through all of it. So, if she calls you, keep in mind that she means well. I know she can be intense."

"She can be, I agree. But I am glad to hear she stood up for you. Do you also know what she wants to tell me about you?"

"Probably that I'm not somebody for something casual. I never have been, and now even less, and that I haven't dated since my break-up, so if it's just some fun you're looking for, I'm not the right person."

"Okay. First of all, thank you so much for telling me all this and letting me get to know you a little better."

A nervous laugh carried over the line. "I honestly don't know why I told you all that. We don't even know each other."

"No, we don't. But even if I sound crazy, I think – or at least hope – we both felt something when we met earlier."

"I... yeah, you're right," the vet admitted shyly.

"I'm glad to hear that. So, secondly, and that's what I'd tell Scarlette, too: yes, I'd really like to go out with you, Michelle. And while every once in a while I enjoy a simple hook-up, usually I try to at least go on a date with a person before anything happens. If during the date it seems we're both looking for something casual, yeah, I'm okay with that. But if I date somebody and it feels like we have a real connection, then I'll happily see where things go and take my time to get to know the other person. I'm not somebody who's purely looking to get people into bed, and I'm always upfront about things, I can promise you that."

Leroy sighed a little before continuing, "Scarlette is probably worried because lately I haven't felt that connection with anybody, so it was more fun and games now and then at parties. And since she hasn't seen me in a longer relationship so far, it makes sense that she'd want to let me know to be honest with you from the start."

"Yes, that's true. So you really want to go out with me, hmm?" Slowly, the confidence slipped back into Michelle's voice.

Leroy hummed, then chuckled and took a quick screenshot of his phone. "Okay, since I promised honesty from the start, let me tell you I might not have been completely truthful when I told you how I saved your contact. Check your messages, I just sent you the real entry."

The few seconds of silence following Leroy's request were quickly replaced by Michelle coughing and the sound of liquid being spilled and a mumble of, "Shit," before he got back to the lieutenant. "Seriously?" The grin on his face carried in his voice as well.

"Sorry, I didn't know you were on your coffee break. But

yes, seriously. Have you ever looked at yourself in the mirror, Michelle?"

"That's very flattering, thank you, Leroy. And I think you're cute, too, by the way. I have a thing for redheads."

"I'm happy to hear that. And I would love to keep flirting with you over the phone, but unfortunately I have to go. I hate to cut this short, but I have a notification to deliver, and several more interviews on my list."

"Damn, I'm sorry. That can't be easy."

"It isn't, no. Though I'm pretty sure you know how it is to be the bearer of bad news. But let me tell you: talking to you made my day considerably better. Thanks for that."

"I do. And you're very welcome. I better let you go, then. What about dinner tomorrow? We can discuss when and where via text later."

"Sounds perfect, doc."

"Great. Talk to you later."

"Yeah, talk to you later."

Leroy pocketed his phone and managed a smile even with the upcoming notification. It was nice to get a pleasant surprise for once.

He knocked on Amanda Gilbert's apartment door half an hour later, the small euphoric high of scoring a date with a gorgeous guy gone after battling New York traffic.

She opened the door after he identified himself, and once she saw him, a silent tear rolled down her cheek. "It's him, isn't it? You're here to tell me my son is dead, that the tattoo you were asking about before was really his."

"Mrs. Gilbert, I am very sorry to tell you that our investigation has confirmed that your son is dead. He was killed two nights ago."

The older woman shook and bit her lip, but then took a deep breath. "Ah, come with me. I think I need to sit down for this."

She led him into the living room, along a wall of family photos, and sank down heavily in a comfortable-looking armchair, gesturing to Leroy to take the couch.

She visibly fought for composure, then looked at the lieutenant. "Can you tell me what happened? Can I see him?"

"Mrs. Gilbert..."

But she interrupted him. "No, of course not. Sorry, I know you're still investigating, you can't talk about it. I've been living with a cop long enough to know that."

"I'm sorry, but yes, we are still investigating. Was your husband a cop? Is he the one in the picture in the hallway?" In passing, Leroy had seen a few pictures of a younger policeman in a street uniform, and later an older man in dress blues.

"He was indeed, yes that's him. He died six years ago, pancreatic cancer. He was a detective upstate before we moved here after his diagnosis to get better treatment for him. He was a wonderful husband, a great father. Cory got his sense for right and wrong from him."

"I'm very sorry."

"Thank you. And even more so, because I can hear in your voice that you're sincere with your condolences. For a lot of people, it's just a hollow phrase. I know you'll look into Cory's death and do your best to solve it. It wasn't just an accident, was it?"

"No, ma'am, it wasn't."

"And since you haven't told me I can see him, you're still waiting for autopsy results, or... Oh my god, it was his arm at the Aquarium, right? I heard about it on the news, but mostly ignored the story and didn't pay attention. It was reported before you first came here, and I was on the phone when it aired. But the photo you showed me just showed the wrist with the tattoo." Mrs. Gilbert might have been in her sixties, but her mind was still sharp, and it was currently doing its best to keep her focused on details to keep the grief at bay.

She has learned a lot by being married to a cop, has learned to listen to what wasn't being said, Leroy thought and admired her for it, even though he cursed the fact in that moment as well. Telling a mother her son was dead was bad enough, telling her they haven't found most of him yet made it so much worse, because there would be one inevitable question – and he could see it manifesting on her face before she even asked it.

"But... Lieutenant, are you sure he's dead, then? I know you found an arm, and he would have lost a lot of blood, but maybe he's, I don't know, unconscious somewhere? Maybe there was an accident, and he just can't call for help."

He hated to break her heart once again. "Ma'am, I wish I could tell you that's a possibility. But our medical examiner has confirmed that the arm was removed after Cory's death."

"I see. Have you found him? No, forget I asked, you can't tell me. But where are my manners? Can I offer you a coffee?" He could see she was getting closer to her breaking point, her hands clasped, knuckles white. It hurt him, but he had to ask her some questions before she got overwhelmed.

"No, ma'am, I'm fine. Thank you. Can you tell me, when was the last time you spoke with Cory?" He got out his notebook and looked at her with sorrow for a mother's pain in his eyes.

"It must have been three nights ago. Yes. He called to tell me he'd be meeting a writer the next day. Apparently that writer found Cory and his plans interesting and was thinking about writing a book or biography about him. I think the name was Tyler or something like that. I'm sure you'll find a calendar entry in Cory's phone. He is... he was a wonderful son, but god forbid if he had to remember an appointment without writing it down.

"Anyway, we talked about the book for a bit, and then he said he couldn't make it to our dinner the next day and asked to postpone it a few days. You see, we usually meet once a week to have dinner together. He wants to make sure I'm okay, and I love to hear about his days."

She must have realized her use of present tense herself, because she shook her head. "Now I will never hear about his days again."

"Mrs. Gilbert, I know this is hard, but do you know why Cory had to cancel?"

"He only said a colleague asked if he could help move something."

"Any chance he mentioned a name? Or if it was a colleague from the Aquarium or the fishing company?"

"No, I'm sorry. But that was Cory. If he could help somebody, he would. And with me being at home most of the time, it was never a problem to reschedule in the past. Sometimes things come up, you know. A cold, an assignment for his college courses, a friend needing help, things like that. It didn't happen often over the years, but life happens."

"It does, yes. It sounds like Cory was well-liked. Do you know whether there was somebody he didn't get along with?"

Mrs. Gilbert took her time to genuinely consider the question, but then shook her head. "No, nobody comes to mind. Like you said, he was well-liked."

"What about work? Do you know what his boss was thinking about Cory's plans to set up his own fishing company?"

"Oh, he was very supportive recently. Cory told me in the beginning, his boss – that's Jake Russel – was skeptical and thought Cory would never get a company going, would never be a competitor. But with all the new regulations, reduced quotas, and so on, he actually asked Cory to explain his plans in more detail. The last Cory told me was that Jake was either thinking about turning his own company around and getting Cory on board as a partner, or even selling the old company and opening a new one together with Cory. Fishermen don't have it easy, but Cory saw a future that could still keep them in business, and Jake understood that if he wanted to survive in that line of work, he needed to be looking further ahead than just the next catch."

"Okay. And the Aquarium? Has Cory ever mentioned any problems there?"

"No, none at all. Everybody liked him, and he was a great help to the vet there, apparently. With him always working on some paper or another for college, he often closely watched the animals, so he could report it to the vet if he spotted something unusual. He was just such a good man," she finished and began to silently cry.

Leroy put his notebook away and took a deep breath himself. "Mrs. Gilbert, again, I'm so sorry for your loss, and to put you through all this. Can I call somebody for you?"

"No, but thank you. I will let you out, and then knock on my neighbor's door. She's a good friend of mine, I'll sit with her for a while."

She walked to the door with him, then laid a hand on his arm. "Lieutenant, thank you. I know notifications aren't easy for the person who has to deliver them either, and you have been very kind to me."

"It's the least I could do. My team and I will do everything we can to solve this case. It's never enough, I know."

"But it'll hopefully be a bit of closure. So, thank you again."

"Of course. Call me, if you remember anything else, or if you need anything."

"I will. Goodbye, Lieutenant."

"Goodbye, Mrs. Gilbert."

When he was walking down the first flight of stairs, he heard her sobs break free and a door being opened.

Leroy made it down to his car, called Luke to update him and ask him to try to access Cory's calendar asap. He managed to set up an interview with Cory's boss at the Aquarium for that day and another with his boss at the fishing company as a video call the next day since the man was out on sea for two more days.

Then he called Michelle. "Hey."

"Hey, Leroy. What's up?"

"Ah, can we reschedule our date?"

"Sure. I know you're busy. Do you think the day after tomorrow would be better?"

"Actually, do you have time tonight? I have another interview, some paperwork to write up, but after that I could use something positive."

"The notification was that bad, hm?"

"In a way, yes. That woman lost her son, and yet she was so graceful, tried to help with the investigation. Gosh, she even tried to console me. Her husband was a detective, and she knew how hard it can be for the cops to do a notification.

"Please, Michelle, don't think I just want to meet you as a distraction or expect you to cheer me up. But I meant what I said, you brightened my day earlier, and I would really be happy to hold on to something good. You seem like a great guy, and I would love to go out with you."

"Leroy, you don't have to apologize for wanting something positive to end an otherwise shitty day. Work-life-balance is a thing, you know. I have worked at an emergency clinic in the past. Believe me, I know something about not being able to let go of a case. So yes, I would be happy to meet you later. Shall we say eight? Do you think that will work for you?"

Leroy sighed with relief. "Yeah, that sounds great. I know an amazing Greek place, is that okay?"

"That's perfect. Send me the details and we can meet there."

"I will. And I'll call them for a reservation. I'm looking forward to seeing you later."

"So am I."

Chapter Ten

Luke put his phone down after talking to Leroy and was just getting up for another cup of coffee when he heard the first thunder crawl through the canyons formed by New York's buildings. The last few days had been nice, but earlier he had heard a warning of a stormfront rolling in.

He found Julia in the kitchen, seemingly looking for a coffee as well, and hugged her from behind. "Hey, baby."

"Hey." She grabbed a second mug and filled it while talking to him. "How are your warrants coming along? Last time I walked by the office door you were mumbling to yourself about the, and I quote, 'goddamn, fucking paperwork, we want to catch a killer, not steal somebody's stupid bank password.' Was the security footage helpful?"

Luke rested his chin on July's shoulder to give her a kiss on the cheek before letting her go again. "I'm pretty much done with the paperwork for now. But I needed to fill out even more, because the footage was tempered with, so I need to access the Aquarium's system. The location software I had running only told me Cory's laptop was at his apartment the last time it was used. I'll have to pick it up from the lab because I need to get into his calendar. I hope they're done processing it already. His phone hasn't pinged any tower since the night of his murder, and the last one it connected to was close to the East River, so unfortunately, I don't think we'll find it again."

"If it was thrown in the river? Highly unlikely," July agreed with a sigh.

"Yeah. His smartwatch has run out of battery, but I know CSU found it in his locker at the Aquarium, so it's in Evidence, or more likely still at the lab, too," Luke finished with an eye roll.

"That's the worst part, right? Knowing what you want to do but having to wait for other people to finish their part of the job first."

"Exactly. I'll give them a call in a minute, check if I can pick up the laptop and the watch today. What about your work?"

"Well, the NYPD now looks efficient and dedicated to solving every case again, even if it's a stolen horse."

"Ah, what?"

"I figured, even though we managed to twist the whole shark story around and people are actually saying how well the dive was handled now, the city needs to see that cops are friendly to each and every creature. And lucky for your PR department, there was a recent case where a neighbor stole the service horse – well, miniature horse – belonging to his elderly neighbor. The man needs the horse because his eyesight is deteriorating. The guy who stole it lives a few houses down the street, and his daughter desperately wanted a horse, and it was her birthday. You get the idea."

"Yeah."

"Long story short, when some of your colleagues found the horse and brought it back, there were tons of photos being taken, and after contacting the old man, your PR people got him to agree to be shown on the NYPD's website and social accounts.

The picture got about two thousand likes within the first half hour. I rest my case."

Luke stared at his fiancée, blinked a few times, and laughed. "Oh god, they'll never let you go again. They might throw you in a cell just to keep you."

"Hm, luckily I know a cop who can help me break out of jail, then," July giggled and leaned into Luke for a kiss, but parted after a moment.

"I wish we could keep going with that," Luke whispered against Julia's lips.

"Yeah, so do I. But work calls for both of us. Since the NYPD is making good press right now, I was transferred an emergency client."

"Emergency client?"

"Yes. Apparently I'm some miracle worker now, and I'm supposed to save a lawyer's face in public after footage of him in a sex dungeon leaked."

"Not ideal, I admit that, but it's not the 1950s anymore, is it?"

"Oh, you're right. Still not the easiest fix, but possible. The thing is, in the footage he's taking part in a gay orgy, while he builds his law practice on 'good Christian values' if you get my meaning."

"He comes across as a homophobic asshole only representing straight couples?"

"Exactly that. The guy would pay us a fortune to save his reputation, but I really don't want to."

"Well, it's leaked footage, right? Without his consent, obviously."

"Yeah."

"Are the cops already investigating?"

"Yes, as far as I know."

"Give me a few minutes to call the lab, then I'll find out who is handling that case. You should get a call from one of my colleagues soon, telling you that you unfortunately are not allowed to interfere in that client's case, because the open investigation can't have more people getting involved in the situation, or it would become nearly impossible to find out where this originated."

"That's..."

"A total lie? Yes, but you'll have an excuse not to work for that client. Tell the cop calling you that you understand, and that he needs to tell your boss the same, then transfer the call to Keith. I'll make sure somebody on the case who can deal with a foul mood talks to your boss."

"There's no end to how much I love you."

"Same goes."

They had only been talking a few minutes, but outside it had become almost pitch black and raindrops were banging against the windows.

"Okay, I really should call the lab. If I can pick the stuff up, I want to get out and back before the storm gets worse."

"Good point. Good luck, babe," July said and grabbed her coffee on her way out of the kitchen and to her own office.

Good luck, indeed, Luke thought while strolling back to his workspace with a mug in hand. CSU and the lab usually did a great job, but they were notoriously understaffed. Not that Luke wouldn't know all about that, but it was a pain having to wait for them to finish, nonetheless.

He wasn't surprised when the lab told him it would take a few hours longer to process the laptop and watch for his case. But with a little pushing and nagging, he managed to get the young man doing the work to promise to have everything ready for pick-up by tomorrow morning. It wasn't exactly fair to exploit the man's youthful eagerness, so Luke made a note to bring along a coffee when swinging by the lab. But Luke knew the shine would dull soon enough for the guy; long hours, pressure from the cops waiting for their results, no recognition from the public. There were reasons many of the techs working for the city weren't a walking ray of sunshine by the end of their careers.

At least the calls to help July to get out of helping her problem client were more successful, and he could hear her phone ringing a few minutes later.

For now, he checked the case folder and the sheet with the tasks he and Leroy were dividing between each other, made a few notes, and marked the people he'd contact to interview, starting with the woman Cory had dated, Nicole Lane.

She answered the phone on the third ring, and Luke was forced to hold the phone away from his ear for a second before he could adjust the volume. A toddler was wailing loudly, and the girl's mother sounded desperate when she spoke. "Yes, hello?"

"Ms. Lane, hello. This is Detective Preston from the NYPD."

"Yeah, I remember. You called about Cory. Can you give me a minute? I need to set down my daughter. She's sick and has been crying for hours, and I promised her she could watch her favorite movie after dinner."

"Yes, of course." He heard her putting the phone down and talking sweetly to the crying child. She might be needing a break, and her nerves were probably raw, but from what he could make out over the phone, she didn't let it affect the loving care for her kid.

She picked up the phone again a moment later after she had seemingly walked into another room. "Okay, *Toy Story* saves the day again. That movie is almost as old as I am, but she loves it. Anyway, what can I do for you, Detective?"

"Ms. Lane, I'm sorry to do this over the phone, but you said you've been staying with your mother since last week."

"Yes. She had a knee operation and needs help, I'm still in Wisconsin. So, have you found Cory?"

"I'm very sorry, Ms. Lane, but I have to inform you that Cory Gilbert was killed two nights ago."

The information needed a second to sink in, then Luke heard a stifled sob on the other end.

"Oh god. How? Was there an accident?"

"We are still investigating the details, but it appears he was murdered."

"What? Who would want to kill Cory? He was a nice guy, didn't hurt anybody, always tried to help people."

Luke listened closely to every pitch in her voice, every shaky breath she took. He hadn't lied, he didn't like doing this over the phone. It was a terrible way to be told somebody close had died with only the cold plastic of the phone to hang on to for the person receiving the news. And from a cop's perspective, it robbed him of the chance to judge a person's facial expressions and body language.

His gut told him she was truly shaken, but he had to go through the motions and interview her, nonetheless. "Ms. Lane, I have to ask you a few questions, are you up for that now or should we schedule an interview for tomorrow?"

The woman took a deep, shuddering breath. "Ah, no, please let's do this now. My daughter is distracted right now, and my mother is already asleep: her pain meds make her sleepy. But tomorrow she has several doctors' appointments, and I'll have to drive her."

"All right. Let me know, if you need a break, okay?"

"Yes, okay."

"Good."

Usually, he would have asked her for an alibi, but since her mother lived in an area with poor cell service, he had already spoken to Nicole the day after the murder on her mother's landline after his initial call to Nicole's mobile had been almost unintelligible. There was no way she could have made the drive back to her mother's house in time after the murder, and he had double-checked the address to which the landline belonged with the phone company.

"Do you have an idea where Cory might have been or what he might have been doing two nights ago?"

"Sorry, no. Like I said when we talked the first time, we hadn't been talking or texting for a few days, so I didn't know if he had any special plans."

"Do you know anyone who might want to hurt Cory?"

"No, absolutely not. Like I said, he was a nice guy. I mean it. He got along well with his colleagues at the fishing company, the people at the Aquarium, too. Even his fellow students, though most of them are younger than him. So yeah, he wasn't close friends with them, due to the age difference, but they got along fine during class."

"Okay. Last time we spoke you said your relationship with Cory was slowly coming to an end. I know this is personal, but can you tell me why that is, if he was a nice guy from what you say?" He had quickly checked what he could of her financial status already, so he didn't assume she had ordered a hit, but he had to be thorough.

"Um, yeah, sure. Look, I liked him, he liked me. But we were both just too busy to find enough time to really get to know each other. Yes, I can tell you he was well-liked, I can tell you he loved his mother and had regular dinners with her, I can tell you where he worked. But that's pretty much it. We had been seeing each other for a few weeks, but that hardly means we had a date every day. And I'm not blaming him alone for that. I had to cancel several dates myself, because my babysitter called in sick, or like last week, when we had planned to go out, but I was here taking care of my mom. So we hardly knew each other's deepest, darkest secrets. I couldn't even tell you his favorite food if you asked me.

"And the times we did go out, we had fun, yes. But I also came to understand that he probably never would give up fishing. I mean, he studied to make it more sustainable, so he could open his own company. I admire how passionate he's about it, but it also means he'd be out at sea a lot. I have a kid to think about. Even if I would've been able to live with not seeing him for longer periods, or get used to a fisherman's ungodly schedule, my daughter would, at some point, love him, because she loves pretty much everybody, and she's too young to understand why he would be leaving us behind constantly . There's a reason why she hadn't met him."

Nicole let out a sigh. "God, I sound so heartless. Like I begrudged him his ambition, his success so far. I don't. But we just weren't meant to be."

"You don't sound heartless. I understand you. You're a mother, you have to put your daughter first. And as a cop, I can tell you, it's better to see early on that things won't work, than dragging it out until there's bad blood between the parties."

A sad chuckle made Luke hope he had stopped her from spiraling deeper into self-loathing.

"Yeah, you're probably right. You must see the worst results of that more often than anybody should. So, no, there was no bad blood between Cory and me. We just slowly texted less and less, had less dates, and I think either he or I would have probably officially ended things the next time we'd have seen each other."

"Okay. What about your daughter's father? Did he object to you dating, in general, or Cory specifically?"

"No. He isn't in the picture. He knows his daughter exists, he pays the mandatory child support, but that's about it. He's a pilot and lives in Vegas, and that sums up his personality. I love my daughter more than anything, she's my world, but she wasn't exactly planned. I had a one-night stand with her father because he looked hot, and the condom broke. I took the morning after pill, but somehow the little worm still managed to nestle herself inside me. When I realized I was pregnant, I decided to keep the baby. I knew her father's full name, because he bragged about his job and how he was a captain for a big airline using his full title. I googled and found him easy enough. He wasn't happy about the letter he got from my lawyer, but he's always paid on time; the bare minimum, but it's better than nothing. I try to save all of it for Malory's education, so it's tough at the moment, but I want her to be able to do what she wants later, whatever that will be."

"Malory is a lucky girl with you as her mother, Ms. Lane."

"Thank you, Detective. Hmm, now that we're talking about partners... I think Cory mentioned a professor once had given him an unfair grade on a paper a while back. At first, I thought Cory was just complaining about it like any other student, you know? But he told me the rest of the story. It turned out, Cory had talked to the professor's wife for five minutes, because she worked at the college, too and had problems with her car one day. Cory had helped her, and the professor had seen the tail end of the conversation – that is his wife smiling at Cory and thanking him. That professor apparently had serious jealousy issues, and he graded Cory's paper negatively. Another student had had the same issue in the past and told Cory about it. Some other lecturer knew how the professor could be, and Cory asked him to check his paper and possibly grade it again. It was the last paper of the course, and he wouldn't have that professor again, so he didn't see the problem in asking somebody else. It wasn't a paper necessary to pass the course, and the other lecturer made sure that there was a comment in Cory's student file that, after a second opinion, the paper should be graded better. The grade wasn't officially changed, because it wasn't the other man's course, but Cory was content that he could refer to the comment."

"Do you have any names for me?"

"No, I'm sorry."

"No problem. If there's a comment in his student file, we'll find the persons involved easily enough. Do you know how the professor took it?"

"He wasn't happy, but in the end he huffed and puffed a little about students having no respect for authority, but then turned around and just left. At least that's the story how Cory told it to me. But honestly, that's the only time I know about that Cory had trouble with anybody."

"This is still helpful. Thank you very much, Ms. Lane."

"No problem. Things between me and Cory might not have worked out, but I still liked him a lot. He didn't deserve what happened to him. I hope you find who did this."

"We'll do our best. Can I contact you at this number again in case any other questions come up?"

"Yes. My mother will need my assistance for a couple more weeks. I'm lucky enough that I can work from home at both my jobs, so I'll stay here with her for the whole time."

"All right. Thank you for your time, Ms. Lane. Goodbye."

"Of course, Detective. Goodbye."

Luke hung up and wrote up his summary of the interview for his report, then added checking with the college to the to-do list.

He had planned to speak to some more people, but couldn't reach anybody. When he looked outside the window, he knew why. The storm was pushing into the city full force, the rain already mixing with hail, lightning exploding in the sky every couple of minutes. People were on their way home, trying to get there before the city drowned in total chaos. And if they were home already, they were probably trying to find a sheltered parking spot for their cars. He was grateful for his spot in the parking garage that came with the apartment. Julia had never needed it for a car of her own with her office close enough to walk to, but luckily she'd also never started to rent the spot to somebody else.

Knowing he couldn't do a lot more on his active case at the moment, he took the time to check on a few of his cases that had gone cold over time, but had to admit that, for now, he was just as stuck with those as he had been when he had put them aside to help his colleagues with more recent murders.

For now, he walked back to the kitchen to start making dinner while Julia still seemed to be in a meeting. It wouldn't be as good as when July cooked for them, but he had learned a few things in the last year. He set the table, got out some candles, and waited to hear the sounds of her finishing work to plate the food. He had just poured them a glass of wine when she stepped into the kitchen.

"Mmm... That smells amazing, Luke. And wine and candles, very sweet, thank you."

"You're welcome. It's a night for it with the storm and all."

"Yeah, that's true. So I take it the lab hadn't finished with the laptop when you called them?"

They both sat down at the small table in the corner. It was set up in a small alcove under a window, and with the way the kitchen was laid out, it almost felt like a separate cozy dining room just for them, hiding the view of a cluttered countertop or dishes in the sink that hadn't been put in the dishwasher yet. For guests, they'd often rearrange things in the living room to have dinner there. But if it was just the two of them, they more often than not ate here. The previous tenants had painted the nook in warm colors, had even replaced part of the window panes with a colorful stained glass inlay. It had clearly been a violation of their contract, but the old couple had lived for decades in the apartment before moving to an assisted living home, and when Julia had seen the sun shine through the glass when going through the apartment with the landlord, she had asked not to change it back.

"No, but I wasn't really surprised. I'll get everything in the morning. I reached the girlfriend, kinda ex-girlfriend, though, and she told me an interesting story about one of Cory's professors. I'll see what he has to tell me. Did everything work out regarding the hypocritical asshole of a client?"

"Oh, yeah. Keith was supremely pissed when he called me after talking to Detective Ramirez himself, but I just let him rant for a bit with the volume on low. Works like a charm every time he's in a bad mood."

"Cheeky."

"Maybe. But if you ever sat through one of his tantrums, you'd understand that it's just self-preservation," Julia countered with a chuckle.

As a newly engaged couple, they naturally ended up talking about and getting lost in wedding plans. They had been talking for a bit, when July cleared the table and came back with two bowls and a container of a mascarpone cream dessert they still had in the fridge from Bea's visit the day before. Luke quickly forgot what they had been discussing when he saw Julia licking her fingers clean after scooping the cream from its container into the bowls and winking at him. Like any man could resist the love of his life sucking lasciviously on fingers that he knew from experience could drive him crazy.

He didn't give her a chance to sit back in her chair. Instead, he pulled her onto his lap and popped two buttons of her blouse, then dipped his finger in some cream and dragged it across the curve of her breasts with a grin. "Oops."

Her laugh echoed through the kitchen and made Luke feel like a king. He knew July had dealt with enough idiots in the past who had reduced her to nothing more than a blond bombshell they wanted to get into bed. To know he was the one whom she trusted, who made her laugh, who had a connection with her nobody else had before, and whom she willingly gave herself to again and again, was humbling and exhilarating all at once.

July nuzzled his neck, then playfully bit his earlobe. "So we won't be eating the mascarpone cream out of the bowls like normal people?"

"Nope," Luke said and after quickly blowing out the candles stood up with her in his arms. July managed to grab a bowl and giggled all the way to the bedroom.

Spreading dessert on each other and nibbling and licking it off led to both of them panting in no time. And when one of July's moans became a needy groan, Luke realized one of his fingers had accidentally slipped further down between her butt cheeks while he filled her throbbing heat with another.

Interesting, he thought and kept going for a little longer.

July groaned again with Luke's one finger curling inside her and the other still gently stroking and ever so lightly pushing. It was a strange, new sensation, and Julia felt exposed in a way she never had before. But the sparks slowly crawling up her spine stopped her from guiding Luke's hand away.

When she couldn't wait any longer, she rolled him over and rode him until they were both breathless, until they both fell into the void of their combined climax.

A few minutes later, they were cuddling in comfortable silence, with Luke actually dozing off for a moment in the warm, cozy glow of the fairy lights they had switched on when they had fallen onto the bed earlier.

Julia took that time to go over her reactions during their lovemaking earlier. A part of her felt ashamed about how greedy she had sounded. But at that moment, it had felt like nothing she had experienced before. Her nervous system had been bombarded with this different stimulation. And although she wanted to deny it, she knew some of her shame also came from the picture of what was "normal" and "accepted" by society at large.

But she knew someone who couldn't care less about society's opinion on what was allowed to bring pleasure and who had always helped her to trust more in herself and her own feelings.

Smiling, July grabbed her tablet from her nightstand and sent a quick text to Scarlette.

Julia:
Hey! Are you still in the city?

Scarlette:
Yeah. Josh called us shortly before we wanted to leave. Seems like part of the road into Hope is flooded. We'll be staying here for a bit.

Julia:
Would you be available for girl talk and possibly some more unusual (for me) shopping tomorrow or the day after?

Scarlette:
Of course, sweetie. I'm just not sure about the shopping tomorrow with the blackout.

Julia:
Blackout?

Scarlette:
Don't tell me you haven't noticed. You guys must have been pretty busy. I mean, so were we, but when the bedroom was as dark as night all of a sudden, it was kind of obvious.

Julia looked around in confusion and realized that the rest of the apartment was completely dark, without even lights from the outside shining in.

Julia:
Oh... Yeah, looks like we're hit, too.

Scarlette:
All of the city is. The storm has hit a lot harder than expected. How did you not know?

Julia:
We were busy, like you said. And we had the fairy lights on, the rechargeable ones. My tablet is charged, there's still cell service to text with you. Half my brain is still melted, don't expect me to come to any reasonable conclusions!

July knew Scarlette would burst into laughter over the last sentence, and she grinned herself when she read the reply.

Scarlette:

Well, that's good to know. Seems like I don't have to sit Luke down for an anatomy lesson before the big wedding night, if he's doing such a good job ;)
Anyway, girl talk and shopping sound awesome, but maybe we should schedule that for when the power comes back online.

Julia:

Oh, yes, he's doing a very good job, don't worry ;)
But yes, let's wait for the power to be restored. Which also means we should stop texting for now. But I'm glad to know you're okay. Talk asap! Love you!

Scarlette:

Yep, would be better.
I'm happy you're safe, too. Talk soon! Love you, too!

With that being settled, July slowly woke up Luke to let him know about the blackout.

Hearing about it, Luke was glad he had reflexively checked and saved every open document again before heading to the kitchen earlier. He had left his computer running in case an important email came in, but visiting his grandparents in rural Pennsylvania as a kid had also ingrained in him how easy it was to lose power during a storm. Of course he knew chances for that to happen were less likely here in NYC, and he was mercilessly teased for it by some colleagues and friends, but on a day like this he knew exactly why he didn't care about their light-hearted digs.

Chapter Eleven

The precinct was even more chaotic than usual, and the mood seemed as charged as the air outside. Leroy savored the fact that he could leave after his interview with Cory's boss, his duties as supervisor of his squad done before the man had come in. The brass was mostly gone or was busy preparing for any eventuality with the storm taking a hold of the city, so nobody would be asking for an update tonight.

The interview itself hadn't been helpful other than confirming that Cory had been well-liked by everybody, diligent when it came to his job, and when he had a few minutes' time during a break, he'd often been sitting in the café to work on his college papers. Other than that, it didn't yield new information.

Leroy walked Cory's boss out of the precinct, and knowing his detective was very much capable of running an investigation, he decided he could check on Luke's progress in the morning – had he found anything groundbreaking, he would've called. He got into his car to fight the crazy streets, so he'd be at the restaurant in time for his date. The thought of seeing Michelle made him smile despite the long, somber day.

He'd hardly been waiting five minutes, when a waiter appeared to show Michelle to the table. Leroy got to his feet and hoped he wasn't overstepping as he slightly leaned forward to give the other man a hug. He was delighted that Michelle appeared to have the same thought, and they casually embraced each other.

"Hi," Leroy greeted his date.

"Hey."

They both settled in their seats, and Leroy couldn't stop the smile spreading on his face. Michelle was beautiful; the candle light made his skin shimmer even more golden and his eyes seemed impossibly rich and luminant. He had changed out of what he had worn earlier and now was clad in a dark purple button-down shirt and black jeans.

"You look amazing."

"Thank you. I got lucky and had enough time for a quick stop at home before coming here."

"That's lucky indeed. I solemnly swear to do better next time, too. Today I was glad to even make it here by car."

Michelle chuckled and let his gaze wander over Leroy. "I knew why I took the subway. And don't worry, I like you fine just like that. I just really hope it's still raining later and that you haven't brought an umbrella," the vet teased with a look at his date's white t-shirt.

Leroy felt a blush spread on his cheeks. He glanced out the window. "Yeah, with this storm, you might get lucky. So, did you find the place okay?"

"Yeah, I did. Your directions helped, because the entrance is indeed a little hidden, but it wasn't a problem."

They were interrupted by a waiter asking for their drink orders, and both decided to start with a coke. It was a weekday and Michelle had an early appointment coming in for a second opinion and Leroy was driving, and knowing that the owner would probably spot them sometime during the evening and recognize Leroy, they'd most likely get at least one ouzo on the house.

After their drinks had been brought over and they had ordered their food, Leroy picked up his glass for a small toast. "To a relaxed, cheerful evening. Cheers."

"Cheers," Michelle replied and clinked his glass. He studied Leroy for a second, then sighed. "Okay, I hate myself for this, and I know you probably can't talk about it, but I have to ask before we start with happier topics. Was the whole surgery this morning useful? Other than saving a shark's life, of course. Has the leg helped at all in the case?"

Leroy giggled, and after a moment's hesitation slid his hand across the table to run his fingers along Michelle's knuckles. "It's natural to be curious, believe me. It's probably part of what makes you a great veterinarian – you want to find out what's causing a problem. And you had the shark's life in your hands, I get why you want to know if it was worth it. So, yeah, you're right, I can't talk about the case in detail. But it helped that we could get the leg to our ME. She could confirm a few facts and also partially rule out some things. We still have a lot to do, talk to a lot of people, wait for more results, and of course hopefully find the rest of the victim. But things are moving forward."

"Okay, that sounds good. Thanks."

"Sure. Have you heard anything about the shark?"

"Yeah, I got an email from the Aquarium's vet. He says the shark is doing fine. They'll keep it in a separate tank for a little while to make sure the wound doesn't get infected and the shark is fit enough to join the group again without being singled out as weak, but otherwise, it's all good."

"I'm happy to hear that. Now, tell me about you, Michelle."

"What do you want to know?"

Leroy studied Michelle for a second, tilting his head a little.

"Where are you from? Your accent isn't born and bred New York."

"It isn't, hm?"

"No, there's music to it, a softness you don't find in people who have grown up here."

Surprising himself, Michelle turned his hand over, linking his finger's with Leroy's. "You have good ears. Most people don't hear it anymore. But you're right. I was born in New Orleans, my mom and my stepdad still live there. I moved to New York to study and got a job here after university, so I stayed, and I fell in love with the city more and more the longer I stayed."

"I like it, and I'm glad you stayed here so I had a chance to meet you. What are your parents doing in New Orleans? And what about your biological father, if it's okay to ask?"

"Yeah, it is, though it might spoil the mood a little. Ah, my dad was a firefighter, he died in an accident during a rescue when I was four."

"I'm very sorry, Michelle."

"Thank you. I have a few memories of him, and they are happy. I think that's the best I can ask for under the circumstances. It was a lot harder for my mother. They had to work hard for their relationship in the first place, and she loved him a lot, still does in a way. When he died, she was left, not just with a child and raising it on her own, but also part of my dad's family and hers trying to tell her how to raise me."

"How do you mean?" Leroy asked.

"Are you sure you're up for this? It's not the easiest topic."

"I can deal with that. I just want to get to know you."

Michelle nodded and took a sip of his soda before he continued. "Okay then. Most of this is second- or rather thirdhand knowledge. My dad told my mom, and when I was old enough, she told me. But you'll get a picture.

"So, my dad was born in 1964, in what today is the United

Arab Emirates. He grew up in a family lucky enough to have resources to travel and see the world. They were a traditional Islamic family, yes, but also curious and more open-minded than many others in their community. And when my dad got older, I think he was just as curious, and maybe less afraid than others because he had seen many different cultures by then. He believed that things could change everywhere, that people could be more accepting. In a way, he was right, when it came to my grandparents. My grandmother caught him kissing a boy in a hidden corner of their garden when he was seventeen."

"Oh, wow."

"Yeah. And my dad, he was very lucky. My grandparents talked to him, and he told them he liked girls, but also boys. There was hardly any proper vocabulary back then, especially not in the UAE, but they accepted what he told them, because they loved their son so deeply that they couldn't abandon him or punish him. But homosexuality is still officially illegal in the UAE today, so you can imagine how it was back in 1980."

"More than dangerous, I would think."

"Yes. Even today, it's a difficult situation. You could still have people being arrested or prosecuted under certain circumstances, though there haven't been official arrests for some years. But back then? My grandparents were so afraid for their son. They knew it was far from perfect in other parts of the world, as well, but they decided to send their son to the US. Not to banish him, but to protect him. They had friends there from their travels, and they had heard bits and pieces about people fighting for gay people in the US over the years. It wasn't a full picture, but they hoped my dad would be safer there, nonetheless."

Leroy nodded and squeezed Michelle's hand for a second. "They sound like good people who had to make a difficult decision."

"Yeah. Anyway, that's how my dad ended up in the USA. I

don't know if he really lived any freer here when it came to dating men, though."

"You mean because of the AIDS epidemic in the 1980s?"

"Yeah. My grandparents wanted to give him the chance to love whomever he wanted. I hope he could. I know he also trained as a paramedic, so I'm sure he was at least safe, or I don't think I would exist. He wouldn't have put my mom in danger."

"I'm sure you're right. How did they meet?"

A waiter came up to their table, looking at their joined hands with an easy smile. "Sorry to interrupt, but your dinner is here."

Both only then realizing how long they had been holding hands, they let go of each other with shy grins.

After the first bite, Michelle hummed in appreciation. "Oh, wow, you weren't exaggerating, this really is delicious."

"I know. I met the owner during a case, actually."

"Ah, the famous phone entries."

"I told you they come in handy," Leroy said with a wink.

"You did. Okay, to answer your question, my dad was on vacation in New Orleans in 1988 for the Jazz Festival. He roamed the streets and stumbled upon a small stage. On it was a small band and this almost tiny Black woman, dressed strangely and wearing weird make-up. And then she started to sing, and my dad was a goner.

"That's actually one of the few memories of him I have: me sitting on his lap in our living room, my mom playing a record and starting to sing, and my dad ruffling my hair and telling me, 'Your mother has one of the most amazing voices I've ever heard.' And then he put me down and started dancing with her.

"Anyway, when he first saw her on stage, he waited almost all afternoon until she finished and asked her out. They instantly clicked, he moved to New Orleans for her, changed jobs from paramedic to becoming a firefighter because they were more in demand, and I came along two years later."

"That sounds wonderful. Does your mother still sing?"

"Oh, yes. Don't freak, but my mom, she's... very unique. When my dad met her, she was a singer, all right. She was the singer of a voodoo jazz band. She made the best of the tourists coming through the city and had a small voodoo shop by day, selling trinkets and some ingredients for real practitioners. She has never been a practitioner herself – and lots of people gave her trouble for it, saying she had no right to run such a shop – but she didn't care. Honestly, she was a single, Black woman in the 1980s, trying to make a living."

"She apparently did a great job. Running a business is no small thing, even a little shop."

"You're right. But she's always loved to sing, so she joined a voodoo jazz band in '85, singing in the evening or at festivals. It helped to bring in some extra money, too, and create some extra interest in her shop. She still has the shop, she still sings. And when she married my stepdad six years after my dad died, he had just bought a restaurant. They kind of incorporated the shop, made it this whole tourist voodoo experience. People still hate them for it, but they love it."

"Oh, who cares? As long as they are happy with what they do, and they don't hurt anybody, let them run their business. How many people sell crosses or bible verse bumper stickers at gas stations and never set foot in a church, either?" Leroy said with a chuckle.

"Good point. But yeah, to come back to your original question, maybe you can understand why my mom was getting all kinds of input on how to raise me. My paternal grandparents would've loved to see me being raised as a Muslim, even though my dad hadn't been a practicing Muslim, either, since he had arrived in the US. And my mother's parents were Christian to the bone and had already tried to stop her from marrying my dad, saying she needed to marry a Christian boy. The voodoo thing was the cherry on top. But my parents had always agreed they wouldn't force any kind of religion on me. I grew up learning about all kinds of things, my mom talked very openly about everything with me. In the end, I have to say, I'm still an atheist," Michelle admitted with a little laugh.

"They're a lot worse things than being atheist. I never was a believer either."

They both ate for a moment in comfortable silence, sneaking glances at each other, before Michelle studied Leroy.

"So, those weren't the usual first date questions, I have to say."

"I know. But firstly – and that's the cop in me – I have learned that you get to know people a lot better by listening to how they talk about not just themselves but about people close to them. Most people are sincerer when the main focus isn't to present themselves in the best way.

"And secondly, I was curious myself. Please, don't get me wrong or be offended, I know it's a difficult topic for many people to talk about, but you are amazingly beautiful, Michelle, and I was dying to know what ethnicities mixed to create such an intriguing man."

"Don't worry, I'm not that easily offended. I mean, we're here to get to know each other, aren't we? Family background is a part of that. And honestly, I know I'm somewhat unusual looking. Many people have no clue where to put me. Funny story, Scarlette actually guessed it when I interviewed for her initially. She asked if I was Muslim and if I was practicing, and I thought she'd suddenly show some prejudice or find a bogus reason not to hire me."

"And what was it really? I haven't known her to be prejudiced, even though I met her only a little more than a year ago."

"Oh, she was just asking so she would know if she should rent one of the other offices on the floor or rearrange the office she already has so she could offer me a prayer room and give me a quiet place to pray even in the lively office if I wanted to, because she really wanted me on the team and to provide me with everything I might need to feel comfortable."

Leroy laughed. "Yeah, that sounds like her."

"Yep. So, now that I have told you my family story, what's yours? You do sound like New York has been in your blood forever."

"In mine, it has. My family immigrated decades ago, I honestly gave up trying to pinpoint one year, because they came over here in waves. So yes, there are Irish roots, I can't deny them. But – and don't let my family hear this or they'll have a collective heart attack – I consider myself very much a US citizen, a New Yorker."

Michelle laughed, then mimed zipping his lips. "I won't say anything, I promise. Do you have many relatives here in the city?"

"Tons, yes. My parents moved into the suburbs a couple of years ago when they retired, because the city was becoming too stressful for them. But there are still a couple of siblings and lots of cousins around, several aunts and uncles, too. My grandmother refuses to move, so I talked with the family. I live in the apartment next to hers, I take care of her as much as my job allows, but we all chip in to pay for a live-in caretaker, too, because she has diabetes and Alzheimer's so we can't be sure she always remembers to check her blood sugar. We all get an alarm on our phones if her levels are out of control, but we all work, so we need to know there's somebody looking after her."

"That's very sweet. How bad is her Alzheimer's, if you don't mind me asking? I know it can be hard on the family."

"It can, yeah. So far, she still has more good days than bad.

She recognizes me most of the time, she even remembers some birthdays. I've learned she reacts positively to smells and music, so I try to bring her flowers like roses or lavender often, and I play her favorite records for her."

Michelle swallowed hard to fight the lump in his throat. He had to look down to hide the shine of tears in his eyes. Leroy was unbelievably kind and sweet – the days when his grandmother didn't recognize him must be like torture to him. When he found his composure, he looked up and smiled at Leroy. "You seem like a wonderful man. I hope she keeps having many more good days."

"Thank you, Michelle."

"Of course. So, can I ask, large, catholic family, how did they take it when you told them you're into guys?"

"Hm, I'd say most of them took it pretty well. It helps that I also date women, and I think most of them think there's still time for me to find a good woman and settle down, that guys are just some fun for me, not people I'd consider a long-term future with. But they are accepting. The few people who aren't, I just ignore."

"Isn't that painful, or at the very least awkward, at family meetings?"

"Nah, not really. When there's about forty people around, it's easy enough to ignore a few of them. And nobody dares to say anything homophobic, because though we might not kick them out of the family for their opinion in general, we would for being hateful about it. We just don't talk, sit at other ends of the table. It works. It's one of my older uncles, and one older aunt. It's not even that they are deeply disgusted, they just don't understand, and the way their mind works, if they don't under-stand, it must be wrong. But I don't get any bible lectures or anything."

"I'm glad to hear that. When did you tell them?"

"When I was seventeen and had my first crush on a guy. What about you?"

While they were talking, their waiter cleared their table, brought their main course and another coke for both of them.

"I was fifteen when I told my mom and stepdad I'm gay. They reacted pretty much like I expected. They looked at me, looked at each other, shrugged, and my mom asked, 'So, what? We kind of figured by the way you look at the neighbor, sweetie. What does it matter whom you love as long as you're happy? Be careful whom you date, which I would tell you even if you were dating girls. Be responsible and safe, which should go without saying, anyway. I know you will be.' And my stepdad added with a grin, 'I had planned to get you condoms soon. Guess I'll throw in some lube, too.' And that sums up my parents' reaction. There was never a need for them to affirm they still loved me, or how happy they were that I trusted them. We've always talked about everything openly. I was very lucky, I never had a moment of fear before telling them. I mean, my mom had married a bisexual guy from the Middle East and had me with him, I always knew she was open-minded. And I knew my stepdad was okay with it, too. My mom had always been honest with him about my dad, so we knew how he had reacted when she had told him about Dad being bi."

"I'm happy for you. What about your grandparents?"

"My mother's parents both died before I came out; my grandfather had a stroke, and after that my grandmother just gave up, I think. She became fragile, aged ten years in twelve months, and in the end stopped eating and refused care. It wasn't pretty."

"I'm sorry. I didn't want to drag up bad memories."

"They are part of life, Leroy, part of who we are. And it was a long time ago. Truth be told, I never felt a hundred percent accepted by them even as a kid. I mean, they never wanted my mother being with my dad in the first place."

"I can't stand people blaming kids for their parents' choices."

"I know, me neither. But my paternal grandparents are great. Still not entirely happy that I haven't become a Muslim, but otherwise they love me for who I am. We're all still in contact with them, and they actually plan to visit the US next year. They haven't been here in a while and aren't sure how long they'll still be fit enough to travel."

"I hope they'll make it a few more times. You seem to love them a lot, like the rest of your family."

"I really do."

After finishing the last bit of his dinner, Michelle smiled at Leroy again. "You know what?"

"What?"

"I think you're right, talking about family like this instead of typical stuff like movies really is a better way to get to know somebody."

"So, what have you learned about me?"

Their plates were cleared, and Michelle comfortably folded his forearm on the table, leaning a little forward. "I learned that Leroy Porter is a kind man, an exceptional listener with an open mind, a loving person who cares genuinely about the people close to him, somebody not blind to the problems of the world and who knows to appreciate the luck he has when it comes to his family's acceptance, who carefully chooses his battles. And he looks even more gorgeous than usual with candlelight shimmering on his face."

Leroy's jaw dropped. "Wow, thank you. I don't know what to say."

When their dessert was brought together with the expected

ouzo, Michelle settled back, his smile still in place. "Why don't you tell me what you've learned about me?"

"I can do that, yes. When I first met you, I thought you were one of the most alluring men I've ever met. And now, I've come to understand Michelle Jenkins is one of the most compassionate people I know, too. He's sweet and thoughtful, he loves deeply, and has an interesting history that has taught him not to be blind to the problems in the world, either, but also to know he got lucky with his family. He is smart and caring and has amazingly skilled hands." Leroy took a deep breath before continuing. "And I really hope he's as gone for me as I already am for him," he managed with a shudder of hope and insecurity.

Michelle took Leroy's hands, beamed at him. "Oh, he is, he's so gone for you. I always thought my mom was crazy when she told me how things with dad just felt perfect, like a puzzle piece falling into place, right from the beginning. But I'm starting to understand what she meant."

"Yeah. I thought the same when I heard Scarlette's and Ty's story for the first time. But sitting here, talking to you, yeah, I get it now."

They kept talking while enjoying their dessert, this time about Michelle's studies, his first job at an emergency clinic, about Leroy studying criminology before getting into the academy and the seminars he sometimes held for the NYPD, about hobbies and other things.

By the time they had finished their meal and had shared one more ouzo, they were holding hands again with Leroy running his thumb across the pulse point in Michelle's wrist.

When Leroy finally snatched up the bill at the end of the evening, Michelle frowned. "Don't even start. You can pay next time, doc."

"Oh, next time, hm?"

"Yeah. You didn't sound like this was the worst date you've ever been on."

"No, it definitely wasn't. Yeah, next time sounds good."

They grabbed their jackets, and Michelle found his umbrella in the stand next to the door. Grinning, he looked Leroy up and down. "I still think I should let you get soaked. Not fair, but you'd look really good."

"And here I was, thinking about asking to give you a ride."

"That's very sweet of you, but the subway station is close, so don't..." Michelle was interrupted by his phone pinging. "I'm sorry. I have it DnD, only important notifications get through. And, yep, that's one of them. They just shut down half of the subway system due to excessive flooding," he sighed after checking his phone.

"Then let me drive you home. It's no problem, I promise."

"Yeah, okay, that would be great. Thank you."

"No problem."

They shared the umbrella, and usually Leroy would have enjoyed the closeness, but the wind pushed enough cold rain sideways to drench them so they just ran to his car as quickly as they could. It was parked in a way that the surrounding buildings sheltered them from the worst of the rain and wind, and once they were next to it, Leroy would've reached for the door handle to open the passenger side's door.

But Michelle turned around with twinkling eyes, still holding the umbrella over their heads. "So, there's this thing everybody always thinks is super romantic."

"And what's that?"

The vet lowered the umbrella with a laugh, drew his date closer with his other hand and pressed his lips against Leroy's. He let him go with a chuckle after a moment. "Kissing in the rain."

Leroy blinked a few raindrops from his lashes, then grinned.

"Hm, yeah. I think that was too short to form an opinion, though," he said and leaned in for another taste.

Both of them sighed into the kiss, and Leroy found Michelle's tongue with his. It didn't take long until they both got greedier, and Michelle dropped his umbrella to let his hands roam across Leroy's soaked shirt with a moan. When they parted this time, Michelle's eyes traveled down and back up. "Oh yeah, you look seriously hot like this."

Leroy threw his head back and laughed. "Thanks. You look very tempting all wet like this, too. And yes, kissing in the rain gets my approval. But I feel like a spring or summer rain would've been a little nicer."

"Keep that in mind for next year, then," Michelle said without thinking. Then he realized the implication. "I didn't mean... I don't expect us to jump right into..."

But Leroy just leaned down, picked up the umbrella and, holding it above their heads again, lowered his lips to Michelle's mouth once more. "I really hope we'll still be together then, yes. Please expect us to jump into a relationship, Michelle, because I really like the thought of being your boyfriend. And I will definitely keep it in mind. But now let me get you home so you can get out of those wet clothes, or Scarlette will kick my ass when you have to call in sick tomorrow."

A little overwhelmed, it took Michelle a second to process the words, but then he ran his arms around Leroy's waist and gave him a happy kiss. "Okay. And I really like that thought, too."

Leroy gently stepped out of Michelle's hold with a smile and opened the door for him, before kidnapping the umbrella to get to his side with a little protection from the rain.

Chapter Twelve

Barely five minutes into the drive, everything around them suddenly went dark.

"Ah, fuck this," Leroy grumbled.

Michelle thumped his head against the headrest in a form of agreement. "Shit."

"Let's keep going, maybe the power will come back. Can you do me a favor and check if you still have a cell signal, though? The generators usually start up quickly."

"Yeah, give me a second." Michelle fished his phone out of his pocket and, after a quick look, nodded. "Yeah, the signal is still good."

"That's something."

With traffic becoming increasingly erratic with every minute they were on the streets, Michelle let Leroy drive in silence. But when the power wasn't back after another ten minutes, Michelle ran his hands through his hair. "Hey, Leroy, you know what, you better drop me off at Scarlette's office. We will never make it to my place. The last time there was a blackout in my area, when some idiot damaged a main power line while doing construction work, traffic was so bogged down it took four hours to sort everything out. We lost power for about twenty minutes, in the middle of the day. This is going to be so much worse."

"Okay, I can see the chaos. But I can't just drop you at the office. You need a hot shower and new clothes. Even if you have scrubs or something there, there isn't a shower, is there?"

"No, that's true. But, well, as long as you don't have to get to the precinct because of this, you could always take me to your place."

Leroy glanced over and drew up his eyebrows with a little smirk.

"Oh, come on, we don't necessarily have to have sex, but even if we do, I highly doubt either of us would regret it. I mean, we both said we want to be together, right?"

"We did. I just remember our call from earlier and all the things Scarlette might tell me and why I should be careful with you."

"Yes. But this isn't casual, we both know that. And wanting a relationship, wanting something serious, monogamous, doesn't have to mean that I need to follow some made-up rules for how many dates I should go on before sleeping with a guy."

"I can appreciate the way you think," Leroy replied and picked up Michelle's hand for a quick kiss. "And regarding your suggestion, I'd be happy to take you to my place. The precinct has emergency plans, and for once, I'm not part of them."

"Perfect, that's settled, then. But, uh, just to be clear, you're okay with being exclusive from the start, too, right?"

"Yeah, of course. When it's more than just some fun I don't need more than one person. So, should we have the condom talk now while we're stuck in traffic and not ruining a moment anytime later?"

"Sure. Okay, after my ex was gone, I got tested several times, just to be sure. With a cheating idiot, you just never know.

Everything came back negative, and I haven't been with anybody else since. So as long as your tests are negative, too, I'd be okay with skipping the condoms. And here are my last test results," Michelle finished and opened the document on his phone to show it to Leroy.

"Awesome, thanks. I just had my annual physical for my job early last month, and I always have them run an extended panel and cover the extra cost myself. One less doctor's appointment to schedule. All negative, too, and I haven't been with anybody since, either." With the car in front of him coming to a standstill yet again, Leroy reached for his phone and showed Michelle his documentation. "So I'd also be okay without condoms, whenever we decide to have sex."

"Perfect," Michelle beamed and leaned over to give Leroy a quick kiss on the cheek.

The distance to Leroy's place was relatively short from where they were, but New York never disappointed and made it as slow and agonizing as possible. Leroy counted four smaller accidents with drivers yelling at each other, two larger ones seemingly without any injuries but with some of his colleagues at the scene, and one more with EMTs already looking after a patient and a cop talking to somebody else. Everybody stood in ankle-deep water, and Leroy thought it was a wonder nobody was throwing punches, yet.

But he forgot about it as soon as he drove into the garage across the street from his apartment building and climbed out of the car. He quickly checked his phone, saw that a text from the caretaker had come through telling him everything was all right and his grandmother was fast asleep. After a quick thank you reply, he pushed his phone back into his pocket.

"Almost there. Come," he said and held his hand out to Michelle, who took it without hesitation.

Huddled together under the umbrella again, they were just taking the steps up to the red brick building housing Leroy's apartment when they heard two gunshots and answering painful cries echoing from the corner store close by.

"Fuck!" Leroy drew his gun and immediately ran towards the noise, yelling at Michelle to call 911 and give them the address and his name and a request for backup and an ambulance.

Michelle did as asked, then followed Leroy at what he hoped was a safe distance.

Near the store, he first heard Leroy identify himself, then a loud "Shit," when lightning illuminated the street and the inside of the store again.

"Doc, you there? Can you come in here and help me?"

Michelle switched on his phone's flashlight and entered the store, where he found an older man clearly in shock and bleeding slightly from a graze on his arm and Leroy hunched over a man around their age with a larger wound in his leg and lashing out in pain. Dropping to his knees, Michelle pulled some latex gloves out of his pocket, then looked at his boyfriend. "Hold him still, I'll look at the wound."

"Okay."

They switched places, and once Michelle managed to have a closer look, he took a relieved breath. "We need to put pressure on it, but from what I can see there's no damage to the femoral artery. What happened?"

"Over there is Mr. Giraldi, Sr. This here is his son. Taking a wild guess, they both wanted to check on the family store, but didn't know it. They live in different apartment buildings around here. And then they probably both thought the other one was there to loot the store."

"Yes," Giraldi, Jr. confirmed through gritted teeth, while his father just rocked in place, mumbling, "I'm sorry, I didn't see," over and over.

The EMTs miraculously arrived a few minutes later despite the traffic chaos, and Leroy was still talking with them near the ambulance when a patrol car pulled to a stop next to the curb. One of the cops almost flew out of it despite the large beer belly he was proudly presenting, drew his weapon, and yelled at Michelle, who was standing underneath a small awning at the shop's entrance, "On the ground, asshole!"

Before Michelle could even react, Leroy was in front of him. "What the fuck, Hawkins? Put the goddamn gun down!"

"The guy is standing in front of the shop where two people have been shot, with blood on his hands!"

"You moronic, racist fuck! He helped me stabilize one of the men. The men who accidentally shot *each other*! For god's sake, he's wearing surgical gloves, not holding a weapon, so put yours down."

"Maybe he wore them to prevent leaving prints. How would you know, Porter?!"

"Seriously? I tell you how I know, that's my boyfriend, who ran down the street with me to help. For the last time, put the gun down. That's an order from the senior officer on the scene."

Hawkins reluctantly put his gun away, tried to whisper to himself, but his voice carried when he mumbled, "Fucking gays, of course they stick together."

Strangely, that calmed Leroy down, and he actually smiled while addressing the man again. "Thank you, Officer Hawkins. That will earn you a nice record of discrimination, racial profiling, and insubordination in your file. That means you can forget about your detective's exam, and maybe you'll even get a suspension."

Apparently losing any common sense he might've had left,

the officer tried to take a swing at Leroy, but only grazed his shoulder instead of hitting his face.

"And that's assault on a police officer. You very likely just got yourself fired, congrats. That's one less bigoted prick in uniform. Very nice," Leroy told him calmly, hardly breaking a sweat while turning and grabbing Hawkins' arm, twisting it behind his back and putting the man's own cuffs on his wrists. When he had him secured, he walked him to the cruiser and shoved him into the back seat.

"You can't prove any of this in the end, you bastard," Hawkins spat.

"Oh, don't you worry about that. I can, and I will."

Through it all, a wide-eyed young cop watched with his mouth hanging open, seemingly unable to process what was happening in front of him. Leroy walked around the car, studied the other cop. "You are his rookie, right?"

"Yes, sir."

"Okay. Look, I'll call in another patrol. This puts you in a position you shouldn't be in with your training officer in cuffs. But if you can take a lesson from this, let it be this: we're cops to protect people, to serve the law, we're not the law, and we're most certainly not above it. And wearing a uniform doesn't make you untouchable or less of a dick. He's been a pain in everybody's ass for a long time, but nobody could make anything stick. That changes now. I'm sorry he was assigned to you as a training officer. I'll look to it that you'll get somebody worthy of the badge after this."

"Thank you, sir."

After handling everything, Leroy turned to a stunned Michelle. "Are you okay? I'm so sorry I didn't check before. You can and should file a civil complaint, too. He needs to be fired. Did he hurt you physically somehow?" When he didn't say anything, Leroy gently took his hand. "Michelle? Are you all right?"

"Huh? Yes, yes, I am. Don't worry. He's neither the first racist nor homophobic idiot I've dealt with. It sucks, but I know it takes time for things to truly change. But, and I know this is the adrenaline talking, it was incredibly hot how you handled all this."

Leroy chuckled, then leaned his forehead against Michelle's. "Only you. Are you sure you're all right?"

"Yes, I promise. Not exactly ecstatic, but that's definitely not your fault."

"Okay. Then let's get home. I can't write a statement at the moment, anyway."

They walked down the street hand in hand, the rain still pouring down on them. Given that they were completely and utterly soaked by now, they didn't even hurry.

"How are you going to prove it? You told Hawkins you could," Michelle said.

"And I can. I had used my phone to record the Giraldis' first statements when he drew his weapon. I never switched off the recording, so all his bullshit is on tape. Plus, the Giraldis have cameras, one of them pointing to the street where we were all standing."

"Leroy, I know you are a great cop, but have you forgotten that we have a blackout and that cameras need electricity to work?"

"Nope, I haven't. But the Giraldis had a reason to be wary of looters. A few years back, we had a blackout here in the street, too, late one evening, and some guys broke into their store. They know I'm a cop, so they asked me what they could do to prevent it from happening again, or at least help catch any other looters. I gave them recommendations for some security cameras that usually run on power, but also have a backup battery running for up to two days and a larger-than-usual internal storage in case of a power outage. They also store their feeds for six months, and it's all digital files, meaning no accidental taping over a recording. So yes, they will have all this on video, and I am one hundred percent sure they'll happily hand it over to me."

Coming up to Leroy's home, Michelle picked up the umbrella that had gotten tangled up in a bush next to the stairs, then walked up the steps again. "Very nice. Now, let's try to get inside this time, Leroy."

"Good idea, yeah. Oh, and sorry, we'll have to take the stairs all the way up to the fifth floor."

"That's no problem."

The building apparently had a backup generator feeding some emergency lights, and Michelle found the gloomy lighting eerily creepy and strangely cozy at the same time. "Hmm... with the rain and storm outside this really has a film noir vibe."

"Now that you mention it, yeah, it kind of does. I have some nice Irish whiskey upstairs, if you want."

"Ah, there's the family connection to the old homestead," Michelle joked and made Leroy snicker.

"Maybe."

"I'll have the drink later, though. First I have other plans."

"Do you, now?"

They had stopped in front of a door with Leroy reaching for the keys in his pockets again.

"Oh yes," Michelle whispered and heard Leroy gasp, when he snuggled closer and nipped on his earlobe. "You should really open that door."

It took Leroy two tries to get the key into the lock. God, when was the last time his hands had shaken this badly because of another person? Was there even a last time? He didn't think he had ever felt this fascinated by and attracted to somebody else.

Opening the door, he wished he could just turn on the light to get back to Michelle, but for the moment they were faced with darkness only interrupted by lightning running across the sky.

"Give me a minute to get some lights up."

"Can I help you with anything?"

"Keep your phone's flashlight on, that should be okay."

Leroy opened a cupboard in the hallway, took out a few battery powered lanterns, switching them on and turning them to a dim light, and set them out next to several doorways, letting Michelle know where to find the kitchen, the bathroom, and the living room while doing so.

Then he walked down another hallway, losing Michelle along the way.

The vet was captured by the living room and stood there taking in the view. One side was completely constructed as a window front, glass covering every inch from side to side and floor to ceiling. But it didn't stop there. In the middle of the ceiling was a huge skylight, a round, clear center, and around it a crown of inlays seemed to create a sun. The next flash of lightning shining through them confirmed a yellow tint.

"Wow."

Leroy called quietly from somewhere behind him. "Michelle?"

"I'm here."

Soft footsteps came closer – Leroy must've taken off his shoes – but Michelle still stared at the work of art that was the living room, taking in more and more with every second. Comfortable-looking armchairs and a large couch were arranged around a wooden couch table, there were potted plants everywhere, giving the room almost a jungle feeling, and there was even a freaking hammock set up next to the glass front. At least, he thought so. It was hard to tell in the low light of the lantern and only the seconds of lightning.

Arms wrapped around him from behind, and Michelle leaned back with a sigh. "Leroy, oh my god, this is amazing, I've never seen anything like this."

"It's gorgeous, isn't it? I wish I could show you in detail, but we need more light for it. If the storm passes before then, you'll get to see the most beautiful sunrise in the morning. But right now, we really need to get out of these wet clothes."

Michelle would have objected and started to ask questions, but Leroy's hands running up and down his sides, his lips brushing against Michelle's neck provided a convincing reason to shift his focus back to his boyfriend. Turning slowly, he took in the sight of Leroy, out of his scarred leather jacket, with only a wet, white t-shirt plastered against his skin. It made Michelle groan, and he reached for the hem, pulling the shirt up and over Leroy's head.

Leroy's fingers were back on Michelle, opening the buttons of his shirt, pushing it down his arms together with the jacket he was still wearing. Deciding he needed to see more, Leroy took Michelle's hand and pulled him to the bedroom, where he had lit a lamp on a table casting part of the room in a warm orange and had set up a few real candles and a lot of LED candles.

"So you're a hopeless romantic," Michelle whispered into a kiss.

"With the right person, I am."

They stood close to each other, and with the shirt gone, Leroy got an even better look at Michelle. His skin shimmered warmly in the low light and his long lean muscles, honed to perfection by swimming as he had said earlier was one of his hobbies, invited Leroy's touch. His hands gently followed each curve until he could see goosebumps spread across Michelle's skin. "You are absolutely beautiful."

And as his fingers wandered further down, he groaned when he found a row of three dermal anchors with dark green crystals the same color of Michelle's eyes following the lines of the vet's obliques on each side.

"God, and these are so hot," Leroy whispered before kissing Michelle deeply.

"How long have you had them?" he asked after breaking the kiss to get some air back into his lungs.

"A very long time, almost ten years. I'm one of the lucky ones, my body doesn't seem to reject them easily."

"You really are. I got several back when they were just getting popular. Wherever I tried it, they always lasted a maximum of six months before they grew out."

Michelle sighed heavily. "Damn, that's not fair. I would have loved to see you with them. They'd look amazing along your collarbones," he said and kissed Leroy there, gently dragged his teeth along his clavicles.

As a cop, he should be ashamed about the whimper that escaped him, but Leroy couldn't give a damn right then. Instead, he focused on Michelle's hot breath on his skin, the vet's hands exploring every inch of his body. He ran his own hands around Michelle's waist and tugged him closer while capturing his lips once more. Hard length pressed against hard length, making both men moan.

"Take me to bed, Leroy," Michelle mumbled while leisurely working open both their pants.

Leroy's fingers curled around Michelle's butt, squeezing the firm muscles. "Happy to. Any preferences, sweetheart?"

The endearment wasn't planned, but it felt perfectly right to Leroy, and he pressed his lips against Michelle's neck, savoring the other man's taste. Warm, sweet, like dark honey and cinnamon.

"Hmm... No, not in general. Just right now, because I'd love to feel you inside me. Is that okay?"

"Very much so, yes. As long as you promise you'll make love to me soon, too."

"I promise, love."

They fell back into their kiss, all the while losing their last clothes and stumbling towards the bed. Michelle crawled up the sheets, sighing happily when Leroy followed him.

A deep kiss, warm skin on warm skin. Hands roaming, breath catching. And when Leroy lowered himself down, all the things he cherished about making love to a man: a firm chest against his, so much easier to feel his lover's heartbeat; strong muscles promising to give as much as take; a hardness just like his own, arousal so undeniable with him being the reason for it.

His lips wandered down Michelle's throat, and the answering moan made him smile. So his gorgeous vet was very sensitive there, that was good to know.

He slowly kissed and nibbled and licked his way from neck to chest to stomach, grinning whenever his touch made Michelle shiver.

His tongue carefully played around the piercings, then ran down the crease between Michelle's thigh and groin. His lover's smell was exhilarating, and he couldn't stop himself from shifting a little and licking Michelle's full length, hovering at the tip and placing a gentle kiss there.

"God, the smell of you, the taste of you, sweetheart," Leroy whispered, his hands running up Michelle's inner thighs and spreading his legs just a little more, fingertips teasing along hot skin and quivering muscles.

He heard a gasp from the top of the bed when his lips finally closed around Michelle's head, felt fingers grabbing his hair and holding him in place when his lover pumped up his hips.

Leroy took his time sucking Michelle, alternating between gently hollowed cheeks and swallowing him deep. He licked the whole delicious length in front of him, even very carefully played with the frenulum below the crown, which caused Michelle's back to arch off the bed and a shout of "Hell, yes" to echo through the bedroom.

Soon enough, he reached for the bottle of lube on the nightstand and covered his fingers to slowly open his boyfriend.

Michelle was panting, his trembling hands falling to Leroy's shoulders, and he pushed himself further down on Leroy's fingers.

When Leroy had worked his way up to three fingers and added his tongue for a playful lick, a suddenly desperate Michelle dragged him up. "Inside me, now, please, love. Please!"

Leroy smiled down on the other man, gave him a lavish kiss. "As you wish."

He reached for the lube again and felt his own fingers shake when he saw Michelle's eyes following his hands' every move. But Michelle was faster in grabbing the bottle and took it upon himself to cover Leroy generously with it. Leroy had to squeeze his eyes shut and grind his teeth to stop himself from exploding right then and there.

Yeah, his hands definitely are skilled doing this, too, Leroy thought.

Michelle guided him to his entrance, and Leroy oh so slowly pushed inside. Enveloped by heat and pressure, he gradually slid deeper and deeper inside until he was sheathed completely in the other man's body. For a moment, they just stared into each other's eyes, cherishing the connection. Then they began to move together while trading kisses.

Unhurried and sensual at first, their lovemaking soon

became more passionate. Michelle wrapped his legs around Leroy's waist, and his nails left scratches on his back, shining bright red on the light skin. Their fingers linked, and Leroy changed the angle of his thrusts just a little bit until his lover screamed.

Over and over, until Michelle was a whimpering mess.

Every single one of Michelle's nerve endings seemed to burn, heat radiating through his entire body with every one of Leroy's glides in and out of his body. And when Leroy hit the perfect spot once again, Michelle came without the need to touch himself or be touched. He'd never had a man before who fit him so perfectly, filling him so completely, both physically and emotionally.

Leroy felt the heat spill between them like liquid fire, saw Michelle throwing his head back as much as the pillows allowed, every muscle taut and his skin glistening with sweat, and he followed him over the edge with a groan.

He did his best not to crush Michelle beneath him when his own arms gave out and he collapsed onto the bed. Their lips found each other on instinct, even though kissing wasn't a real option with both of them still panting, still shivering.

Coming down from his high, Leroy gently ran his fingers through Michelle's hair. "That was amazing."

"It was, *mon coeur*," Michelle agreed. His accent had gotten thicker the more passionate they had become, and it seemed the mind-boggling orgasm had brought out the deepest of his New Orleans roots.

"Hmm, I like when you call me that," Leroy confessed.

"I'll remember that."

"Good. Should we take a quick shower? And after that, I could try to be a good host. The oven works with gas, I could make you a tea, or maybe even a coffee, I have a moka pot somewhere."

"Sounds perfect, and I wouldn't say no to a tea."

When they were cuddled together in bed again a little bit later, sharing a large mug of tea, Michelle's phone rang. He grabbed it from where he had put it on the nightstand earlier when they had been hanging up their wet clothes after the shower.

"Hey, boss."

"Hey, Michelle. Just making sure all of you are okay. Sorry, I know it's late, but even getting through is kind of a miracle at the moment. Are you all right? Any big problems due to the blackout, do you need anything we could try to get to you?" Scarlette asked.

"Ah, no, I'm good, but thanks for asking."

"Okay. Oh, and I got an email regarding your appointment tomorrow morning. They can't make it. They're not even stuck in the city, but in a small cabin somewhere. Couldn't leave there today, and now most of the road they would have to take is covered in rocks and dirt after a landslide. So you can sleep in. If the power doesn't come back before seven tomorrow morning, consider this the notification that the office will be closed tomorrow, but I'll also try to text updates to everybody."

Michelle was just about to say thanks again and goodbye, when Leroy's phone started ringing, too. Leroy answered the call, then left the bedroom so they wouldn't talk over each other. Of course, Scarlette picked up on it.

"Oops, sounds like you're not alone. I hope I didn't interrupt anything."

"No, you didn't."

"Did you get yourself some private police protection?"

Michelle rolled his eyes, but couldn't stop the smile spreading on his face. "You know, that's not very appropriate for my boss to ask."

"The boss called to ask how you are and let you know about your meeting and a possible office closure. This is the friend asking."

"I know, just kidding. So, yeah, I'm at Leroy's place. I heard you talking to Julia earlier, called Leroy, and somehow things just... happened."

He could hear the smile in her voice. "And is it just some fun or are two giving this a shot?"

"We decided to see where it goes."

"Sweet. You two fit together. Anyway, I don't want to interrupt your fun, and I need to preserve some battery – we didn't exactly bring twenty power banks with us when we came to the city. Have a good night and be safe. Say hi to Leroy."

"Thanks. I will. Have a good night, too."

Leroy came back to the bedroom with a self-satisfied smile on his face.

"What's up?" asked Michelle.

"That was my commander, personally, and of course unofficially, thanking me for finally getting something on Hawkins he can use to get rid of him."

"Very nice."

"Yep. What was Scarlette's call about?"

"Just checking in with her employees and letting me know I don't need to get up too early tomorrow because my clients can't get here. Also, she says hi."

"So everybody will know by tomorrow."

"Yep."

Leroy shrugged. "Sounds good to me."

They snuggled back under the covers, and Leroy told Michelle a little bit about the apartment. How some of his first family members coming to America had actually built it, how several generations had grown up there in many of the apartments of the house, but how they now rented them out. How his grandma used to live in this unit, but then it had become too big for her, stressing her out when her Alzheimer's got worse and she couldn't find things anymore.

"My great-grandfather put in all the glass work, and my grandma loved to plant things and put up a rooftop garden. I'm not as good as she is, but I do my best, so on good days, I can bring her over here to enjoy the flowers because she can't get to the roof anymore."

Michelle took a shaking breath. "I think I just fell in love with you. This is the sweetest thing ever, *mon coeur*."

"That's good, because I think I already fell in love with you this morning when you checked on the shark one last time after the surgery and whispered to her that everything would be all right."

Talking soon became kissing, and kissing turned to pressing close, sliding against each other until they both came with the other's name on their lips. After lovingly cleaning each other and blowing out the real candles, they crawled back into bed and finally fell asleep.

And when Leroy awoke the next morning with Michelle curled around his back, he gently pushed his hips back and sighed at the feel of heat and hardness pressed against him. Michelle kissed his hair, and Leroy tugged on his lover's hand, guiding it to his butt and inviting him to open him after finding the lube they had recklessly discarded somewhere the night before. It didn't take long for Leroy to seek more, and Michelle slowly slid into him, filling him, and caressing Leroy even more with a hand curled around his shaft.

After a morning shower, they were both sitting in the hammock and drinking coffee Leroy had made on the stovetop after they had found the power to still be out. Michelle sighed contently, his head leaning against Leroy's shoulder, his eyes feasting alternately on his almost naked boyfriend and the view outside the windows. This side of the building overlooked a park with a large pond, and Leroy had been right: the sun creeping over the trees, hitting the water, and shining over the eclectic mix of houses making up a neighborhood that was so uniquely New York, was breathtaking.

Back in the bedroom, it seemed like a sin to Michelle to hide Leroy's beautiful body under clothes. He was a little broader than Michelle, his muscles more defined than the vet's lean shape, and the dusting of red curls on his chest, his strongly muscled arms, and his flat stomach were all looking way too inviting, so Michelle grumbled, "You look way better in just your boxers, and better yet naked."

Leroy lifted his chin with a finger, pressed a kiss to his boyfriend's pouting lips. "Thanks. Unfortunately, they don't call that appropriate work attire for a cop, and I have to get to the precinct. We have an emergency generator powering a few things, and I have a video interview scheduled that I urgently need to keep."

"I know. I'm just teasing."

"I know. Do you want to stay here with the office closed? I doubt the subway is running, and a cab or an Uber probably is still a nightmare."

"Are you okay with me staying alone at your place already?"

"Yeah, of course. I don't have a lot of entertainment, but you can pick any book you like, and I think my Kindle might have some power left, too. You can borrow some of my sweats and a t-shirt, that might be more comfortable for the day. And Mr. Giraldi should be back home, too. He knows where I live, he might bring over some food from the store; he told me yesterday he wanted to thank you for taking care of his son."

"Uhm, okay."

They were interrupted by a knock on the door, and when Leroy checked who it was, he found his grandmother and her caretaker there.

"Sorry, she is having a good day and insisted on checking on you when I told her about the blackout," the woman in scrubs explained to Leroy.

"Good morning, Sue. No problem. Good morning, Grandma. Come in."

He guided the old woman to an armchair in the living room while talking to the caretaker. "There's some coffee left on the stove. It should be enough for both of you."

"Oh, thank you."

"No problem."

By now, Michelle had found the clothes they had been discussing and carefully peeked around the corner in a silent question on how Leroy wanted to handle this. The cop curled his finger with a grin on his face.

"Grandma, I want you to meet my new boyfriend. His name is Michelle."

Michelle made his way to the living room and held out his hand to the woman. He could clearly see the sparkle in her eyes he had already come to know lived in Leroy's, too. "Good morning, Mrs. Porter. It's very nice to meet you."

"Good morning. And please call me Muireann. If you're Leroy's boyfriend, you're practically family."

"Well, in that case, Muireann, thank you. You have a wonderful grandson."

"I do. Do you have time for a chat? I was told there was all kinds of madness going on outside."

"It turns out, I do have some time, yes. You are not wrong, it's a little chaotic, but not too bad outside. Why don't I walk Leroy to the door, and after that we can have our little chat? I'm sure you have some great stories to tell me about him."

"You're a good lad. Yes, let's do that. Leroy, my boy, you made a good choice. He's very sweet, and also very good-looking. Now, be careful today. I love you."

Leroy leaned down to kiss her cheek, and smiled at her. "Thank you. I love you, too, Grandma."

At the door, Leroy drew Michelle into a sweet embrace. "Sorry to leave you with her like this."

"Are you crazy? She's great, I like her already. And don't worry, if she gets worse, I won't take it personally, and her caretaker is here, too. We'll be fine. You go to work now and find a killer. And like your grandma said, be careful. I'll see you later."

"Okay, yes. See you later."

They parted ways with a long kiss, and Michelle almost danced his way back to the living room.

Chapter Thirteen

L ast night had been perfect to get rid of a body. The rain alone had kept people inside, but the blackout on top of it could only be described as a gift of fate. A torso left here, a head placed there. Everything had been planned differently at first; this wasn't a happy occasion, but at least nature was lending a helping hand, and such a gift should not be wasted.

Okay, the blackout had created more chaos than expected, the streets had become a nightmare in no time. But the annoyance had been worth it. With the body gone, nobody would ever make the connection.

And Cory wouldn't stir up trouble anymore. No more interruptions to the operation, just smooth sailing from here on out. *It was his own fault, really, right?* Why had he been up that night in the first place? And then he had been bold enough to snoop around after that. What had he been thinking? Sure, he had been a nice guy with some big ideas. Changing fishing routes, casting nets at different times to avoid this fish species or another. Who knew, maybe he had been on the right track. But then he had to ruin it for himself, and now this was what was left of him.

Now things would get back to normal. Now it was just a question of time until the cops found the body and came to their conclusions.

Chapter Fourteen

Unbeknownst to each other, Luke's day started almost as nicely as Leroy's had when July ran her hand down his body and under the blanket to wake him up, and then crawled on top of him, taking him inside with a moan.

But even sumptuous lovemaking in the morning couldn't keep him in a good mood when he read a text from the lab telling him that due to the blackout they unfortunately couldn't finish processing his evidence yet. It wasn't a surprise, and he knew he could hardly do anything with the electronics himself until the city restored the power supply, but it was giving a killer a bigger chance of getting away.

Over a glass of orange juice, he instead coordinated with Leroy over the phone. Updating each other, they decided his lieutenant would run the interview alone as planned, and Luke would grab Cory's paper notebooks from the lab. These had been processed already, and knowing about the incident at college, the cops hoped to find some clues as to what might have been going on.

Luke left Julia with a kiss and wished her a relaxing day off. After all, without power hardly any of her clients had been

120

posting since right after the blackout, with most of them trying to conserve their phones' batteries as long as possible, too.

He was hardly out of the garage – luckily, they had a spot on the upper level of the two-story structure under their building and their level wasn't flooded – when he realized he wasn't the only one jonesing for coffee. The morning crowd wasn't as large as usual, but it was enough to make an impression. People either sleep-walked like zombies or were yelling at each other more aggressively than was normal even for a morning in New York.

Just before he arrived at the lab, a push notification via the city's emergency network on his phone brought some positive news: Power was supposed to be restored to the first neighborhoods in a few hours. While it would take longer to bring the whole city back online, it was something that would help first responders immensely. He had seen many unlucky uniforms on the streets while driving, and even with the water still standing in the streets, ambulances were doing their best to hurry to where they were needed. The first daylight had also brought maintenance crews out to clear water from basements and streets. The storm would be an expensive one for the city, no doubt.

But electricity at the very least would mean less angry people, fewer calls for ambulances to homes with residents needing a substitute for their non-functioning medical equipment, and electrical pumps to help clear out the water.

For what it was worth, the weather had been so terrible last night that he hardly saw any evidence of looted stores or homes.

Badging his way into the lab, he was surprised how many people were already there, most of them running around frantically. He made out the guy he had been talking to the day before and stepped into his way. "Hi. Tobin, right?"

"Yeah. Oh, wait, are you Detective Preston?"

"Yeah, that's me."

The young man in front of him squirmed. "Man, I'm so sorry, but I don't know when we can get you the electronics you asked for. We had an incident last night."

"What happened? Did somebody break in?"

"No. But one of the trees outside was ripped out of the ground and crashed into a window in the lab. We have a lot of water damage there, and your electronics were close to the window."

"Ah, shit." That explained people scrambling to save whatever they could.

"Look, we processed everything, I took prints, we tested for all kinds of residue, I took pictures. What I couldn't do yet was write it up, because the power went out just when I opened the file. And like I said, the evidence is soaked."

Luke scratched his neck. "Okay, I was actually here for the paper notebooks you guys collected from the victim's locker at work and his apartment. You added those to the file already, I managed to check yesterday."

"Yes, exactly. And since they've been processed, they were already in storage waiting for you. They should be fine."

"Perfect. Look, is there any chance I can still take the electronics with me? I'm a tech geek myself, if it's just drying them and salvaging whatever possible, I can do that myself, if you can add your findings to the file later without the pieces here."

Tobin seemed unsure about it, so when his supervisor passed by them, he stopped her. "Melinda, Detective Preston here has an unusual request," he said and explained the situation.

The woman looked at Luke and grinned. "Ah, it's fine, Luke knows what he's doing. Just make sure, both of you, you fill out all the paper forms, including the exact state of the electronics, soaking wet and all, for chain of custody. We'll have to add it to the system later, but we really need all the documentation. And

I wouldn't do this for a lot of people, but I know Luke is as diligent as they come."

Luke smiled at her. "You're my star, Melinda."

"Oh, I know. And congrats on your engagement, by the way."

"Thanks. I see, not even a blackout stops gossip in law enforcement."

"Oh god, no! We run on gossip, you know that. Leroy managed to get Hawkins arrested, by the way."

"Seriously? He didn't say on the phone. I'll grill him about it in person later."

"Do that. I gotta run. Bye!"

She was gone in a second, and Tobin shrugged. "If the boss says it's all right, I'll happily get you your evidence. Let's go."

Luke fought his way to the precinct to check in with Leroy and let him know about the electronics. But when he entered his bullpen, he had to smile despite the annoying setback.

His colleagues had decorated his desk with streamers and balloons, and had left him a bottle of champagne and a "Congratulations" card. He took a photo for July, thanked those colleagues who had made it to the office so far, and made a mental note to bring along something to snack on for the break room once the city was back to normal.

Leroy was already conducting his interview, so Luke let him be and settled with the notebooks on a free desk close to a window. The bullpen just wasn't designed to work without artificial light.

After half an hour, he knew marine biology wasn't a field he'd ever strive in should anything prevent him from being a cop before his retirement. But the notes confirmed the picture he had so far of Cory: detailed notes, with a focus on his studies, no doodles except course related sketches. He took his work and his studies seriously. The only thing standing out every few pages were some numbers scribbled in the margins of which Luke couldn't make sense of at the moment.

When he looked up from the papers again, Leroy was leaning against the desk and studying the notebooks himself. "Anything useful?"

"Nothing about the incident. But I think these numbers could be something, I'm just not sure what, yet. What about his boss?"

"He gave me the same picture as everybody else. Cory was serious about what he was doing, he was dependable, always helpful, maybe a bit stressed – he has seen him wander around the ship some nights when out at sea, like he couldn't sleep. He didn't know anybody who'd want to hurt Cory. The only one sometimes talking shit over a beer is the captain of one of the other ships. Cory's boss thinks the guy's probably worried about his job. Says he's just a hired captain without any say in the company, and the owner might be selling sooner than later, should Cory's work yield results leading to companies having to invest to keep up. I'll follow up on it, but I thought Cory was years away from implementing new techniques or really starting his own company."

"He was, yes. But it wouldn't be the first time somebody got killed just to stop an idea from spreading in the first place."

"That's true. In any case, I'll have a look at the guy and talk to him. Are you going back to school?"

"Yeah, but the campus is closed today due to the blackout and repair of other storm damages. It's on my list first thing tomorrow. At the moment, I'll keep having a look at this, get home and start on drying Cory's electronics, and hope with the power coming back up later that I'll have my warrants to get into the Aquarium's system."

When Leroy drew up his eyebrows in question, Luke told him about the incident at the lab.

"Of course, why wouldn't a tree crash into a window and ruin our evidence?" Leroy let out in an exasperated huff.

"Maybe it's the universe balancing the scales. We've got good things going otherwise, so we need to be hit with some crap during the investigation. I mean, I got engaged, and you finally managed to put Hawkins on the spot for all his bullshit, and you got a new boyfriend."

"Aside from the fact that I worry about you talking about things like cosmic balance, I'm not surprised in the least that you already know all that," Leroy said and playfully punched Luke on the shoulder.

"Like I would ever seriously mean that part. All good with Michelle?"

"Yeah. My grandmother met him this morning and practically adopted him into the family already."

"Welcome to my world. Whenever we visit my parents, they basically ignore the fact that I'm one of their biological children and spoil their new daughter."

"Be glad they all get along so well. One of my sisters-in-law hates my mother. One Thanksgiving they threw cranberry sauce at each other until my dad took the bowls from them and dumped them into the garbage."

Luke couldn't stop the laughter escaping him. "Whenever I hear a new story about your family, I think I want to be a fly on the wall at a family gathering one of these days."

"Just come by. Everybody would think you're just somebody else's new partner. I guarantee you, nobody would even ask. Bring along a kid, and you'd be invisible."

"Maybe someday," Luke said but didn't specify which statement he was talking about exactly.

They parted ways after another look at the case files

together, both following their own leads again for the rest of the day.

Which meant Luke was stuck in traffic once again on his way back to his apartment when his phone rang. Checking the display, he answered it a second later, "Hey, Rose."

"Hello, Luke. How did you and Julia survive the blackout?"

"Okay, actually. What about you?"

"Not too bad, either. I'll have to toss a few things from the fridge when I get home, because I don't want to end up with food poisoning from my burger patties. But otherwise, it's all good."

"I'm glad to hear that. What can I do for you?"

"It's more what I can do for you. I had a chance to look at the DNA comparison. Your leg and arm are definitely from the same man."

"Thanks for confirming it, Rose. How come you guys have power?"

"Luke, we are one of the places in this city with the best emergency generators. Nobody wants the morgue to start heating up, especially in the summer, but even now we try to avoid that at all costs."

"Good point."

"Oh, and Leroy also dropped off a small, shiny piece with the leg which apparently was also in the shark's stomach. Initially, I thought maybe it was an artificial fingernail, but the form and material are wrong. With all the chaos going on, it took me a little longer than usual, but after I could finally take a closer look at it, the thing it reminds me most of is fish scales — which would make sense given a shark's diet, but like I said, it's artificial. It's weird."

"Huh, that's strange, yes. But it's good information. Thank

you for calling me, I have no idea when I can get back online and check the server."

"I figured. Talk to you soon, Luke."

"Yep. Bye, Rose."

I have been summoned. You, too!
Bea called everybody to have dinner at the restaurant this evening. They can't use anything that was in the fridges for paying guests. Anything that might be dangerous will be tossed, of course, but we're all supposed to help eat the rest so all the good food isn't wasted.
I'm already at the restaurant helping with the preparations. Hopefully, we'll have electricity later, but just in case, I already took some of our candles and battery powered lamps along.
Do what you can for work and then get here.
I love you!

Following orders, he set up the electronics in his office and gave the dehumidifier he had hooked up to a closed box for cases like this a hopeful look. "Please have power."

He flipped the switch, and for a moment heard nothing but the same looming silence from before. But then the device started to buzz while starting up, then droned steadily, and a few lights in the apartment flickered on as well.

"Fuck, yes, finally!"

In the apartments around him he could hear more ecstatic

cheers like his own, and in an apartment on the other side of the street somebody opened a window and blasted AC DC's *Power Up* album loudly into the streets. Any other day, people would've complained, but today a few even started to sing along to the rock backdrop. You just had to love New York sometimes.

Knowing it was a longshot, Luke opened his laptop to check on his warrants. Luck wasn't on his side this time, which didn't come as a huge surprise. By tomorrow he would have them. He knew it, but patience wasn't his biggest virtue. A quick look online at the city's emergency information website showed him that even with the warrants he probably wouldn't have been able to get anything done regarding the security tapes. The Aquarium wasn't scheduled to get power back until later, and he assumed any emergency generators they had were currently being used to keep the animals in their care alive.

The only thing he could've already started was a request for social media user data. On the other hand, he was hoping to possibly shorten the list before contacting the platforms. He knew from experience that the longer the list they sent out, the more the companies tried to block any request, dragging out the process sometimes as far as taking it to court. For a cop just doing his job, it sucked. Could he understand the companies' need to protect their clients' privacy? Sure. On the other hand he wondered, more often than not, what people were willing to freely share online, while at the same time claiming to be concerned about everybody spying on them, or complaining when somebody broke into their house right when they were on vacation. And how was it the damn police couldn't do anything?!

Focusing on what he could do, he updated the case file with Rose's findings and made sure the dehumidifier was doing its job without any issues.

After that, he called it a night for the job and checked on all appliances in the apartment. It seemed they had gotten lucky nothing had been damaged, neither by the sudden outage nor by the power being switched back on for the whole apartment at once. Some of the circuits were old, he would have preferred to switch them on one after the other, but without knowing the exact schedule it hadn't been possible. Satisfied even without his warrants, he grabbed his jacket from the hook by the door and made his way to his car to join his fiancée for the impromptu dinner party.

Chapter Fifteen

At the restaurant, July thought she hadn't exaggerated in her note to Luke. Beatrice had indeed summoned her — and half an army of family and friends along with her. Everybody had brought candles or lamps, flashlights and fairy lights with batteries, even some glow sticks. Scarlette's dad, Marco, had done his best to get some lights for the kitchen, and was now working there with his mother, Bea, and several of his siblings. Meanwhile, Scarlette's mom, Cynthia, was commandeering a group of teenagers and children to set up lights everywhere in the dining area. Other people, including some of Scarlette's employees, were doing their best to set the tables. Observing it for a moment, Julia thought it was a well-orchestrated ballet of pure and utter chaos with people bumping into each other, cutlery scattering on the floor, and some of the younger kids fighting lightsaber battles with the glow sticks.

Then she saw Scarlette beelining it in her direction, stopping shortly to crouch next to a young girl and saying to her with a grin, "No, no, what did I tell you, Lily? A lightsaber is all fun and games, but force-choking people is a lot more effective and can be done from a safe distance," before finally stopping next to the door leading to the larger wine cellar, looking at the waiting Julia.

"I don't know why, but somehow I'm constantly relieved you and Ty won't have kids."

"Oh, come on, that's just teaching her to be mindful of resources, like time, strength, limbs..." Scarlette replied with a laugh.

"Uh-huh, yeah, sure. I was told you needed a helping hand or two to get some wine upstairs."

"Yep. And I requested you. I thought we could squeeze in some girl talk at the very least, even if shopping is still off the table," Scarlette explained.

"Sounds good."

Scarlette grabbed a lantern and carefully made her way down the steps with Julia following her. At the bottom of the stairs, both women picked up a basket each – stashed there specifically to easily bring up several bottles – and wandered down the packed shelves.

"Okay, tell me what you want to talk about. I doubt it's about business or geopolitical developments and the desire to buy an island far away from all the craziness. Though that *would* be unusual shopping, even for me, and we tend to have interesting discussions about these topics. But it sounded more personal. You don't have any doubts about the wedding or something, right? It didn't sound like it."

Julia shook her head. "No, absolutely not. It's, ah... uhm..."

Studying her friend for a moment, Scarlette saw a flush bloom on July's cheeks even in the dim light of the lantern. "Oh, this has to be good. From the way you fumble your words and the look on your face, I bet it's about sex. What is it? Did Luke ask you to do some roleplay? Bondage? Do you want to get him a 3D model of your vulva to attach it to a masturbator as a wedding gift?"

Julia stared at Scarlette for a full ten seconds, slowly blinking and silent, opened her mouth as if she wanted to say something just to close it again, then tried once more a second later. "Yes, it's about sex, no, it's not about roleplay or bondage, and why the hell would I want to give him that as a wedding gift if he can have the original?"

Yes, Julia had learned over the years she could speak frankly with Scarlette about everything, and she had become a lot bolder, but Scarlette was still more easygoing when it came to actually saying things out loud.

"Well, what if you are away for work, or he is? He could still have a part of you for some solo fun then. Or what if you're on your period you don't feel like it's a great day to have sex? Helping him out can still be fun for you both."

"Okay, yeah, valid points. But no, it's not that. When we had sex yesterday, one of his fingers touched a little lower than usual. I don't think it was on purpose and it has never happened before, but it actually felt really good. So I was thinking, maybe that would be something to look into. But I have zero idea where to start."

"Aww, finally you start believing me that anal can be fun. I knew it would take a guy you trust completely."

"Seriously, that's your response?"

Scarlette giggled and bumped her hip against July's. "Yep. Don't tell me you expected anything else."

Julia sighed, but it ended in a low laugh. "No, not really. Anyway, any pointers?"

"Sure. First of all, did Luke realize what he was doing?"

"Yeah, I think so."

"And you liked it."

July nodded. "Uh, yeah. I don't know how to describe it, but I ended up making sounds I never made before. There was this tingling sensation up my back, and it didn't feel dirty or kinky or anything, it just felt…" She seemed lost for words and shrugged.

"It felt primal, like it woke up a long-dormant part of your brain, and it reduced you to the cavewoman still buried in there in the best possible way?" Scarlette suggested.

"Holy shit, yeah, that describes it really well."

"It can feel like that, yes. Try combining it with an air pulse vibrator, it's epic. But that's for the advanced seminar, and we'll leave pegging for the pro lesson, if Luke is ever interested. But for now, let's go back to beginners.

"First of all, no it doesn't need to feel dirty or kinky or anything. Biologically speaking, it's a part of your body with a large amount of nerve endings. It's normal that it's a sensitive area. And it's near a person's sex organs, so if those are stimulated and then there's more contact somewhere close, the area is even more sensitive because there's a higher blood flow and the nervous system is hyper-reactive, to explain it without going into even more detail. And if people would understand the biology behind it, half of that 'that's only for gay people' bullshit would die, but that's a whole different story."

"Yeah, true. But even knowing all that, doesn't it hurt? I mean outside stimulation is one thing, penetration is different."

Scarlette set the lantern in the middle of the room and started collecting a few bottles of different red wines while swaying her head side to side. "Done right, usually it doesn't hurt, or at least not a lot. There might be a sting, but it shouldn't be truly painful. If it is, you probably aren't ready, either because you aren't in the right frame of mind to relax or because you haven't been prepped properly."

Julia went to the shelves on the other side and picked out some whites, filling her own basket. "And what's the best way to be prepped? I know there are tons of plugs and stuff, and that's why I was talking about shopping with you, because I think I'd be completely overwhelmed."

"To be fair, I think in the beginning everybody is overwhelmed," Scarlette said with a wink. "But you're right, there are a lot of things out there. And I can only say, you'll have to try. Preferences are totally different for everybody, and what works best, too. Personally, I don't mind wearing a toy anally while having vaginal sex. It's a different feeling for the guy, too, and it can push the penis nicely against the G-spot."

Looking over her shoulder, Scarlette pointed at another shelf. "Bring a bottle of champagne, too, we have a battery powered cooler for single bottles upstairs," she said, and then continued like there hadn't been any interruption to the actual topic of conversation. "But when it comes to prepping for anal sex, I like fingers better, there's more control, and it's of course a more natural feeling. Start with one, very slowly and gently at first. Most of the time, when you're up to two or three and the glide feels good, you're okay to let the guy in.

"It will still feel different, it will feel bigger. And it will be weird the first time. There are a few things truly important things when it comes to anal sex: One, patience. Go slow, inch by inch. Give your body time to adjust. As the passive part, *you* say how fast or slow things go, no matter what the guy thinks should be okay.

"Two, lube. I can't stress this enough. Lube is your best friend here. And not just at the beginning. Feel free to use more when it starts to dry mid-intercourse."

"Yeah, I kinda figured."

"I thought so. But you might think it's enough. Just add some more. You can always get cleaned up and do laundry later, but not using enough lube and ruining the experience for you just because you don't want it to drip on the sheets is an avoidable mistake.

"The other things should be kind of self-explanatory. Use condoms, at the very least with a guy whose status you don't know. Which isn't an issue with Luke, I know. If you feel better, even though you don't use them anymore in general, feel free to get some anyway, sometimes the glide is easier with a condom and lube than skin and lube.

"Last but not least, condoms are also a good idea if you might want to go back from anal to vaginal to finish but don't want to clean in-between. Because even if you're clean inside as long as you don't feel like you really need a bathroom in a minute, there's still a lot of bacteria you don't want to bring into your vagina."

"Makes sense, yes."

"Yep. And that's pretty much it. Except for, talk. Both of you. Communicate what feels good, what feels weird, when you need to slow down, when you feel ready for more. Believe me, the very first time, you'll probably clench shut with the initial pressure. That's okay! It is a weird feeling, if you aren't used to it. But it does get better, and then it can be really amazing. But there will be days you won't feel like it. I mean, it's not like Ty and I have anal sex every second day or something, but when the mood strikes, it's a lot of fun in whatever constellation you try it. Which reminds me of one more thing in case you and Luke ever switch it up: short fingernails are a must."

"Right. Hm, I don't know if Luke would like it, but well, like you said, we'll need to be talking anyway."

"Yep." Scarlette checked both their baskets and nodded. "We should be good with these. Let's get back upstairs."

"Okay. And thanks."

"Sure, no problem. Still want to go shopping?"

"Ah, maybe in the future. For now, I think I might try it without toys."

"Do you have lube at home? Or do you want me to get some from my car?"

"Yeah, we have some. We sometimes use it before or after my period."

"Makes sense, the tissue undergoes a lot of changes during a woman's cycle, sometimes lube makes everything a little smoother."

"Exactly. And why the hell do you have lube in your car?"

"Because I packed some toys and the lube at home before coming to the city. And then my car was at the office most of the time, so I didn't bring it upstairs to our apartment, yet."

They both took the last step upstairs, just to be greeted by a smirking Tyler. "You lead some interesting conversations without me, Sparks. And I'm looking forward to the drive home already."

Grinning, Scarlette stepped around him with a quick kiss. "Me, too, Link. Me, too."

Looking around, Julia saw even more people had arrived, and a second later her gaze landed on Luke opening the door of the restaurant. His face lit up when he saw her, and he strode right towards her.

He gave her a kiss, then brushed a strand of her blond curls which had come loose back behind her ear. "Hey."

"Hey. I see you found my note."

"Yep. And I come bearing good news: our neighborhood got back power shortly before I left home."

"Awesome!"

Luke said hi to Scarlette and Ty as well, but after that any more updates for July had to wait, because aside from several people coming over to congratulate him personally on his engagement, he heard his name being called from the kitchen.

"Luke, I know that's you who just came in. Come here and say hello. And bring Tyler, you two can start carrying out some food," Beatrice ordered. The woman was in her eighties, but she still loved to keep everybody on their toes.

"Yes, ma'am," Luke yelled back with a laugh and dragged Ty along, leaving their women to set the wine bottles down on the tables.

Once they were finished with their tasks, July and Luke were ushered to a larger table and handed some champagne by Scarlette. "Since we couldn't have a drink at your actual engagement," she said with a wink, but as usual with her family, she quickly left again to keep an eye on the food to make sure it was distributed equally among the tables and nobody hogged any favorites.

July and Luke were talking quietly among themselves and Luke was absentmindedly scribbling down the numbers from Cory's notebook when somebody gave Julia a hug from behind. "Congrats, July! To you, too, Luke," Michelle said and laid a hand on the detective's shoulder, giving it a squeeze.

"Michelle! Hey! And thank you." July got up to give her friend a proper hug, then looked over his shoulder. "Hey, Leroy."

"Hi, Julia."

Luke turned around and after thanking and greeting the other two men, too, he scanned the rest of the room. "Okay, I have no clue if there's any rhyme or reason to the seating order. Just sit with us. I shouldn't be surprised that Bea called you, too, hm?"

Leroy shook his head and grinned. "No, absolutely not. And I'm not even surprised she only called Michelle and told him to bring me along," Leroy said and put his arm around his boyfriend's waist.

"No, you shouldn't be," Bea said, suddenly standing next to

Leroy. "You are well aware that I know almost everything going on in the family. And you also know by now you're just as much part of this family as any blood relatives. By the way, you two just won me fifty dollars, thank you." She looked between Leroy and Michelle. "I told my nephew you two would be a sure thing if you ever ran into each other; he didn't see it."

Leroy cocked his head with a smirk. "You had a betting pool on Michelle and me? You know gambling is illegal, right Beatrice?"

"Boy, what are you going to do, throw a sweet, old lady in jail?"

Next to him, Michelle giggled, and Leroy could only shake his head again with a sigh. "No, I guess not. But thank you for inviting us."

"You're welcome. Now, sit down and help us eat all this food. And later, you'll take some leftovers back home for your grandmother." She didn't brook any argument and left their table as fast as she had appeared.

With Luke making some room on the table, Michelle caught a glance of what he had been jotting down on his napkin. "Huh, I've never seen anybody writing it like this."

Luke looked down at the numbers and back up. "What do you mean? Do you have any idea what they're supposed to be?"

Michelle shrugged. "Well, I thought they looked like coordinates, just written in a weird way. I've never seen anybody writing them like a plus sign, usually it's one long line of digits. Aren't they?" He studied the numbers a moment longer. "I would think this is longitude," he said as his finger traced a vertical column of numbers, "and then this is latitude," he concluded while pointing to the horizontal line of numbers.

"I don't know. But if they turn out to be, you just helped me out a lot. Thanks, Michelle."

"Sure, no problem."

It didn't take long until Tyler and Scarlette sat down with the four of them and began talking about the upcoming Halloween party. The two cops at the table quickly updated each other on everything case-related – mainly the electronics drying safely at Luke and July's apartment and Leroy's possible suspect having an unshakable alibi with having been at sea the last five days – then joined the others in the general discussion.

"You guys know you need to show up in a couple costume now, right?" Julia teased Leroy and Michelle.

"You gotta be kidding me," Leroy huffed, but Michelle suddenly gasped and grabbed his lover's forearm on the table.

"No, that's awesome. I have a great idea," he said and whispered something into Leroy's ear that made him laugh.

"Yeah, okay, that sounds great."

Scarlette's inquiring glance was met with a challenging grin from Leroy and Michelle. "Forget it, we're not telling you. But I'm sure you'll love it," Michelle brushed her off with a chuckle.

Over the course of dinner, conversation flowed from the party to July asking about the renovations of the old villa on the West Coast Scarlette and Tyler had bought after the blackmail case that had brought them together last year had been closed.

"It's going slowly, but we expected that. There's a lot of bureaucracy slowing things down due to the age and heritage status of the house. Luckily, we want to restore it, not change it, so the Heritage Society over there is helping out where they can."

"And you still want to make it a museum-slash-homage to your ancestors?" Leroy asked. He had heard some bits and pieces about the work being done, but wasn't as deeply involved as others like July.

Scarlette nodded. "Oh, yeah. Mainly, it will be a museum focused on the silent film industry back in the day and its stars. But it will also have a section showcasing the society and the problems of the era like prohibition, and – given how everything started with the blackmail all that time ago – the struggles the queer community was facing at the time."

"Sparks is right, we are in contact with some excellent historians who are already working on everything, so once the building is ready to be used again, we can set things up quickly," Tyler added.

"Let me know before things start happening. I wanna have a publicity strategy ready and in line with your agent, Ty," July said.

"Yeah, no problem. I'm just not sure you won't be neck-deep in wedding preparation by then. But we'll keep you apprised."

"Link has a point. I need some details here: Have you already started on any wedding plans? Can we help with anything?" Scarlette asked and pulled over a clean napkin and the pen Luke had left lying on the table earlier so she could take some notes.

But Julia shook her head. "No, to be honest, with the case and then the blackout, there hasn't been a lot of time to discuss anything. We think end of spring, early summer, but that's about it. Oh, and Luke's brother was at home when we told Luke's parents. He said he'd get in contact with you, Ty, regarding a bachelor party when the time comes."

"Nice, that should be fun," Tyler grinned while playing absentmindedly with his wife's hair.

The group was just getting ready to bombard the couple with more questions when suddenly the lights in the restaurant flickered on. Everybody in the dining room clapped and cheered. Of course, dinner had been great, and the whole clan – no matter whether family or friend – had taken the chance to make the best of an annoying situation. Impromptu gatherings were rarely this large. But they were always fun, and there was always enough to update each other on. Yet, with the power back up, everybody was anxious to get home and check if every-thing was all right.

Nonetheless, Bea commanded in her usual good-natured manner that everybody eat up first, and help clean up – after all, she planned to be open for paying guests again the next day.

Chapter Sixteen

Outside, the city was bustling. People were literally dancing in the streets while using buckets to scoop water out of their basements, and several coffee shops had apparent customers helping the owners to open up despite the evening hour. Almost twenty-four hours without power meant many New Yorkers hadn't had any coffee in just that long and were longing for their fix.

Michelle was sitting next to Leroy in the car and observed the city scene passing by his window. "There's no other place I know where people would bash in each other's heads over practically nothing every other day and yet come together now to help each other without hesitation. Admittedly, not without the ulterior motive of getting coffee, but still."

"That's New York for you."

"It is. I still feel bad for showing up at the restaurant in sweats, though. I have never done that before. And I don't care that enough people find that totally appropriate attire for going out by now. I don't."

"Sweetheart, I understand you. But it was an extended family meeting, not even a normal private party. Half the kids were running around in their PJs. You were fine, and I really like how you look in my clothes."

"Good point."

Leroy reached over to pick up Michelle's hand and bring it to his lips. "So, do I take you home and we schedule another date, or can I convince you to either let me sleep at your apartment or pack a few things and come back to my place?"

Michelle took a moment to consider the question. "Hmm... You know," he finally said, "I think I should repay the hospitality you offered. My place isn't as amazing as yours, but I have a very comfortable bed."

"Sold," Leroy answered with a chuckle.

Wrapped up in each other's arms, they were stumbling into Michelle's apartment a little later. Taking a step backwards, Michelle almost slipped on a piece of paper. He looked down at the folded note on the floor that somebody must've slipped under the door. "What the..." he mumbled and reluctantly let go of Leroy to pick it up.

Sorry. If there's any damage, please give me a call.
My dad fell during the blackout and couldn't turn off the tap.
He told me to let you know he's okay. He's not entirely, he broke
his leg.
But it could've been worse.
He'll be staying with us for a while.
C. Davidson

"Oh no, poor Mr. Davidson," Michelle mumbled with a concerned voice.

"Who is he?" Leroy asked and read the note over Michelle's shoulder.

"My upstairs neighbor. He's in his nineties, but he's still fit – mentally and physically. Or was, it seems. I hope his leg isn't too badly broken."

Reading his boyfriend, Leroy stepped in front of Michelle and cupped his cheek. "It's not your fault, sweetheart."

Michelle puffed out a heavy exhale. "Yeah, I know. And I know I didn't have a chance to easily get here last night, it probably was mayhem. I'll give his son a quick call, it's not too late."

"Okay. Mind if I have a look around?"

"No, feel free to check everything out."

Strolling through the apartment, Leroy felt comfortable right away. The kitchen was New York's usual small size, but Michelle used it as efficiently as possible with high cupboards, spice glasses mounted underneath the wall-mounted cabinets above his counter, a pegboard on a cupboard's free side, and some rails with hooks for utensils along the wall behind the sink and stove. And from what Leroy could see, everything in the kitchen was high-quality equipment – not exactly a surprise given Michelle's mother and stepdad owned a restaurant.

The living room was cozy with a couch to sink into, a small side table, and a wall with lots of records and a record player hooked up to a set of good speakers. Going through the record collection, Leroy found some classic rock, but also a lot of jazz and blues. Most of the floorspace was clear, so Leroy assumed Michelle liked to dance. A collection of old photos of famous jazz singers was hanging on the walls next to both sides of the couch, but right in the middle on the wall above it was a large picture of a gorgeous woman on stage with a band next to her. Her head was tilted back, her long dark curls tumbling down her back, and she was mid-song. The photographer had managed to catch her eyes, and Leroy could clearly see whom Michelle had gotten his striking eyes from.

One bedroom had been converted to an office with lots of veterinary books and magazines covering a wall, some vintage drawings of organs framed and hung up, and a display cabinet showcasing some instruments and even the skeleton of a small animal, probably a rabbit going by the skull. On one wall was a wardrobe, revealing itself to be a murphy bed in a dark wood cabinet, so that the office could also function as a guest room.

All of the apartment was painted in bold colors of dark red and blue, deep teal, and in the bedroom a green that was almost the same as Michelle's eyes.

The whole apartment was a perfect reflection of who Michelle was and where he came from, with more pictures of his mother, his biological father, his stepdad, and his grandparents mixed with photos of friends, and some of himself working with some animals hanging on the walls in the hallway.

Leroy heard Michelle still quietly talking with his neighbor's son. But the promise of a comfortable bed was luring Leroy deeper into the bedroom. He had taken off his shoes, and after a few steps his feet stepped onto a wet carpet. So far he had only gone with the light from the hallway, but now he took a step back to flick the wall switch, and sighed. "Ah, damn. Michelle?"

Michelle walked down the hallway with a question in his eyes.

"Sorry to interrupt, but I'd say there's indeed some damage."

Taking in the scene in front of him, the vet nearly dropped his phone. "Oh, no... Uh, Mr. Davidson, I'm so sorry, I really just wanted to know how your dad is doing. But we just saw that there's at least one room where the water leaked through the ceiling. It looks like most of my bedroom is flooded. Can I get back to you?"

Michelle listened for a moment, then nodded even though it wasn't a video call. "Okay, yes, we'll do that. Look, we can handle this between the two of us and the insurance and the landlord. Don't stress your dad even more with this. This is just stuff, I'm just glad he's otherwise okay. Tell him I say hi and I'm sorry I wasn't home. I'll get back to you soon. Goodbye."

After hanging up, Michelle sagged against Leroy. "Fuck this."

"I know, baby. Let's take some pictures, and then clear out what we can."

"Yeah. You know, Mr. Davidson was about to take a bath, the tub was running, and he just wanted to grab a glass of wine and a book. He was on his way back to the bathroom when everything went dark. He tripped on a corner of the carpet, fell, and broke his leg and couldn't get up. His son came by hours later, when he finally got through the traffic chaos here, and found his dad. By then, the tub had been overflowing for hours. And the worst part is, his dad is mute after he was injured in the war and his larynx was severely damaged. It's a miracle they could save him; but he never regained his voice, so he couldn't even call for help, and his phone had been in the bathroom, so no video call to his son, either."

"Shit. How is his leg?"

"Luckily it was a clean break. He's old, so healing will take time, but he didn't need surgery or anything. I'll have to call him tomorrow personally."

"How do you two communicate? It sounds like you know him better than most people know their neighbors."

"Ah, I just check on him from time to time, and we talk in the hallway. Sometimes I bring his groceries along when it's heavy stuff like bottles. He's a sweet old man, and his family is good people. When he couldn't talk anymore, all of them learned ASL so he wouldn't have to scribble everything down.

When I moved here and met him, I started to pick up on it, and then put some effort into it. By now, I'm pretty fluent, too."

Leroy stared at his boyfriend in awe. "You're amazing," he declared and leaned in for a tender kiss. "Now let's clean up a bit, and I guess then I'd better take you back to my place after all. Waterbeds are fun, but not like this."

Michelle managed a sad chuckle. "Yeah, you're right. Guess I'll have to call Scarlette and let her know I can't make it to work tomorrow. I'll have to get back here and get a company to dry the place, and the landlord will want to have a look, too. None of this will happen tonight, though."

Leroy nodded and gave Michelle another small kiss, before stepping back and looking around for a place to start.

They worked for an hour, with Leroy tossing some things that couldn't be saved from the nightstand, stripping the bed, and propping up the mattress and Michelle making a few calls and then packing a bag for the next few days. This would take time.

Finally, they made their way back downstairs to Leroy's car. Leroy put Michelle's luggage in the trunk, and Michelle took the garbage bags they had filled and quickly stepped around the corner. "I'll be right back."

Seeing a small, furry bundle next to the dumpster, Michelle dropped the garbage bags and fished a pair of gloves out of his jacket pocket. He had some in almost all his jackets, it just so happened – he didn't even consciously put them in there. Now he carefully reached out for the cat on the ground. Though he was fairly sure the animal was dead, it was hard to be certain in the dim light of the alley, and he didn't need a cat bite on top of everything else that had happened.

But no, the small orange cat was dead, and after a look at the splintered and partially ripped claws, Michelle thought she had likely been hit by a car, from the looks of the body possibly sometime last night. She hadn't been there all that long. Usually he would curse the driver, but with the storm going on, the person might not even have noticed the accident. Still, Michelle couldn't leave her lying there like this, so he opened the garbage bags, emptied one into the other – now almost overflowing – and put the cat in the empty bag. Leroy wouldn't mind making a quick stop at Scarlette's office. They didn't run an official clinic there, but they had a small medical area to check those animals that needed to be taken from their owners right away. And the small area also included their freezer for animals they had to put down.

This day had taken a turn for the worse quickly. Talking with Leroy's grandmother had been wonderful. And when she had been exhausted just after lunch, her caretaker had taken her to her own apartment, and Michelle had explored Leroy's place a bit more, had fixed himself some more coffee and found a book to read – it turned out Leroy's fantasy collection was huge and was rivaled by an almost-as-large romance section on his book-shelves.

Dinner had been awesome; he loved the whole Langella clan and was incredibly grateful that Scarlette had invited him to the restaurant almost from the beginning when he had started working for her.

Taking Leroy home after dinner sounded like a perfect way to end the evening, but then things had gone very wrong. Now he had a dead cat next to him on the ground, a flooded bedroom, and garbage bags he needed to squeeze into the probably already full dumpster.

Just get it over with and enjoy the rest of...

But Michelle's thoughts came to a crashing halt when he opened the lid of the dumpster and had a look inside.

Chapter Seventeen

"Oh god... Leroy!" Michelle yelled for his boyfriend, his eyes still glued to the scene in front of him.

In the dumpster, on top of countless garbage bags, lay the headless, naked torso of a man. The skin was pale, a stark contrast to the dark edges where the head and limbs had been removed. Pieces of garbage clung to the torso, but even in his state of surprise Michelle could see there was no fresh blood splattered or smeared around, and signs of decomposition gave him the impression this wasn't somebody who'd been killed an hour or two ago.

Leroy came running around the corner, gun already in hand. "What's wrong?"

Michelle turned his head in Leroy's direction and inhaled deeply, thankful that it wasn't summer, and the smell wasn't as bad as it could be. "I think I just found another part of Cory. Unless there's somebody else cutting up people and dumping them around the city at the moment."

After checking the alley, Leroy holstered his gun and took a step closer to Michelle. From the new angle, he saw immediately that his boyfriend was correct. "Fuck! Yeah, that's Cory's torso. Aside from the tattoo on his wrist, his mother showed me a picture of Cory at some beach getting ready for a dive. The tattoo on his pec matches the one on the torso."

"*Merde.*"

So Michelle's French comes out when he is pissed or unsettled, too, Leroy observed. If the situation hadn't been so bleak, he might've teased his lover for it. As it was, he just filed the information as "adorable" in his mental folder about Michelle. "Yeah. I assume you didn't touch anything, right?"

"No. Only the lid of the dumpster, and I'm wearing gloves. I had to repack the garbage – in the bag on the ground is a dead cat now – and I just wanted to dump the other bag."

"A dead cat?" Leroy raised his eyebrows.

"Yeah. I found her here and wanted to make sure she's properly disposed of... Come to think of it, she was possibly hit by a car, but hasn't been dead all that long. I can tell you, the torso hasn't been in the dumpster long, either. Four buildings use it, somebody would've seen. I really don't think it was there before the blackout. So, maybe you should have a closer look at the cat, too. Yesterday was chaotic, but this alley wouldn't have been that busy. Maybe whoever dumped the torso hit her close by and she crawled here before dying."

"Huh, good thinking. Yeah, let's mark the cat for our ME."

It didn't take long for the team Leroy had called in to arrive at the scene. CSU was going over the dumpster and the surroundings. An ME arrived with a couple of technicians, but Leroy asked for Rose to be the one to look at the body.

"She won't be in before morning," the coroner told him.

"I know. But I am sure I know whom the torso belongs to, and she's working on that case with Detective Preston and me."

"All right, then. And you want me to take this cat along, too? Are you sure about that?"

"Yes. Please do it, store it with the torso, make a sign, or whatever. I don't want it to disappear in a medical waste bucket by accident."

"Okay." The ME shrugged. "You'll have to explain that to Dr. Miller, not me."

"I will, don't worry."

Meanwhile, uniforms were talking to any residents they could find in the four buildings Michelle had indicated to Leroy were sharing the dumpster and searching the area for anything possibly related to the body dump.

When Michelle came back downstairs with two vats of coffee and some paper cups for everybody a while later, Leroy knew his boyfriend had just made friends for life.

One of the uniforms called over to his superior when Michelle reached the edge of the area cordoned off with crime scene tape.

"Hey, boss, please tell me he's telling the truth and you know him. I could really use the coffee, and if you can confirm his story, I'd be very tempted to have one."

Leroy couldn't begrudge the guy the wish. The storm might have passed, but dampness clung to the city, and the October winds made for a chilly evening. Considering most of the uniforms had probably been out on the streets trying to keep people calm during the day until the power had come back up, Leroy could imagine how the guy must feel.

"Yeah, he's my boyfriend, he lives here, you can trust him. I'm just not sure about his coffee-making skills, yet."

The uniform filled a cup with steaming hot, black gold and after a sip, he sighed appreciatively. "I'd keep him around, boss. The coffee is great."

"Good to know."

Michelle was allowed to slip underneath the tape and strolled over to Leroy. "Here, have some. I felt a little useless. You already took my statement, and I was slowly going crazy staring at my soaked bedroom."

"I get why. Good news is, this shouldn't take too much longer. CSU is almost done, and many of your neighbors aren't at home right now. I suppose a lot of them are shopping now that the lights are back on, and some might have gone out of the city to spend some time with friends or family. I have some people on my team who decided their wives should get out of the city too because they have small babies, so for them having power is pretty much essential."

"Hm, yeah, I can imagine."

Drawn in by the lure of fresh coffee, teams of uniforms came back from canvassing, all reporting the same. So far, nobody had witnessed anything, and to hopefully get a better picture, a second round of door-to-doors would be necessary.

Resigned, Leroy finally called it a night about forty minutes later when the last of the uniforms came back without any useful information. "All right, we'll pick up on this tomorrow. Grab a last coffee, everyone."

A moment later, Leroy stared in disbelief at his boyfriend who was handing out more cups when it seemed like he was on a first name basis with half the uniforms already. "How?"

"Oh, come on, I met you yesterday, we got together hours later. People just like me, love."

"They do, and so do I, I'll agree with that. But to be clear, I'm not inviting all of them into this relationship or even just the bedroom, just because they think you're hot."

Michelle almost choked on his own coffee. "What?"

"I knew I'd get you with that," Leroy said with a smirk and held the car door open for Michelle, then rounded the car, slid into the driver's seat. "You're mine now."

"Oh, I know, just as you're mine."

Leroy stole himself a kiss, then asked with a grin, "My place still okay? Or would you rather we sleep in your guest room? Fair warning, I'll have to get up early. So if you don't want me to potentially wake you up, we can also go our separate ways for tonight. I don't think you need to be concerned about the torso being dropped here. It's strange, but in this case I think it's really just a weird coincidence. The only people who know about your involvement are the ones on the vet team, and we checked all their alibis for the night of the murder. They're all cleared."

Michelle almost melted. "You're very sweet and very considerate, Leroy. But yes, I'd still very much like to go home with you. And don't worry, I'll have to get up early, too. Which means you should start the car now, so we can get home and make the most of what's left of this evening," he added with a teasing smile while his hand wandered up the inside of Leroy's thigh.

The cop cleared his throat and shifted a little in his seat to get more comfortable within the confines of the suddenly strained fabric of his jeans. "Ah, yeah, okay, good idea."

Chapter Eighteen

S unshine glaring on Luke's screen didn't help brighten his mood. After Leroy's update last night, Luke had checked on Cory's electronics. The dehumidifier was doing its job, but it would take time.

Now it was morning, and he still didn't have the warrants for the social media accounts or the Aquarium's security system. But it wouldn't do him any good to get mad; he knew better than that. Instead, he got up and poured himself another coffee, this time into his travel mug, wrote a note for July because she was in a meeting and he didn't want to interrupt, and left to get to Cory's college campus.

Upon his arrival, he was faced with a similar scene like the one he had seen at the evidence lab the day before. Countless people in lab coats were accompanied by what seemed to be student aides, and all of them were loudly talking over each other. From what he could make out, many experiments had been interrupted by the blackout, some apparently at a critical stage.

Yep, I know why I didn't follow through with the college path any longer than necessary, he thought. He knew he was a damn good cop, yet still, when he had started dating Julia, he secretly had been insecure after getting to know her better. Yes, he had gone to college and gotten his Bachelor's of Science in Information Technology with additional courses in Computer Technology and Internet Security. But four years had definitely been enough for him. He had always known he wanted to be a cop, it just played into his hand that police work became more and more entangled with IT every day and he had also always loved tech. So he had wanted to have a degree that would help him get a good position in the police force. And yet, college itself just wasn't for him. He wasn't patient enough for the experiments he was hearing about now in passing, and imagining forcing himself to go through those lengths just to have a blackout possibly destroy weeks or months of work? Definitely not something he would want to have to deal with.

Then there was Julia. She had studied longer, had a Master's of Public Relations and Bachelor's degrees in Marketing and Communication, along with courses about Social Media and Applied Mathematics to understand the underlying algorithms.

She was easily the most amazing person he had ever met; no wonder he had fallen for her very much as soon as he had seen her. He was incredibly lucky and thankful that she didn't care about degrees and social status like other people, or he wouldn't have had the smallest chance with her. He was far from stupid, but he wasn't a scholar either. And yet, with all their differences, they had so much in common as well, and they were building a life together every day, were planning to get married.

I must've done something right, he thought with a small smile, before schooling his facial expressions since he had just reached the Administration Office.

He stepped out of the office half an hour later to stroll to his car and counted the visit mostly a success. Given the investigation into Cory's death, the clerk had given Luke access to his student file without a problem. It had only confirmed previous statements about the man's work ethics and academic successes.

It had also included a comment about a second opinion about the grading of one of Cory's papers complete with the name of the lecturer giving the second opinion and a note stating, "*Additional opinion requested and granted after incident with Prof. Frederik Samson, see respective personnel file.*"

Unfortunately, this was where the administration clerk couldn't help him any further, because regulations forced her to ask for a warrant to hand out personnel records.

But lucky for Luke, the woman was a huge gossip – what she couldn't hand out officially, she dished out freely over the fresh cup of coffee she got herself during his stay.

After a lengthy, detailed description of the argument between Cory and the professor of his anatomy course, she went on to tell Luke about "all those other times when Professor Samson was arguing with people at the end." She was clearly on a roll, so Luke let her go on.

It turned out, Professor Samson had left the faculty two and a half months earlier, after being diagnosed with a brain tumor which had affected his behavior leading up to the diagnosis. If the clerk was right, he and his wife had relocated to San Francisco about two months ago after a surgeon had heard about his case from a colleague and was hopeful she could remove the tumor.

That was a start. He had a name, a new state of residence. For now, he should be able to find the professor and give him a call.

He'd nonetheless request a warrant to verify facts, just as he would request warrants for the professor's bank statements and the ones for the captain Leroy had been looking at. Just because they provided alibis that showed them unable to kill Cory personally didn't mean they couldn't have paid somebody to do it.

Before getting into his car, Luke checked his emails once again, but his other warrants still hadn't come through. Grumbling, he sat behind the wheel, sent a quick update to Leroy, confirming that he'd request Leroy's warrant as well like they had discussed last evening, then made his way back to his apartment to work from there.

Back home, he found July talking with her earbuds in her ears, her phone in her back pocket, and one of his whiteboards rolled into the middle of their living room. "No, let's not do that. You'll want to highlight every borough separately, or everybody will complain that they aren't the first picture of the post."

When she turned around and spotted Luke, she grinned and waved briefly, before turning back to the large map of the city she had sketched with key words written for each borough. From what Luke could see, she was helping the PR department with a positive portrayal of the aftermath of the storm and blackout.

Since he didn't want to interrupt, he stepped into his office and shut the door behind himself after grabbing a chocolate bar from their kitchen. After filling out the paperwork for the new warrants, he started a search for Professor Samson. It probably would take a few minutes, so he decided to use the time and work with the input Michelle had given him last evening regarding the numbers in Cory's notebook.

He tried a few different ways to input them, but finally came up with multiple locations, all at sea. Which made sense, given Cory's field of study and his job. But it didn't tell Luke why he had written down those coordinates. Checking several maps didn't give him any more information. It didn't look like anything was out there other than the open sea. Luke uploaded the information to the case file and added a note that he or Leroy would have to talk to Cory's boss again to ask whether he knew anything about these coordinates.

Switching to the other window open on his laptop, he saw that his search for Cory's former teacher had been successful. He found a phone number for Professor Samson and picked up his phone.

It rang a few times, before somebody picked up. "This is Frederik Samson's phone," a female voice answered anxiously. In the background, Luke heard chatter and some sharper yells alongside the beeping of medical equipment and the clatter of a cart with some trays being pushed.

"Hello. I'm Detective Luke Preston with the NYPD. Am I speaking with Mrs. Samson?"

"Yes. What's this about? I'm sorry, but you called at a bad time. I'm at the hospital, my husband is having surgery right now; if this isn't about something too important, would it be possible for you to call at another time?"

He couldn't exactly blame her for wanting to get rid of him under the circumstances. "Mrs. Samson, I'm sorry to disturb you at such a difficult time. I understand that you have other priorities at the moment, but I'm investigating the recent murder of one of your husband's former students."

For a moment, there was only stunned silence before Mrs. Samson spoke again. "Good god. I'm very sorry to hear that. But I don't know exactly how I or my husband could help you."

"The murdered student is Cory Gilbert. I believe there was an incident involving the three of you in the past."

"Oh, no. Poor Mr. Gilbert. But, Detective Preston, whatever connection you are looking for here, it's not there. Yes, Mr.

Gilbert helped me out one day, and my Frederik got agitated about it. And yes, after that, they had a minor dispute about the grading of a paper. You will find all that in my husband's personnel file, I believe." She took a deep breath before continuing. "Here's what's not in the file, though: In the time before the incident my husband had become more and more paranoid, more spiteful, sometimes even delusional. But it was something he mostly was able to hide at work. At home it showed more openly. One day he accused our neighbor of poisoning our cat. We don't have a cat."

"I'm sorry, that must have been a difficult time for you," Luke told her with a kind voice.

"Yes, it has been, indeed. But, Detective, this has been going on for quite some time. You said the murder was committed recently. Believe me, my husband hasn't been in any condition to kill somebody, or even travel back to New York, for a while now. At least I assume that's where Mr. Gilbert was killed, given that you work for the NYPD."

"It is."

"As I said, it couldn't have been my husband. Nor me, if you are thinking about looking in that direction. I have been taking care of Frederik around the clock for weeks and months now. And more importantly, neither of us would have a reason to kill Mr. Gilbert. Yes, the incident happened. But after the diagnosis, they added that to the entry in my husband's file and made sure he wouldn't lose the health benefits his job was offering. And even with those, his treatment here in San Francisco is costing us a fortune. Anyway, everybody understood what had happened and the cause for it, and as far as I know, Mr. Gilbert got another opinion for his paper and was content with that solution. Ah, excuse me a second."

Luke heard the phone's speaker being covered and a

muffled conversation taking place, while he jotted down some notes.

A few moments later, Mrs. Samson got back to him. "Sorry, that was my husband's surgeon. She told me the surgery went well. If you don't have any other questions, I'd love to go see Frederik now."

Luke scanned his notes again before he answered her. But he knew what he wanted to do next. "No, that's all for now. Should anything else come up, I'll get back to you. Thank you for your time and help, Mrs. Samson. I wish your husband a speedy recovery."

"Thank you. Goodbye, Detective Preston."

"Goodbye."

After hanging up, Luke reopened the Samsons' social media accounts – sometimes he was grateful for how careless people were with their private lives – and made a list of several friends and family members still in New York whom he planned to speak to. If Mrs. Samson had told the truth, her husband seemed unlikely to be the reason for Cory's murder and even less likely to be the killer (though being an anatomy professor would've explained his skills with a knife) but he would verify her story nonetheless.

Three calls later, he bumped Professor Samson down the suspect list. He would still check financial records once the warrants came through, but he had gotten the exact same picture from family members that Mrs. Samson had given him. It didn't sound like the professor had been able to plan a murder or organize a hit, and in his rare lucid moments had apparently even regretted the whole incident with Cory.

Luke checked the electronics after his last call, but found they still needed more time to dry. Yet his mood brightened when he heard the notification for an incoming email and saw that his warrant for the social media user data and the Aquarium's security system had come through.

He sent the user list he had already prepared and the respective paperwork with the warrant to the social media platforms and gave them a quick call to make sure this would be handled as a priority.

Then he packed a few things and headed for the apartment door to get to the Aquarium. Hopefully, he'd find something useful there.

Chapter Nineteen

Leroy decided he could most definitely get used to waking up next to a naked Michelle. After switching off his alarm and, with that triggering a routine to turn on the ceiling lamp to a low, warm white, he let his gaze wander over the smooth skin of his boyfriend's chest, his abs, the irresistible shimmer of his piercings, and back up to that beautiful face that was a perfect mix of Michelle's combined heritage, with the high cheekbones and the narrower chin from his father, the angles given a softer touch by his mother's side just like the slightly fuller lips and, of course, those striking green eyes now looking lovingly at him.

"Good morning, sweetheart."

"Good morning, *mon coeur*."

Smiling, Leroy leaned over and brought his lips to Michelle's for a sweet morning kiss. "I'm sorry that I have to get up so early. You can go back to sleep, if you want to."

But Michelle shook his head. "No, it's all right, love. I understand why you need to get to work. And even though Scarlette had no problem with giving me the day off when I called her last night, I still have enough to do myself. Let me see if my landlord got back to me," Michelle replied and reached for his phone. "Okay, so my landlord said he could get to my place this afternoon. And he asked not to contact a company to dry the place just yet. Since it leaked through the ceiling, it's not just my stuff but also the building that has some damage, so he will arrange everything."

"You trust him to do that? I rarely hear good things about landlords in this city."

"I know. But he's actually doing a good job. And I understand his reasoning in this case. It will be fine. But depending on how extensive the damage is, I might have to stay here for a bit."

Leroy gave him a huge grin. "Michelle, you know that's no problem at all."

"Perfect. So, I was thinking, now that I only have to be at my place in the afternoon, I could head to the precinct with you, file that civil complaint against Hawkins. If I can ride with you, I'll find my way once I'm there, and you can get to work."

"Sounds good to me."

Michelle knew they should get out of bed, but he couldn't stop himself from running his fingers through Leroy's hair. "How much time do we have before we need to leave?"

"That depends. If you're happy with home-brewed and not a stop at a coffee shop, it'll buy us some more time."

"I prefer home-brewed coffee anyway."

"Great. Then you'll just have to let me get up to switch on the coffee machine so it can do its magic."

The vet drew up an eyebrow. "What, no smart integration yet?"

"Ha ha. It's on the list, believe me. And yes, I know, Scarlette got me hooked on all that stuff, I'm the first to admit that."

Now, Michelle giggled. "Don't worry, love, she did the same to me. And I'm grateful. Even just waking up with such a nice light instead of a bright, cold one is very nice, and pretty close to how my morning light setting looks, too," he said with a wink.

"Now get out of bed, get the coffee going, then come back here and get me going."

Leroy had probably never made his way to the kitchen and back faster. And when he stepped into the bedroom again, his breath caught, and all his blood left his brain to pool further down.

Michelle had pushed the blanket away, and was sitting against the headboard with one knee drawn up a little, his eyes closed, and his lips parted in a lustful sigh. One hand ran over his chest, with the other he slowly stroked his hard length.

Leroy groaned deeply and cupped himself.

"Do you like what you see, *mon coeur?*" Michelle asked teasingly and opened his eyes to look his boyfriend up and down.

"Do you really have to ask?" Leroy countered and let go of himself so Michelle could see exactly what he was doing to him.

"You look delicious."

"You, too, sweetheart."

Michelle smiled smugly. "Then get over here so we can each have a taste."

Eagerly crawling onto the bed, Leroy mentally shook his head. He felt like a teenager again, excited to get his hands, his mouth on his lover. And yet, this also felt vastly different from any simple teenage lust. There was a rightness to being with Michelle, to the taste of his lips now on his own, that he had never experienced with another person before. An epiphany bloomed within him: the knowledge, and with it the comfort, that this would be permanent. Softly sighing, he broke the kiss and looked into Michelle's eyes. "This is going to last. We are going to last." It wasn't even a question.

Michelle took a sharp inhale, before his hands cupped Leroy's face and he nodded. "Yes, we are. You just felt that, too, hm?"

"Yeah." Gently brushing a strand of hair from Michelle's forehead, Leroy smiled serenely. "I love you, Michelle."

His lover's lips quivered, and a sheen of happy tears filled his eyes. "I love you, too, Leroy," Michelle whispered back with a smile of his own.

They sunk back into another deep kiss, but when their bodies pressed together and Michelle felt Leroy's arousal against his own, he playfully nipped at Leroy's bottom lip. "And I love kissing you, but that wasn't the taste I was talking about before."

Leroy grinned at his boyfriend and rolled his hips to make them both moan before sliding away from Michelle. "Good point," he said and began moving them into a comfortable position on their sides until their groins were in each other's faces.

Humming, Michelle ran his hand around Leroy's hip and down to his butt to draw him closer, and opened his mouth invitingly. He loved Leroy's taste, the sweetness of his skin combined with the salty flavor of his lust, loved the feeling of Leroy inside his mouth and the moans he drew from his lover with his lips and tongue. It was just as thrilling as the heat, the wet glide of Leroy's mouth on him.

They moved their heads together, both slowly starting to thrust their hips as well. Low moans grew louder, the vibrations traveling through them making them both crazy. At some point, their hands found each other, and with their fingers intertwined, their movements became more and more urgent, until they both climaxed, each savoring the taste of the other.

When they cuddled a little longer afterwards than they should, they had to rush through their morning routine and fill the coffee into travel mugs, but neither of them could really regret it.

• • •

At the precinct, Michelle would've asked around about the right person to talk to about the complaint, but Leroy shook his head and took his hand. "Come upstairs with me. I have to go over the reports from the uniforms and their canvass yesterday, but I'll call somebody to take your statement in my office. Otherwise you might have to wait for hours; there's still a lot of extra work going on after the blackout."

"Sure, if you don't mind, we can do it like that." Michelle smiled and stepped onto the elevator with Leroy, then quickly checked his phone when he got a text. "Ah, perfect."

"Hm?"

"Scarlette texted. While I enjoy very much having you as my personal chauffeur, my car will be ready to be picked up later today. It's a company car and was due for its routine check-up. I actually left it at the shop after the surgery. It should've been ready yesterday, but like you said, the blackout fucked up a lot of things."

The elevator door opened again, and when they stepped out, neither of them noticed they were still holding hands. One of the detectives looked up and grinned when he saw them together. "Yo, boss, if you bring your boyfriend, does that mean I can bring my girl along to work, too?"

Leroy smirked at the young man. "Sure, Takagi, if she can help us get rid of Hawkins, or extract critical evidence from a shark's stomach, she's more than welcome to tag along. And what the hell are you still doing here? Wasn't your shift over hours ago?"

"It was, but it turned into a stakeout. We got in a few minutes ago; I wanted to write it up."

"Has anything game-changing happened?"

"No, not yet. Olson and his partner took over from us."

Leroy nodded. "Then write it up later. Tell Thompson the same, and then get home and get some sleep, both of you."

"Okay, thanks, boss."

"Sure," Leroy said, and given that the bullpen had already seen them coming in holding hands, he kept his fingers linked with Michelle while leading him to his office.

Inside, Michelle turned to Leroy and studied him for a moment. "I don't think I've ever been with a guy as unconcerned with PDA as you."

"Hm, I admit usually I wouldn't be like this at work, simply because it's not very professional. But this case is crazy, the last few days with the storm have been crazy, so right now, I don't care. But when it comes to the PDA with a guy part, I don't give a damn. Seriously, if anybody has a problem with me being in love with a man, with you, they can fuck off. I know that's not how most people see it, but let's face it: nobody can please everybody. There will always be people that find a reason to hate somebody else for whatever reason, be it skin color, religion, sexual orientation, or anything else. So why the hell would I even care about their opinion? And I've never had a problem standing up to people confronting me."

"True, you're good at that. So you don't mind your detective's comment about you bringing your boyfriend?"

"No, why would I? There was no judgment there. That's just the normal, good-natured teasing around here. He'd ask exactly the same if you were a woman. I'm not saying there are no assholes around the precinct – you've met Hawkins, after all. But there'll always be assholes somewhere, being dicks about whatever. This department is good, though."

Leroy leaned against his desk and ran his hands around Michelle's waist, not caring if anybody walked in or saw them through the glass. Sometimes it was nice to be the boss.

"Look, I know it's often happening out of a sense of protecting oneself, but many of our fellow members of the queer community have also interpreted genuine questions that were asked out of simple interest or the usual teasing among friends or colleagues as pure hatred right away. And at the risk of seeming naive, let me also say, if we as queer people want equality, want to be seen as the normal people that we are, it should also be okay for straight friends to ask us the same questions they'd ask other straight people or joke in the same way they would about a hetero couple."

He could see Michelle wanted to object, so Leroy held up a hand. "Before you say anything, let me tell you that yes, I do very well understand that the queer community has endured terrible things for a very long time, and that we're still facing a lot of shitty opinions and unfortunately also violence from assholes often enough. And I know it's human nature to hear the negative opinions so much louder, to even ignore any positive voices over it. I also believe that – at least at the moment – most, but unfortunately not all, members of the queer community are working on truly furthering understanding, but that some few people rather just take the easy way to point fingers and blame straight people in general. And generalization never works, does it? Let me ask you this: What happens when a straight person asks you how many guys you've slept with last week?"

"I get pissed. Not every gay man has tons of different partners."

"Exactly. And yet, if a gay guy asked you the same question, you'd probably be a lot less pissed. He'd be allowed to, because he is like you, at least in a way, even if he did just the same as a straight person and assumed you're into the hookup culture just because you're gay. It's kind of a reversed *Animal Farm* situation of 'some animals are more equal than others,' while all we should want is for *everybody* to be truly equal. Isn't that just as biased on our side? Again, I understand where it comes from, I do. I just think going into every situation anxious and with the preconception that *all* straight people still hate us unfortunately often leads to a tense mood that in the end leads to misunderstandings and possible arguments. In my opinion, it's just more useful to give people a chance to show me how they react, and if they turn out to be assholes, I can still tell them to fuck off. But we aren't any better than the people we complain about if we constantly keep up our own prejudices and see snide comments when they're not always meant to be taken that way."

Michelle took a long moment to truly consider what Leroy had just said, then answered him, "I have to admit, I never looked at it from that perspective. And I know you aren't naive, I know you see the problems. But yes, I can see your point when it comes to both sides not being without prejudice. I mean, I've had a friend, just a friend, years ago, who's bi as well. At some point he moved away, and we haven't stayed in contact. But I remember how annoyed he was with the straight *and* the queer community. Whenever he hooked up with a guy, straight guys would ask him how he could give up on boobs and all, and whenever he was with a girl, our gay friends asked him how he could live without guys and what was so great about women, anyway. And when he was in longer relationships, both sides all but ignored that he was bi at all and started calling him straight or gay depending on the partner, basically saying without hooking up with one gender or the other, he wasn't attracted to men or women anymore. Even for me, it sometimes felt like both sides didn't even allow him to call himself bi anymore; in the worst cases they were insinuating he'd just experiment – which, come on, isn't even a bad thing, as long as everybody involved knows what's going on and is okay with it – or simply wouldn't know what he liked. So, yeah, I know the queer community isn't perfect either."

Leroy tugged Michelle even closer and laid his forehead against his boyfriend's shoulder. Chuckling, he turned his head and mumbled against Michelle's neck. "Yeah, don't even get me started on that topic. Bottom line is, we're all human, we're all just people. Some are good people, some aren't, and I react accordingly to their behavior. But I don't hide who I am or whom I love from anybody."

Michelle smiled and pressed a kiss to Leroy's temple. "I like that very much, *mon coeur*. Usually, neither do I. I just wasn't sure how you usually handle it with your team, though I'm not surprised given how you introduced me to the uniforms and Hawkins as your boyfriend without hesitation. Which brings us back to the depressing topic of civil complaints and murder."

Leory let out a grim moan. "I know. Let's get started then."

He walked behind his desk and picked up his phone to call a colleague to take Michelle's statement, and at the same time switched on his computer.

Michelle finally took a moment to have a look around. Though Leroy's office wasn't huge, it had a small table with two chairs in addition to Leroy's desk and a few file cabinets. Pointing at the table, Michelle raised his eyebrows in a silent question. Leroy nodded and kept talking on the phone for a moment longer.

After that, it didn't take long for Leroy's colleague to knock on the office door. And when she entered, Leroy greeted her, but then excused himself and put in his earphones to listen to some music while reading the reports, so he wouldn't be distracted by the conversation.

Michelle retold the events on the evening of the blackout from the point he and Leroy had arrived at the lieutenant's front door, then repeated a few things when the woman had a follow-up question. But all in all, it was a quick interview and the officer left them with a cheery smile on her face soon after they had finished. It seemed to Michelle that pretty much everybody wanted to see Hawkins kicked out. After what the man had dared to do and say to him and Leroy, Michelle was more than happy to help make that happen.

Leroy looked away from his screen and took out his earphones. He had a pen in one hand and tapped it against the table.

"What is it?" Michelle wanted to know.

"Not sure. Something about the neighbors. Nobody saw anything, it's not one of the statements. But there's something, and right now it makes my brain itch, because I can't put my finger on it. I'll have a look at the rest of the file..." But he was interrupted by his phone. Seeing the name on the display, he smiled when he answered. "Hey, Rose."

Michelle waited quietly. He knew Leroy was busy enough, so he'd leave him alone after the call. His complaint had been filed, and he was sure he could busy himself until later that day. *I could look into getting our Halloween costumes, for one,* he thought, and was just about to get his things together and leave his boyfriend's office when he heard his name and looked in surprise at Leroy.

"Rose, wait, I'll put you on speaker. Michelle is here with me, he found her," Leroy said to the caller while gesturing to Michelle to join him at his desk.

After some quick instructions, Rose was discussing external and internal trauma indicators with Michelle, and Leroy got the feeling that the two doctors understood each other well enough, even when they switched from human to cat and back. At some point, they were going over potential X-rays that could be taken to confirm the suspicion of the car accident. And though Rose was positive she and her assistant could manage, she stopped talking for a moment, before speaking up again. "You know what, doc, if your day allows, you can always come here and help us with the cat. From what I've seen in the case file when adding my findings, you have the clearance. As long as I don't let you work on the human body, it would be all right. Not that I doubt your skills to know your way about human anatomy, but the court might object, since you did study veterinary medicine."

Michelle chuckled. "Don't worry, most of the time I find people gross. There's a reason why I chose vet med. The torso is all yours."

"Perfect. Leroy, does that work for you? If you want to come by, too, I can also go over what I've found so far in regards to the torso."

"Yeah, that sounds good. I'll bring Michelle along. We should be there soon."

"Perfect. See you two in a bit. Bye."

At the morgue, Leroy glanced over at Michelle before stepping inside the building. "Are you sure you're okay with this?"

Michelle stopped walking for a moment, looking at Leroy with his head cocked. "You know, it's very sweet that you want to make sure I'm okay and protect me. But Leroy, love, I'll be fine. During my anatomy lessons as a student, I was shoulder-deep in the abdomen of a dead horse to extract its liver after we had removed the intestines first. I already helped you get Cory's leg out of a shark, I found his torso. And finding that by surprise was more of a shock than this more clinical setting will be."

Now even more concerned, Leroy gently took Michelle's hand. "Shit, I didn't think about that. Are you really okay? I should've offered to let you talk to the department's psychologist."

"Baby, sweetheart, I swear to you, I'm all right. It was a surprise, somewhat of a shock, but I'm not traumatized," Michelle said, then went on, when he saw Leroy still frowning and probably mentally kicking himself. "I promise. Your worry warms my heart, it does. But I know myself well enough to tell you I'm okay. Trust me to know myself, and to always be honest with you, okay?"

The last of Leroy's frown disappeared and he leaned in for a soft kiss. "Okay. Shall we, then?"

"Yes, let's do this."

Back to his professional self, Leroy badged them in a moment later and guided Michelle through the maze of corridors that made up the realm of the city's medical examiners. Aside from a few offices, a break room, and a small waiting area, Michelle also saw several smaller rooms set up with round tables and chairs. Some were even furnished with a more comforting setup with couches, and in one he thought he spotted a corner with toys for smaller kids. All of them had tissue boxes sitting on the tables or a shelf, and in most there was a small fridge with some bottles of water or juice. It seemed the team at the morgue was trying to make things as easy as possible for the relatives of their guests.

When they came closer to the medical bay of the facility, lights turned from a warmer white to an even brighter, colder white, walls became tiled, and there was no trace of any carpet on the floor anymore. Michelle made out the door to a viewing area, so people didn't have to step into the autopsy area for identifications. He suspected it was also easier to have cops waiting there and observe an autopsy than have them underfoot next to the table.

"How many autopsies have you witnessed?" Michelle calmly asked Leroy. He didn't have to ask whether Leroy attended them at all; he knew his partner well enough for that already.

"As many as I can. And if I can't make it to the autopsy itself, like in this case, I try to at least once make it here to talk to the ME personally, and see the body myself."

Michelle nodded. "You're a good man, and a good cop. Let's see what we can do to find justice for Cory."

Leroy nodded and pushed the large metal doors open, then held one side open for Michelle to slip through.

They found Rose studying another body on one of several height-adjustable tables and dictating her findings into a voice recorder. Looking at the rest of the area, it seemed the ME's office did their best to accommodate Rose as much as possible. Not only had they supplied her with autopsy tables she could work on from her wheelchair, several desks were adjustable as well. He wasn't surprised: from his talk with her earlier, she sounded highly skilled and competent, and had she been a vet, he would've wanted her on his team as well.

When she heard them come in, she looked up and stopped her recording. "Well, hello there. Leroy, you bring me the sweetest gifts. I had no idea you were so good-looking, doc."

Leroy cleared his throat loudly. "He's not playing for your team, Rose."

Her bright grin stayed in place. "Well, in that case, Ken will be very grateful to you. I asked him to give Michelle a hand later, anyway."

"Forget it. Michelle is also mine," the cop grumbled good-naturedly.

Next to Leroy, Michelle giggled. "Michelle is also standing right here and can speak for himself. And I will gladly accept the help, but I'll have to disappoint Ken when it comes to anything else. But we didn't want to interrupt your work on your other case, Rose."

The call earlier had been enough to have them on a first name basis, and even though the patients around him weren't his usual clientele, not to mention the fact that they were dead, he felt comfortable enough in the medical surroundings to join in on the banter.

"Oh, don't worry about it. Mr. Shafer here came in a few minutes ago, I only just started the external description. I can pick that back up later. He is a case of an unattended death, likely due to old age, not a homicide. Unless I find something strange, that is. But as of now, his case is important, of course, but not as time-sensitive as a murder case with a killer still on the loose."

"Okay."

"Come over here, you two," Rose said and made her way over to another table. She drew away the cover and revealed Cory's torso.

When both men were standing next to her, she began to tell them the details of her examination. "So, I have to say it again, though you know it. Officially, I cannot tell you yet that the torso belongs to the limbs you and Luke brought me. We started the DNA analysis, once I have the results, I'll update the file. Unofficially, yes, skin and hair coloring match, so DNA will likely confirm this to be Cory Gilbert's torso. Even the tattoo matches the one on his wrist in color and style, so I assume he had it done by the same artist both times. His chest tattoo seems to be older, seeing as it's faded more than the one on the wrist, even though his wrist probably was more often exposed to sunlight."

"I know you have to say it, Rose. Given that I have seen a photo of this tattoo, I agree with you that even without DNA results yet, this is very likely Cory's torso," Leroy told her.

"Good to know that we agree," she replied with a wink, then kept talking. "All right. Medically, Mr. Gilbert was a healthy male. His liver showed no signs of excessive drinking, most of his other organs were in a good condition. His lungs showed minor deposits of particulate matter. Without an in-depth examination, I'd say those were in line with what probably all of us show from living in a city; maybe the levels were slightly elevated for him, but I suppose his job on a boat with heavy machinery might have contributed to that. Either way, it wasn't what killed him."

"I would've been surprised if that had been the case," Leroy said matter-of-factly.

"You and me both," Michelle added with a nod.

"Make that three of us," Rose said, then gestured back to the torso. "I can also tell you Mr. Gilbert was in a good physical condition. He was well-trained, but he also must have taken care of himself during his work. I couldn't see any of the skeletal deformations often seen in people doing lots of manual labor and heavy lifting. He must have been careful to lift with his back straight, using mostly his legs. And though his hand has a few callouses, I feel confident to say he probably wore his gloves most of the time. His foot shows no deformation either, he most likely wore high-quality work boots."

"It would fit with everything we've learned about him so far."

"Yes, I thought so. Now that you brought me the torso I have internal organs for a more detailed tox screen. That is still running, so I can't tell you any results, yet. But to be honest, I don't think there will be anything. Looking at the condition of the body parts I already have, and the fact that the limbs were removed post-mortem, my best guess is, once you find his head, we'll know more about his cause of death. Because his torso doesn't show any other mortal injuries other than the ones where his arms and legs were cut off. I found a few older bruises, but they were consistent with injuries I've seen on other fishermen in the past."

Leroy exhaled heavily. "I was kind of afraid of these results after seeing the torso yesterday. Please tell me you found some-thing else. I noticed you started with the internal findings, that's not your usual style, Rose."

"You're a good student, Leroy. And you're right. The body itself doesn't give away that much. But I found some other things that might help you. There was a tiny piece of metal in the wound on his right hip. Without something to compare it to, I can't say anything for certain, but my best guess is, that it's part of the serrated blade that was used to cut off the limbs. I also found a small piece of plastic – could be foil, could be from a garbage bag, I still need to have the lab take a closer look. And on top of that, I found a few shreds of fiber stuck to the neck wound. Again, these need further examination as well. My preliminary guess would be fibers from a carpet in a trunk or footwell of a car, because they look like many others I've found on bodies, but let me stress that this is really just a guess."

Pleased, Leroy beamed at the ME. "That's still awesome, Rose. Thank you so much. Now we have some things to compare when we get to the point where we can arrest a suspect."

"I thought you would like that. I wanted this visit to end on a happy note, as happy as it can be at least."

"Good thinking. So I take it that's really all you have for me at the moment."

"Yes. You know how this goes: Bring me the head, and I can hopefully tell you more."

"That's good enough for me right now."

Leroy's gaze wandered to Michelle. "I take it you will do the post-mortem on the cat now?"

"If that's all right with Rose, yes."

The woman looked from one man to the other. "It's all right for me. Say goodbye to each other outside the doors, though. I'll let Ken know to meet you there now, Michelle. That way I can keep working on Mr. Shafer without your conversation and smooching in the background of my recording," she said and stuck out her tongue at them.

Laughing, Leroy dragged his boyfriend back into the hallway and waved goodbye to Rose on the way.

With the doors closed behind them, Leroy looked at Michelle. "Are you okay with me leaving you here? I did see some new notes from Luke in the case file just before we came here, and I had planned to take some of it over from him so he has time for the electronics and the security footage – his warrant should come through there soon."

"Sure. You can get back to the precinct, no problem. When I'm done here, I'll head to the shop and get my car; it's actually not that far from here. Then I'll get home and wait for my landlord. You've got a job to do, and I have enough on my schedule, too. I'll be fine, I'm a big boy." Michelle knew it was a mistake as soon as the words had left his lips.

Leroy's eyes darkened and he took a deep breath. "Yes, you definitely are," he said and ran his hand around Michelle's neck to draw him in for a fierce kiss. "And I intend to feel every last bit of you inside me tonight."

God, Leroy would be the death of him, and Michelle knew he would die a happy man. His knees were weak, and he pressed his lips against Leroy's again with a low moan, his hands clinging to his lover's arms for some support.

They were interrupted when somebody giggled behind them. "Oops, sorry, guys."

Leroy broke the kiss and ran his thumb over Michelle's cheek. "I guess that's my cue to leave. I'll see you tonight. I love you."

Michelle smiled a dreamy smile. "Yeah, until tonight. I love you, too."

With Leroy leaving, the vet focused on the other man. He was maybe five years older than Michelle, wore a pair of light blue scrubs, and had a pair of glasses pushed up onto his head. "Hey. Sorry about that," Michelle finally said.

"Hi. No problem. I feel like I should be the one apologizing again for ruining the moment."

"No, absolutely not. We got carried away, we didn't exactly plan an extended goodbye like that."

"How long have you been together?"

"A few days."

The other man guffawed. "Ah, young love. Can't blame you. I was thinking about asking Leroy out more than once, but somehow we never were single at the same time. Looks like I'm out of luck again, with both of you. I take it you're Dr. Jenkins."

"I am, but Michelle is fine. Ken, I presume?"

"That's me. Should we get started on the poor cat, then?"

"Yes, let's do that."

Chapter Twenty

At the Aquarium, Luke was happy to see that he didn't have to deal with the same security guard Leroy had spoken to before. And given the grumbles coming from the guy's supervisor, who was now setting Luke up in the main office so he could check the system and download the recordings, Luke wasn't sure the sorry excuse for a security guard from the night of Cory's murder would still have a job after this was over.

It didn't take long for Luke to get started, and his first check confirmed one of his suspicions: the night when the sharks were fed parts of Cory's body, somebody had gotten into the Aquarium using Cory's own keycard. There was no data showing that the card was swiped on the way out again, but one of the side doors' logs showed it had been opened about fifteen minutes after Cory's card had keyed somebody in. So whoever it was hadn't stayed around for long to see the sharks dine.

Luke downloaded the log entries, then moved on to downloading the security feed including all background data, not just the raw video feed. A quick look at the original footage proved it wasn't just the feed he had been sent that had been tampered with. And looking at the system data, there were some anomalies hinting at a remote hack. So most likely he wouldn't find the odd thumb drive lying around.

On top of all that, he downloaded the video feed of the last few weeks. Leroy had talked about Cory's boss at the fishing company stating that Cory had seemed somewhat restless lately. Maybe it would help to observe Cory here at the Aquarium as well.

Once he had everything he wanted, he packed his things and went to look for Cory's boss at the Aquarium to ask him a few more questions.

The man seemed eager to help, and Luke wasn't surprised. Julia had told him that the Aquarium was still suffering from a lot of bad press. Solving this case and being shown to be helpful was important if they wanted to get back on track with their ticket sales.

In the end, Luke learned, it hadn't been completely out of the ordinary for Cory to come by at night, even if he hadn't worked that day or even week. His research and project planning included the improvement of fishing techniques with regard to the circadian rhythm of different species so that fishing companies would possibly be able to prevent unnecessary bycatch. He knew unintentionally catching unwanted fish, whether for their size, species or even sex, was a big problem in commercial fishing and came not only with a bad public opinion, but also with ecological problems and sometimes even fishing bans. He had hoped to improve existing strategies for bycatch reduction. That was why he sometimes had spent a late evening or even a night at the Aquarium studying nocturnal species. The Aquarium didn't have a problem with it, and had simply asked Cory to let the security guard on duty on any of those nights know that he was there. So whenever the keycard logs were checked and somebody had seen Cory's code, nobody had been surprised. But with the investigation going on, they had refrained from going over the logs themselves during the last few days.

Luke left the Aquarium with the new information and the need to bring in the security guard working at the night of Cory's murder for further questioning. In his car, he made a call to organize two uniforms to pick up the security guard, then called Leroy. They decided to meet up at the precinct to lead the interview together. After that, Luke would get back home to work in a quieter environment on what he had collected at the Aquarium and the electronics still drying, and Leroy would take over the social media accounts and the bank accounts of the professor and the other captain.

The city had gone mostly back to normal, though Luke still saw more than enough people cleaning up the aftermath of the storm, and signs in shop windows advertising discounts on products that hadn't been cooled during the blackout.

When he finally arrived at the precinct, he was surprised by the elated mood his colleagues were in despite all the recent extra work. "What's up with you guys?"

One of his fellow detectives swiveled his chair around to face Luke. "Oh, we hope we can trust the current gossip dribbling down from the brass. You know about the boss and Hawkins butting heads?"

"Yeah, I do."

"So, the lieutenant put in an internal complaint, and today he brought his boyfriend along who filed a civil complaint as well. Word is, this has made his way as far up as the freaking Chief of Police. Internal Affairs is looking into it right now, and if it turns out there's some hard evidence, it doesn't look good for Hawkins at all. The guy is a pest, lazy as hell, and giving all of us a bad rep. We're discussing a small gift for the lieutenant, should he really manage to get Hawkins kicked out."

"Nice, count me in," Luke said with a grin before heading toward his own desk in the bullpen.

He was still updating the case file when a uniform appeared next to him. "Detective Preston."

"Officer Hayes. What can I do for you?"

"It's about the man you asked us to pick up."

"Did you bring him in?"

The officer huffed out an annoyed breath. "Oh, we brought him in, just not to the precinct. When we arrived at this apartment, his neighbors were just ready to call us, anyway. His TV had been running on full volume for hours, and when they knocked to complain, he yelled at them and threatened to bash their heads in with a bottle. Just before we arrived, they heard something crash together with a loud thud and a groan."

"I assume you gained access to check on him."

"We did. Your man is a piece of work. Turns out he was more than black-out drunk. He tripped over the TV cable, the TV crashed, and he fell to the floor, where he passed out completely from severe alcohol poisoning. We called an ambulance; he's currently at the hospital and being treated. My colleague stayed with him for now, but the doctors told us that he'll likely be unconscious for the next twelve hours at the least. They fear he might even slip into a real coma. His liver seems to be failing. That's the last I've heard."

Luke shook his head. "Everything else would've been too easy to hope for, hm? Thank you, Hayes. Please send me the hospital details, I'll get in touch with them, and if you let me know who's currently at the hospital, I can coordinate with your partner. Good job securing him, though."

"Thanks. And I'll send you everything right away."

With Hayes gone again, Luke finished his entry, quickly talked to the hospital and the uniform still guarding the unconscious security guard, and then got up to grab a coffee from the break room. It was more of a black slush than coffee, but he was annoyed enough to ignore that fact. Walking back to his desk, he saw Leroy leaning against it. Luke held up his hand in a silent question, but Leroy shook his head and showed his own travel mug.

Once Luke sat back down in his chair, Leroy smiled at him. "Thanks for the offer, but I refilled mine before I left the morgue."

Luke shrugged and grinned at Leroy. "I get why. They have damn good coffee there."

"They do," Leroy agreed and took another sip.

"So, I was going to call you once I was back at my desk. You're here earlier than I expected. Sorry to be the bearer of bad news, but our interview has been canceled."

"Why?"

"Funny thing, it turns out being extremely drunk and tripping over a cable do not mix well," Luke began in a sarcastic tone and then told Leroy the full story.

When he was finished, Leroy groaned in annoyance. "What an idiot. Okay, we'll reschedule the interview to whenever he wakes up. Let's stick to the rest of the plan. I'll check the money and accounts; you get home to have a look at the tape."

"Yeah, okay, let's do..." Luke was interrupted by his ringing phone. After checking the number, he looked at Leroy. "It's Dispatch."

He picked up, and after listening for a moment, he let the caller know he'd put the call on speaker so Leroy could listen as well. "Okay. Hello, Lieutenant."

"Hello."

"As I was saying to Detective Preston, we got a call about a head turning up in a flooded basement. I already sent uniforms to secure the scene, but I was on the night when you called in the torso, and I figured this might be related. Detective Preston is listed as lead on the case, though."

"He is. You did the right thing calling him. But we're working on it together. Thank you for calling us first. If it turns out this isn't related to our case, we can still hand it over, but chances are high it could be part of our case. Send us both the address, please."

"Will do."

A few moments after hanging up, both Luke's and Leroy's phones pinged with a message and the details. Leroy cursed.

"What?"

"That's close to Michelle's place and to where the torso was dumped."

Luke nodded. He wouldn't feel comfortable with something like this happening close to the person he loved, either. And after he had seen how Leroy and Michelle interacted, how Leroy looked at the veterinarian, he didn't doubt for a second that those two were already head over heels in love.

"Then let's get there, see what's going on, and make sure Michelle is okay."

"Yeah."

Usually, they would have taken one car, but this time they arrived separately to allow Luke to get home easily after processing the scene, if possible.

Stepping out of the car, Luke shot Leroy a resigned glance when they both heard somebody retching. One of the uniforms standing near the crime scene tape and keeping an eye on the crowd that had already formed came over to their cars and, after greeting them, looked at Leroy. "Deja-vú."

"Indeed." Seeing Luke's confused look, Leroy explained, "We worked the scene the night Michelle found the torso."

"Ah, okay."

"How's your boyfriend doing with that, Lieutenant?"

"He's okay. Thanks for asking."

"Sure thing. I guess you want to know what's going on here today, though."

Both Luke and Leroy nodded and checked their surroundings as the officer began to tell them the details. "We got a call about an hour ago. The poor guy over there still puking his guts out every few minutes is Randy Wagner. When he caught his breath for a moment, he told us he was sent here by his boss to pump out yet another still-flooded basement after the storm. Everything was fine, until the pump stopped. He went back down into the basement to check if something was blocking the hose. When he picked it up, there was a human head still stuck to it from the pump's suction. He dropped everything, ran back upstairs and onto the sidewalk screaming, and ever since then is vomiting every few minutes. Well, more like dry heaving by now. A passer-by, Anna Kupka, heard him scream, managed to get some minor details out of him, and called the cops. That's her over there, trying to calm him down. She said she's an ER nurse, and talking to her helped to distract him, so I decided that although it's not strictly protocol, I'd let them sit there together."

"Good call," Luke and Leroy answered in unison.

The officer nodded and continued his report. "We secured the scene, CSU and the ME are here, and we already have uniforms canvassing the area and knocking on doors. It's one of the buildings we've been checking since the last time, too. I don't know if you managed to check that part of the file yet. But the second round of door-to-doors for the torso didn't yield any new information."

"Yes, we saw. You did a good job, thanks. We'll take it from here."

"Thanks. No problem. If you need anything, let me know." With that, the cop stepped back to his position to keep guarding the onlookers.

A quick glance inside the basement confirmed the teams were still busy working down there, so Luke and Leroy made their way over to the unlucky finder. Randy Wagner was twenty, and this was his first real job after helping out at his father's coffee shop after high school. He looked like he had aged ten years within the last hour. They managed about five minutes of talking to Randy, but as soon as they started carefully questioning him about finding the head, the man blanched and ended up with his own head between his knees, gagging once again. They accepted that they wouldn't get a lot out of him like that, and Luke stepped to the side for a moment to discuss the situation with his lieutenant.

"Leroy, what do you think about calling in the department's psychologist? I don't even think he knows anything, but I'd feel like crap if we didn't offer him some sort of support."

"Same. The poor lad might be traumatized for life."

"Yeah. Look, check on him, wrap up what you can, and I'll make the call."

"Yes, good plan."

It wasn't much, but they at least had learned that Randy had started to pump the water out of the shared laundry area of the basement and that the private basement compartments the building offered so far were all still locked. Luke made the call and after that made his way over to the CSU and ME teams again. When they glared at him, he held his hands up in surrender.

"I come in peace. I'm not here for a lot of details, I just wanted to ask if you can confirm that all the private basement compartments are locked, and the head likely had been some-where in the shared area before it turned up like this."

One of the technicians looked up from taking pictures of the hose to which the head had stuck before. "They are, yes. And so far, it doesn't look like any of them have openings through which the head would fit. But there's still enough water down there that I can't tell you that for sure. But my guess at this point is, that yes, the head probably had been somewhere in the laundry area when the pump was started."

"Okay, thank you. I'll leave you guys to it."

Luke risked a glance at the ME, but the stony expression on the young woman's face stopped him from even opening his mouth. He knew she and the CSU team were right – they all had to do their jobs properly, and that took time. He shouldn't rush them. But as the one investigating a case, striving to bring all angles together to find a murderer, naturally, he was always looking to get as much information as possible as quickly as possible. Sighing, he leaned against his car and typed a short note for the case file on his phone.

A surprisingly short time after his call, the precinct's psychologist arrived at the scene, and Luke greeted the man and gave him a few details. Together, they walked over to the others. Leroy and Luke thanked Mrs. Kupka again before letting her go, while the psychologist guided Randy to a quieter corner and began talking to him in a calming manner.

Luke and Leroy looked at each other, and Leroy sighed. "You know what, you can head home and get started on screening the surveillance footage. I'll take the scene from here. It's no use for both of us to wait around."

"And once you're done here, you can check on Michelle?"

"Yeah, I won't lie, that's a bonus. He has a meeting with his landlord at his apartment before heading back to my place. And with more body parts showing up around here, I'd feel better knowing he's safe."

Luke squeezed Leroy's shoulder. "I can completely understand that. Okay, let's do it like that, and say hi to Michelle from me. I'll be on my way, then."

"I will. Okay."

Chapter Twenty-One

Back at home, Luke started his computer and made his way into the kitchen to grab a proper coffee. He might have become a coffee snob since he had gotten together with Julia and her supply of delicious Italian coffee from Scarlette's family, but he figured there were far worse vices he could indulge in. He was just about to step into his office when he felt his fiancée's hand on his arm. "Hey, Luke."

"Hey, July."

They caught each other up on their day so far for a minute or two, but Luke still had enough work to do, just like Julia. She got on her tiptoes, pressed a kiss to his cheek. "Good luck, I hope you find something useful. And I have a surprise for you later."

"Really now?"

"Yep."

"Do I get a hint?"

"Nope, definitely not. Now get back to work," she replied with a cheeky smile and vanished back to her own office.

Following her order, he sat behind his desk and decided he would give the electronics a little longer to dry while he was going over the surveillance videos and system data.

It was tedious work, but he managed to isolate the signature of a signal interfering with the Aquarium's security system. He couldn't pinpoint exactly what kind of device had been used for it, but he could see a list of affected systems. Aside from the video feed and door alarms, it seemed somebody also had switched on the webcam in the Security office, possibly keeping an eye on the guard (which made Luke shudder, remembering what the guy had been up to for hours).

Luke had seen a lot of hacked systems over the years, but whatever he tried, he couldn't get more information from the data in front of him. It gave him a bad feeling: something was seriously off here. This was more than the typical hack half of the teenagers nowadays could pull off if they put in a little work. To get deeper into this, he'd need to book a spot at the tech lab at the precinct, maybe grab one of the specialists there to help him out. He was good, but they were on a whole other level.

Knowing he wouldn't get any further as it was, he switched to the video footage. The footage of the night of Cory's murder was still useless, but going over the weeks before helped Luke to get a personal picture of Cory. It confirmed what he and Leroy had been told by everybody. He saw Cory helping with cleaning some of the smaller tanks, lending a hand during a medical procedure on one of the fish, and preparing buckets for feeding. He moved confidently, evidently knowing what he was doing, and yet always approached the tanks slow enough for the fish to not be surprised too much. Two nights also showed Cory sitting on the floor in front of one of the larger tanks, observing its residents and taking notes on his laptop, which was set to a low screen brightness so it wouldn't disturb the fish.

It made Luke angry to see how dedicated Cory had been, and to know his life had been cut short seemingly without any reason.

Finally, Luke had a look at the footage of the café area. He had thought that if he could find a motive for the murder – and the somewhat public disposal of Cory's remains – it would be tied to something happening at the Aquarium, something between him and a colleague more likely during their work, not while Cory was taking a break and was studying alone like his boss had said.

For a long while, all Luke saw was indeed Cory sitting at a table near the large entertainment pool, his back to the water, where one of his colleagues was putting on a show in her mermaid costume. He had observed a similar scene a few times when he finally began to recognize a pattern. It wasn't all the time that Cory was sitting close to the tank, and he was never facing it when he did. Skipping through the footage again, Luke realized Cory only sat at the tank when one specific colleague was putting on her show. His first thought would've been an affair, or some flirting at least, but then Cory would've been facing her, not be staring at his notes. And studying the footage in more detail, Luke found Cory wasn't the only one interested in his notes. His colleague was repeatedly swimming close by, looking over Cory's shoulder at the pages as well. Luke couldn't make out what exactly they were looking at, but when Cory picked up a pen and repeated a motion, Luke thought the biologist was likely drawing a circle. Then it hit Luke that the notebook on screen was one of the exact ones he had lying around. Flipping through them quickly, he saw a date had been circled on a page – a page with coordinates scribbled below the date Cory had written down and circled.

Checking the date against a calendar, he saw the day had been a Sunday, so this wasn't a date to remember when the lecture the notes next to the date had been taken, but most likely was in connection to the coordinates, and his colleague seemed to be trying to read everything despite the water and glass wall. Something strange was clearly going on here.

He reached for his phone and called the Aquarium's director asking for the complete roster for the days Cory was shown with the mermaid in question. Asking only for the different mermaids could get out too easily and give people a warning.

The director was cooperative, and Luke received an email with the rosters within minutes. Comparing it against his list of employees and their job descriptions from the first day of the investigation, he found the one he wanted to talk to quickly. And reading her name, something seemed familiar about it. Too familiar to ignore. Hoping, but not expecting too much, he opened the search field in the case file and typed in her name. When the match came up, he cursed and reached for his phone again.

"Leroy, are you still at the scene?"

"I was just about to leave. We had the water pumped out of the basement after all, CSU found some hair that could belong to Cory and some blood behind the dryer. They assume the head had been hidden there before the movement of the water dislodged it. With the basement flooded, nobody had been down here since the storm, so nobody saw it. Why?"

"Apartment 4E, Erin Graham. She works at the Aquarium as one of the mermaid actresses. I've seen her on the surveillance footage swimming close to Cory and reading his notes – very likely the pages with the coordinates. We need to talk to her."

There was a moment of silence, then Luke heard a quiet thud like Leroy was kicking a wall. "Shit, yes, that's it. I knew it. Something was bothering me when I was going over the reports of the door-to-doors after the torso was found, but I couldn't pinpoint it. The building here shares the dumpster with Michelle's building. I must've seen her name on the list, but I didn't actively make the connection with this case. I'll find her and bring her to the precinct."

"Let me know when you have her and you're on the way. I don't have it too far, I'll be there quickly. For now, I'll look at the footage again for more details and run a background check on her."

"Okay."

After hanging up, Luke initiated the search for Erin Graham and went over the videos once again while the program was gathering data. The surveillance footage didn't give up any more details, even after looking it over repeatedly. He looked for another connection between Cory and Erin, any footage that might show them arriving or leaving the Aquarium together or handing each other anything, but didn't find any instances like that either. Another look at Julia's spreadsheet with the social media contacts showed only a loose connection between them as far as publicly visible.

Hoping the electronics wouldn't disappoint, Luke decided to try Cory's laptop. It didn't come as a surprise that it was password protected, given that he had used it at college and work and would've wanted to protect his company plans. Unfortunately, that meant it would take longer to get into it and see if he might've stayed logged into his social media apps.

Luke prepared everything to get access to the laptop, then picked up Cory's watch. Most people protected their laptops, even their phones, but hardly anybody remembered to be as vigilant with their other connected devices like their smartwatches.

Switching it on, Luke seemed to finally have some luck. The watch appeared to be working fine, and there was no screen lock set up. Checking the installed apps, his enthusiasm died a little, though. Cory hadn't used his watch as extensively as some other people, there were no messenger apps or music apps. Mainly, he found the pre-installed fitness apps for counting daily steps, a heart rate monitor, a sleep tracker. On top of that, the watch didn't run on its own data plan, but had been connected to Cory's phone via Bluetooth in the past, so most of the apps were trying to connect to the phone again, showing no recent data. But Luke felt a jolt of excitement when he swiped to the calendar tile. It hadn't tried to sync just yet, and he read an entry saying "Help Ariel" on the evening of Cory's murder. But without opening the calendar on Cory's computer, he couldn't get any more information from the watch.

Luke updated the case file with the latest information nonetheless, and while doing so, his eyes landed on an interesting detail from one of the reports in the file that connected neatly with the video he had been watching earlier.

Still, he couldn't have a closer look without Cory's laptop unlocked. It was frustrating to feel like he was close to something but being unable to work on it just yet. At least he still had a background check he could look at.

He opened the window with Erin Graham's information and began studying it. At a first glance, it seemed like a typical story, even if it was an unhappy one. She was an only child, both her parents had unfortunately been killed when the apartment building they had lived in had caught fire while Erin had been away at college. No other close relatives, and from the looks of it, she was currently single. She had graduated five years ago. She had studied English and Music and had been part of the college's swim team. After graduation she had been working as an editor for a small indie music magazine, which had been discontinued a few months ago. Now she was working at the Aquarium to pay off her remaining student loan. No large online presence, but she had the usual social media accounts, following her alma mater, the magazine she had been working for, some colleagues he had seen on Julia's spreadsheet already.

No criminal record. No driver's license, so not even a parking ticket. Just a woman trying to get by.

And yet, call it instinct or intuition, something told Luke to take a closer look. He began with her social media and found the accounts to be relatively new, all maybe a few months old. Some pictures showed her morning coffee, others showed her in the water with her costume, some more were taken of her record collection. Ordinary, nothing exciting. The only thing a little odd was that several had been posted on the same days, then days of silence. Not completely unheard of, though. Maybe she was following her own social media regime, only logging in every once in a while.

He followed a link to her former magazine, but both the social media account and the website only showed a "Sorry, we've gone out of business" notice now. He didn't find any contact information, and googling only yielded one or two very short articles. Which also was the case for other indie magazines, so it wasn't entirely suspicious. Still, it didn't sit right with him for some reason.

Her alma mater was more active and up to date. Running a search on the website, he found a picture of Erin Graham in a swimsuit. She was in a pool, hooking her arms on the edge and smiling at the camera. It was the only picture he found of her, though. And the longer he looked at it, the more he felt something was wrong with the picture. Yes, the swimsuit had the same color as the ones her teammates had been wearing in other photos. But this picture felt different from the others. She was alone in it, and hardly any of the other team members had close-ups on the website. Yes, she was pretty enough. Luke assumed that might make her a good candidate to be used to generate more interest in the team. But the picture was taken in a way that it was impossible to determine where it had even been taken. It could've been any other pool. And the coloring, the composition of the picture, it all felt like somebody else had taken this picture. Of course, the photographer could've changed, but it seemed like her college usually had the same person taking pictures of the team. Looking at the website in more detail seemed to confirm Luke's feeling that somebody might have added this photo and the description without the college's knowledge.

With an uneasy feeling, Luke had to satisfy his curiosity and began to look for the apartment fire that had claimed Erin Graham's parents' lives. He found a police report on a fire in the small town her parents had lived in, and a larger article about it, both claiming three people had died. When he kept looking for information in some smaller newspapers and in the obituaries of the following weeks, though, he found only references to one person, a seventy year old lady, dying and her funeral being held.

Going over everything once more, Luke felt like he was staring at a ghost when he studied Erin Graham's background check and her ID photo.

None of it made sense. Why was a mermaid entertainer staring at coordinates a fisherman had scribbled down? Why was there possible physical evidence connecting her and Cory's body? Why did she feel like she wasn't real?

He couldn't and wouldn't make assumptions, but hoped all the little pieces might point him in the right direction. No matter what, all of it would make for an interesting interview with Erin Graham once Leroy would bring her to the precinct.

Chapter Twenty-Two

Luke stood next to Leroy in the observation room, finishing the discussion of their strategy and having a first look at Erin Graham in the flesh sitting in the interview room through the one-way mirror.

"Cory's captain hasn't gotten back to you yet about the coordinates, right?" Luke asked while studying the woman in the adjacent room. Right now, she didn't seem completely relaxed to him, but not all that nervous, either.

"No, unfortunately not. But reception is spotty as far out as they are, the video interview was difficult enough. I hope to hear from him soon. But we still have enough to talk about with her, I'd say."

"That's for sure. Shall we?"

"Yes."

The cops entered the interview room, and the woman sat up a little straighter. She had her brown hair in a ponytail, and a loosely fitting sweatshirt covered the fit body Luke had seen in the water before on tape. Cory had been fit as well, but if she had surprised him, Luke could see how she could've overpowered him. Toying with the paper coffee mug in front of her, she gave them a friendly yet a little confused smile. She had been mirandarized, but so far didn't look concerned.

"Ms. Graham, thanks again for coming here with me and talking to us. This is my partner Detective Preston," Leroy said and took one of the two chairs facing the woman.

She nodded and shifted her gaze to Luke. "Ah, yes, of course. Hello, Detective. This is about Cory, isn't it? It's horrible what happened. But I don't know how I could help you, to be honest."

Luke sat in the chair next to Leroy's and nodded, with a smile on his face for now. "Hello, Ms. Graham. Yes, this is about Cory Gilbert's death. Can you tell us how well you knew Mr. Gilbert?"

She shrugged and sighed a little. "Not all that well. We've been coworkers for the past few months, but we worked in different areas. I'm doing a mermaid show in the entertainment pool in the cafeteria, Cory works... worked with the vets and keepers, taking care of the animals."

"But you met each other backstage in the employee areas, didn't you?" Leroy asked.

Nodding, the woman looked between the two cops. "Yeah, sure, every once in a while we ran into each other. We said hi to each other, there was some small talk. We were friendly, but it wasn't like we were actual friends."

"And anything more than friends?" Leroy wanted to know.

Now Erin shook her head. "No, nothing like that either. From what I heard, Cory had a girlfriend. He didn't seem like the type to cheat."

"And would you have been interested, had he been?" Leroy kept digging. He and Luke had agreed on him taking these questions, while Luke would take over later.

"No."

"I thought he seemed nice."

"Well, first of all, had he been open to it, he hardly would've been nice. And second, I'm into women, so he was definitely not my type," she admitted with a shy smile.

"Fair point," Leroy agreed, then took a moment to consult the file folder in front of him. He knew the details, but he also knew about the effect of a short pause at the right moment.

"Can you tell us where you were the evening before Cory's arm was found?"

Genuine surprise and worry flickered over her face. "What? You don't think I have anything to do with this, do you? I couldn't..."

Leroy eased back in his chair, his body language a little more relaxed again.

"We don't think anything at the moment. We're just looking to find out more about Cory and what he had been up to before his arm was found, so anybody who has seen him before could help us," he told her.

"I guess so. But I didn't see him that evening. I think the last shift where we were together at the Aquarium at the same time was a couple of days before that."

"Okay, but you haven't answered my question. Where were you that evening?" Leroy asked again.

"I visited my girlfriend. I've been staying with her the last few days, actually."

Nodding, Leroy reached for the coffee mug he had brought along. After taking a sip, he set the mug down again and looked back to Erin Graham. "Hm. Is there anything you might need help with? Something you might have asked Cory to give you a hand with?"

"Ah, no, not really. I mean, my girlfriend and I are thinking of moving in together, so I might have asked Cory and some other colleagues for help moving, but that's not something happening right now."

Once again, Leroy nodded. "Things are getting more serious with your girlfriend. That sounds nice."

"Yeah, it is," Erin answered with a smile which didn't entirely reach her eyes. Leroy couldn't blame her. Being interviewed by the cops in connection to murder investigation left hardly anybody completely unfazed, innocent or not. And yet, he understood what Luke had meant when he had told him that something about Erin Graham simply felt off.

Time to try to throw her off a little.

"Ms. Graham, do you have a nickname by any chance? Something your colleagues might call you?"

She tilted her head and looked at Leroy in confusion. "Huh? Ah, kinda, I guess. Sometimes the other girls call me Ren. Short for my name, sort of, but also because I like to listen to the *Footloose* soundtrack while warming up before getting into my costume."

"Really? I would've thought something more along the lines of Ariel."

"Nah, not really. I think I heard the very first girl that worked in the entertainment pool when they opened it got that nickname. She only lasted about a week, though. One of the other girls told me she developed an allergy to the cleaner the Aquarium uses for the pool and had to quit. And when she was gone everybody realized it would be weird to give all the entertainers the same nickname, and after that, I haven't heard anybody being called Ariel anymore."

This time, Luke shot her a question. "So the entry in Mr. Gilbert's calendar to 'help Ariel' didn't refer to you?"

"Uh, no, I never asked Cory for help with anything."

"Do you have any idea whom else he could've meant by 'Ariel'?"

The woman shook her head. "No, really. Like I said, we didn't talk a lot or anything. We were coworkers, but we didn't even do the same work. It's not like we spent a lot of time together."

Now, Luke cocked his head. "Are you interested in marine biology, Ms. Graham?"

Slowly, she seemed to become more confused. "Um, well, I know a few things about the animals we keep at the Aquarium, just in case a guest runs into me and has questions when I'm on my way to or from the entertainment pool."

"No classes about it back in college?"

"No. Look, I was on the swim team back then, I needed a new job after my old company was closed, and I had heard about the Aquarium looking for people to do a show. The money and the hours are okay, and it's not a strip show like probably most of the advertised 'mermaid' acts are, if I had to take a guess. I wasn't hired as a keeper or something like that," she explained in a tone that was a mix of confusion, burgeoning annoyance, and a bit of embarrassment.

Still eyeing her with curiosity and giving away nothing, Luke summarized, "Okay, so you and Mr. Gilbert were simply coworkers, didn't exactly talk with each other, but there was no animosity between the two of you, either. You didn't look for his help, and you have no deeper interest in his field of work."

When he paused to give her a chance to answer, she nodded. "Yes, exactly. Which is why I don't know how I could be of any help, really."

"We will get to that once you tell us why you and Mr. Gilbert seem to have had a standing lunch break meet," Luke said, while Leroy sat back a little to give this part of the interview over to his detective.

There was the tiniest flicker of acknowledgment in her eyes before she shook her head once again. "I don't know what you mean."

"Really? Then maybe you want to explain to us what

exactly you were doing when you swam close to his cafeteria table and were looking at his notes multiple times over the last few weeks."

That brought an expression of honest surprise to her face. "What?"

"Ms. Graham, I have video footage of you and Mr. Gilbert. For the past few weeks, whenever he took a lunch break and you were in the water, he sat close to the tank, and you swam over, looking over his shoulder, studying something in his notebooks. Care to share what was so interesting?"

Obviously trying to gain a moment to form an answer, she brought her mug to her lips to take a sip of her coffee. After setting it back on the table, she looked from Luke to Leroy and back. "I really don't know what you're talking about. I mean, sure, it could be that I swam over to him from time to time. It's a cafeteria, the pool is there to entertain everybody – including a lot of kids. And the kids love knocking on the glass. Let me tell you, it's not just fish that get disturbed by that because it's freaking loud underwater. Cory was there, silently reading, and many parents kept their kids away from him to give him quiet time to study. So yeah, maybe I swam over there subconsciously more often than I realized. But I didn't read in his notebooks. Honestly, how could I? I assume you know how hard it is to see underwater. It's difficult enough to put on the show without goggles, let alone read somebody's notes."

"Hm, see, I was thinking the same. But I did some reading, and I found out that some children in South-East Asia can see a lot better underwater than other people. Those kids basically grow up swimming and diving, and they learn to actively adjust their eyes to see better underwater. There's a scientific paper on it and all, going into details of accommodation and pupil constriction and everything. Not my field of work, either. But what I understood is, that the scientists also worked with kids in Europe, and after some time of training, those kids could improve their underwater vision, too. Now, to me that sounds possible for somebody like you who's been swimming for years and who's diving in a pool several days a week."

That actually made her laugh a little before she answered, "Really? You think I trained myself to see better underwater so I could read Cory's notes? Why? Why would I do that? I don't even a hundred percent know what he studied, so why should I be even interested in those notes?"

Luke shrugged. "You tell me. He also was looking into starting his own company, trying to overhaul old fishing techniques. Maybe a competitor felt threatened and offered to pay you for information about Mr. Gilbert's work. Maybe you pretended to be interested, or that you wanted to help him with the new company. He believed you, you used your time at work to gather information and report it to somebody else."

"That's ridiculous!"

"Is it really? Did Mr. Gilbert find out that you were using him and confronted you about it?" Luke knew this was all pure speculation, wild theorizing. But it began to get her riled up, to bring her into a position where she wanted to defend herself. And those were the times most people slipped up.

"No! Like I said, it was quieter over at his side of the cafeteria. And well, maybe I..." But she didn't finish the sentence, just shrugged.

"Yes?"

"Maybe recently I wasn't so sure I only like women," she answered in barely a whisper and began picking nervously at her fingernails.

"Huh, so his girlfriend wasn't that much of a problem after all?"

"I..."

"Did you flirt with him, ask him out, and he shot you down?"

"No! I swear. I never told him or anything."

"And yet, he clearly pointed something out to you in his notes. Was it a date or time to meet?" Luke knew exactly what Cory had been pointing out, but he also knew not to just give everything away.

"What? No. I don't even know what you mean. He probably just highlighted something or took some additional notes, and maybe that looked like he wanted to show me something."

She isn't doing a bad job coming up with excuses, Luke admitted to himself. But he also knew for sure what he had seen on the video footage. It was time to put a little more pressure on her. "Tell us what happened between the two of you. Did he reject your business ideas, find out you were planning to sell him out, didn't want to date you? There was something going on, clear as day."

"No, no, there wasn't!"

Luke leaned forward, his arms resting on the table, and looked her straight in the eyes. "So you want to tell us it's just a coincidence we found Mr. Gilbert's torso in a dumpster that your building shares with others? And even more of a coincidence that we found his severed head in the basement of your apartment building?"

Erin Graham was either a better actress than he had thought, or this one was really a surprise for her, because she jerked back with her whole body. "What? Oh my god," she mumbled with her hand covering her mouth.

"No explanation for that?"

She merely shook her head.

"Then maybe you can tell us why we found a piece of your costume with one of his legs. There was a plastic scale from your mermaid tail in the shark's stomach together with the leg."

And once Luke had seen the video footage and her outfit in the water, the artificial fish scale Rose had mentioned had made sense.

"Wha... what? That can't be. I didn't... You can't really think I killed Cory. Why would I do that?"

"Then explain all this to us. The evidence points to you. You had some kind connection with Mr. Gilbert, which you aren't telling us the whole truth about."

"I am. I... Somebody must be framing me!" She sounded more desperate with every answer.

"Why?"

"I don't know! You're the cops, figure it out! I didn't kill Cory, somebody wants to make it look like it was me!"

Crossing his arms, Luke leaned back in his chair with a tiny smirk. "And could framing you have anything to do with your backstory being a lie? Your photo on your alma mater's website doesn't fit the rest of the photos and was put there by a hacker. Nobody has heard of the magazine you worked for; I made a few calls on the way here, there's not even one copy of it left *anywhere*. The fire that supposedly killed your parents only killed one elderly woman. Who are you really, Ms. Graham?"

The instant of pure shock vanished from her eyes within a heartbeat, composure and calculation taking over. "I would like to make my phone call now."

Chapter Twenty-Three

Luke and Leroy allowed her the call and posted a uniform to wait in the interview room with her while they went to Leroy's office for a short private conversation.

"Well, that certainly should be interesting," Leroy said.

"Yes, most definitely. I wished we'd had a chance to look into her finances already, but I'm still more than curious what story we'll be told."

"Same. But even without the finances, we have enough for her to be our main suspect at the moment. I would like to hold back on officially charging her for now, though. But even when her lawyer gets her out of here, we can advise her not to leave the city. If she takes off, she'll just be even more suspicious, and we can charge her. Any judge would grant us a warrant for her arrest then. As it is right now, I already filed a request for a warrant for her financial records."

"Good. My gut tells me she'll be the key to solving this, no matter if she turns out to be our killer or an important puzzle piece. Let's focus on her for the rest of the day. I think the social media accounts and the professor's and the captain's deeper financial checks can wait a day."

"I agree. Depending on how this goes, I can still have a look. But I also feel like we're close to something with her."

"Yeah. Oh, did you hear from Michelle? Is he all right?"

"Yes. I asked one of the uniforms to check on him before I left the scene, and give him my keys, because I was pretty sure he'd be home before me. He texted me just before you arrived earlier. He's fine. His apartment is a mess, it'll take time to fix everything, but he packed more things and is staying at my place for now. But no threats or signs that somebody else had been at his apartment, so I think we were right and people don't know he's been working on this case with us."

"That's good. Sucks about his apartment, though."

"Yeah. Though I'm not complaining: I get to have him in my bed for the foreseeable future," Leroy added with a cheeky grin.

Luke chuckled and shook his head. "Can't say I'm surprised. Tell him if he needs anything after, he can ask. I still have some stuff in storage after moving in with July. Maybe I have something he might like."

"Great, thanks. I'll let him know."

Their conversation drifted back to the case, and when Luke came back into Leroy's office with two fresh coffees, an officer stepped in with him to let them know that Erin Graham's lawyer was there.

Stepping into the interview room, Luke came to a sudden stop when he saw the tall, lean woman with sharp features and intelligent gray eyes sitting next to his suspect.

And when the woman's gaze met his and she saw the recognition in his eyes, she inhaled sharply. "Well, fuck."

Leroy drew up his eyebrows, and to Luke's surprise, so did Erin Graham. "I take it you know each other," Leroy said and looked at his detective.

"Yes," Luke answered, then looked back at the women. "And I am surprised to hear you're here as a lawyer."

Thoroughly annoyed now, the woman ran her hand through her short, practically styled hair. "Do me a favor and give us another minute."

"All right, but I can't wait to hear what you have to tell us. Leroy, a word?"

"Oh yes, please."

Back in the observation room Leroy faced Luke. "Tell me she's not your ex or something like that."

Luke shook his head. "No. But I've met her. July's mom threw a birthday party, and she invited a few of her colleagues from the New York office, including Naomi Collins here. I don't know what's going on, and maybe she studied law in the past. But the last time I spoke to her, she was working as an FBI agent."

"Huh, that is interesting, yes. And it looks like she had no clue you were working on this case."

"Yeah, I got that feeling, too."

"Do you want to give July's mom a call?"

"I'll keep it as an option. For now, I want to hear their version first."

Leroy nodded, then raised his chin a little, pointing at the window through which they had seen the women argue. "Looks like you get your wish," he said, when Naomi Collins got up to knock on the mirror on her side.

A moment later, four people were sitting at the table in the interview room, glaring at each other in silence, until Erin Graham finally shook her head. "Fuck, this was *so not* planned. But Naomi tells me you can be trusted."

"She's right," Luke stated simply.

Studying him, assessing him for a long moment, she nodded. "Switch off all recordings, and we need a room where nobody can listen in on us."

"A little cloak and dagger, don't you think?" Leroy threw in.

Graham nodded briskly. "Yes."

Luke and Leroy shared a look, and with a nod, Luke got up. "We'll switch off the recordings. And I can adjust the opacity of the glass so you can see nobody's listening in from there."

It was a compromise for all of them, none of them wanting to give up authority or any advantage, but in the end the women agreed.

When Luke sat back again after getting everything ready, he spread his hands. "Okay. It's just the four of us. Now, tell us what's going on."

Taking a deep breath, Erin Graham sat up straighter. "I didn't lie when I said somebody wants to frame me. I didn't kill Cory. He was my informant. I'm CIA, working undercover. My real name is Rachel Ward. Special Agent Collins and I are working together in a joint effort to stop an international weapon smuggling ring."

While Luke blinked twice in surprise, Leroy drew up his eyebrows. "Seriously?"

"Yes. The operation seems to be relatively new, but when it became clear that some of the business takes place so far off the coast that it borders international waters, and given the fact that we don't know every buyer and the possible use of the weapons yet, the CIA is involved in this."

Leroy scratched his jaw. "Okay, I can understand that. But why isn't the NYPD involved? How come you work closely enough with the FBI on this that Special Agent Collins is your first call instead of your superior? And why are you so damn forthcoming with all of this? The last time I had a case where a federal agency was involved, they did their best to keep us out of everything."

"All good questions," Agent Ward admitted. "Some of them

are related. Let's start with the NYPD's involvement in this case. Actually, some of your colleagues from another precinct got a call from Cory, but he wasn't being taken seriously. That's when he started looking for whom else he could contact, and his search caught our interest. Somebody reached out to him, and we started to set up a team. As to why I called Special Agent Collins, and why we're so forthcoming, those reasons go hand in hand with what I said before."

Agent Ward picked up her coffee for a sip and set it back down with an angry sigh. "I am being framed for Cory Gilbert's murder. The FBI at this stage is mainly working on finding the buyers here in the States. Cory was helping the CIA with details on the sellers."

Luke nodded. "And you being framed likely means somebody on the inside, somebody at the CIA, is working with the sellers. It would make sense; the system of the Aquarium showed signs of a highly sophisticated hack."

"I'm not surprised. And yes, I thought the same: if somebody is sabotaging this investigation, then it's likely somebody from the CIA. Which is why I called my FBI contact first, though I made sure nobody knows Agent Collins is my contact. Another reason why we're so open about this is your girlfriend's mother. SA Collins tells me she is trustworthy, and..." Ward cut herself off.

Luke tilted his head. "Let me guess, because July's mom ran a background check on me?"

A little embarrassed, Ward nodded, and Luke smirked. "You didn't really believe I didn't know that, right? I would've been disappointed if she hadn't done it."

"Good to know. Aside from that, I had an eye on the investigation and had already had you checked as well. Since you recognized SA Collins, we decided we would all benefit from cooperating on this instead of her pretending to be my lawyer like we might've done, had you not recognized her. Aside from keeping the investigation into the smugglers on track, I think all of us want to bring Cory's killer to justice."

"We agree on that," Luke said, and Leroy nodded as well.

"I thought so. Now, to be honest, at the moment we're still debating what's the best way to go on. It might not be the worst idea to keep me here for a while. They might believe their plan worked."

"Which might lead to them making a mistake, or at the very least not being as vigilant as before."

"We hope so, yes."

"We can make that work. We should also be able to create a fake recording of this interview for them to find in the files in case your mole in the CIA hacks into our system here. It's not an easy thing to do, but I imagine for somebody with CIA resources and training, it's not impossible."

"You're probably right, Detective, though it's not my specialty. And the fake recording is a good idea."

"Should we get that out of the way first? We keep it short, I'll upload it with the time stamp adjusted, and after that we head out of here into Lieutenant Porter's office to discuss the case in more detail," Luke offered, and everybody agreed.

It didn't take them too long to come up with a short interview during which Erin Graham pleaded her innocence and timidly asked for a lawyer. Said lawyer showed up and gave the performance of a bored, disillusioned public defender, ending with Luke and Leroy leading the suspect to the holding cells given the physical evidence and location where the torso and head had been found.

Sitting in Leroy's office a while later, Special Agent Collins shuddered. "Urgh, I hate to act like I'm either totally clueless or simply completely disinterested."

"You put on a good show, though," Leroy said and handed her a mug of fresh coffee.

"Thanks. And hey, at least studying law before joining the Bureau was good for something, even if it's just to sound convincing on a fake recording," she said with a small grin.

"That's the spirit. Now, let's talk about the case. Agent Ward, I assume you did indeed know what Cory was pointing to in his notebook."

The woman leaned against the edge of Leroy's desk and nodded. "I did. He was showing me coordinates."

Luke cocked his head once again. "And you could really read them underwater and through the glass?"

"Yes. And before you ask, yes, I actually know the article you mentioned earlier. It's interesting and something I have tried to train myself to do as well. Swimming is a real hobby of mine, and I have made small improvements in my vision so far. But while reading Cory's notes, I was wearing contact lenses that help to correct the different refraction."

"Wait, contact lenses like that exist?"

"They're not widely available. There was a German company producing them a while ago, but the company closed when the demand wasn't high enough. Still, the technology and the scientific basics are out there, and several agencies have worked on improving the lenses even further over the years. So yes, I could read what Cory had written down. And I have a knack for numbers and a very good memory. I usually read the coordinates shortly before the end of a show, then when I got out of the water, I jotted everything down. It seems a little cumbersome, but we wanted to keep our contact to a minimum. Plus, it would've been weird for Cory to sneak into the women's locker room on a regular basis to hide a piece of paper in my locker."

"Agreed. But why not use a secure email or phone connection to text?"

"My superior deemed it too insecure since we don't have a lot of info on the group running things yet. He was afraid of somebody hacking the shipping crew's devices and, by that, giving away how closely we're watching the operation."

"Okay. Can you tell us what the coordinates are for? All we found out so far is that they belong to spots in the middle of nowhere in the open ocean."

Both agents nodded, and Ward explained the details. "Pretty much, yes. They also indicate where Cory's fishing boat stopped when it shouldn't have, and where Cory observed a member of his crew pulling up crates from the ocean in the middle of the night."

"Crates with weapons, I take it," Leroy said while taking notes in his own notebook to keep things out of the electronic files for the moment.

"Yes. Cory was awake studying one night when he felt the boat stopping. He wanted to check what was wrong, and when he was on deck, he saw the pickup happening. He managed to stay hidden and see his colleague opening the crates to check the content."

"Do you know which colleague was involved?"

Ward shook her head. "No. That's the thing. The guy accepting the crates apparently has watched *I Know What You Did Last Summer* one too many times or something. He was covered up with full fishing gear, and given where Cory was hiding, he didn't see the guy's face. And once we got involved, we told him to stop trying to identify the man. We asked him to only get the coordinates where the boat stopped; we were working on finding out if there's a pattern to where the deliveries are being picked up. Somebody had to deposit the weapons after all, and if possible, we want to stop the whole organization, not just the person picking up the weapons."

"Makes sense," Luke said while taking his own notes, but then looked up at the agents. "I hope you understand that while we respect your investigation, we still want Cory's killer behind bars. We won't let him go free just to keep the investigation running."

"We didn't expect that. And as important the investigation is, we both also agree that Cory's killer belongs in jail. I'd say we should discuss a solution when we have the killer in custody," Agent Collins proposed.

"All right. Did Cory say anything about feeling threatened lately? Anything that could help us find his killer?" Leroy asked the agents.

Both of them shook their heads and Ward answered, "No, unfortunately he didn't. He didn't think anybody had even noticed he was taking notes about the coordinates. As I said, the pickups happened during the night, when nobody would notice the boat stopping. Cory told me he had to get on deck, or at least out of his cabin, to get a signal to pinpoint the coordinates, but usually nobody saw him. And if anybody did, he was pretending to text his girlfriend or looking for a signal to check something on his college server, something like that."

"Yes, that fits with what his captain told me about Cory seeming restless and walking around at night sometimes. Though he didn't say anything about the boat stopping," Leroy told the women.

"Yes, those were most likely the nights Cory was trying to log the coordinates. But Cory's safety was important to us. We told him to stop trying to identify the guy and also to wait a little while to get us the coordinates, to only get on deck once the boat was moving again. It would be enough to get us coordinates close to the pickup points, that way once we can determine if there's a pattern, we know which areas to stake out."

"Have you made any progress on that?" Luke asked.

"Not yet. Our data analysts are busy people, as you can imagine."

"I could offer to run it. I know it's tricky given that it's sensitive data from a federal investigation. But if you indeed have somebody on the inside manipulating the investigation, who's to say they didn't get their hands on the data and falsified it before anybody could run it?"

Agent Ward's face spoke volumes. She knew Luke was right on both accounts: she couldn't easily share the data, but she also couldn't be sure it was processed correctly by her colleagues. It was Special Agent Collins who saved her from the ongoing internal debate when she said, "Give him the data. After all, he already knows about several coordinates Cory wrote down, and he will of course have to check the dates against the crew's roster to see with whom Cory was on board those days. Right now, everybody on the crew could be a suspect. The coordinates are part of the murder investigation, and we agreed on cooperation. Our superiors can complain – and probably will – but they can't kick our asses too hard for sharing information pertaining to the murder case."

Ward slowly nodded. "Yeah, nice play. I can live with that. I have a copy secured, Special Agent Collins will have to get it for you, Detective," she added.

"Sounds good. And you are still sure you want to stay the night in a cell here for show?"

"Yes. I've had worse undercover assignments, trust me. A warm cell with clean food and water is fine with me."

They would have talked more, but a call from Rose interrupted them, so the four of them finished with the most important details and Erin Graham was escorted to the holding area.

Special Agent Collins left with a promise of the data in the morning, and Luke and Leroy split as well.

Erin Graham's apartment had been combed through by the crime scene team on Leroy's order, so he said he would take the morgue. Luke would make a quick stop at the apartment as well just in case somebody had eyes on it and, after a walk-through, would make his way home to check if he could access Cory's laptop yet.

It was getting late, and with the newest revelations, they were all ready to call it a day soon, so they would be rested in the morning when they would hopefully make even more progress.

Chapter Twenty-Four

Perfect, everything was going just as planned. The text had confirmed it. The annoying agent had been arrested – well, poor, innocent Erin Graham had been arrested, and was now being held in police custody. The cops had apparently even saved the tearful interview of her claiming to be framed. It seemed staying undercover was truly more important than anything.

All this could have been avoided if Cory hadn't been such a nosy idiot. On the other hand, this meant they could get rid of one agent looking into them. Of course there'd be a replacement, but as always, these things would take time. Surely it wasn't that easy to come up with a new idea fitting the specific criteria of a fishing company now that their inside man was dead. And any new fisherman was of course the first to be suspected of being a new undercover agent. They wouldn't be that obvious, would they? But then again, maybe they thought it would be so obvious that nobody would expect them to do it... Ah, who knew what those agencies were thinking with all their spy games.

Most importantly, Cory was gone, the coordinates they were

analyzing were bullshit – at least if his contact knew what he was doing – and the cops were looking at Erin Graham. And cops being cops, they'd stop digging soon enough. There were enough things pointing to her, and all the cops usually wanted was to close a case to look good.

All this would buy some time to finetune the deliveries and pickups, maybe switch to another company. In that case, even if they sent a new agent to look into this one, they wouldn't find anything anymore. But for now, it would be best to lay low.

Chapter Twenty-Five

Finally pulling into the garage at home, Luke saw a text from Leroy coming in.

Leroy:
Rose hasn't done a complete evaluation of the head yet.
But after a first look, she says she has an idea on the murder weapon.
Possibly a captive bolt pistol. She says the wound pattern fits.
More tests to be done, but I told her it's a good start and to go home for the day.

Smiling, Luke typed an answer before he got out of the car.

Luke:
Fits the fishing company, too.
They might have one to stun large fish.
And good call telling her to finish up for the day, or she'd pull an all-nighter. I'll use my contacts to get her something sweet as a

thank you for all the extra hours she's been doing for this case.
Talk tomorrow.

Leroy:
Good idea! Talk tomorrow.

Upstairs, Luke found Julia on the couch flipping through a wedding magazine, a movie playing in the background. She looked up at him with a smile, then followed his gaze to the magazine. "Hey. My mom. We met for a late lunch, and she handed me this."

"And have you seen anything you like in there?"

"Not really. But finding out what we *don't want* is pretty much as important as figuring out what we want."

"True. Especially once everybody starts telling us what they think would be great."

July shuddered. "Yeah. That's gonna be fun. Do you think Scarlette would be up for telling everybody to leave us alone?"

"Oh, you mean tell everybody to fuck off because we know what we want and can plan our own wedding?"

"Uh-huh, yeah."

Luke laughed. "It's Scarlette, of course she'd be up for that."

Leaning over the couch, Luke gave Julia a kiss and ran his hand through her curls. "How was your day? Aside from lunch with your mom."

"Oh, actually pretty good. Kenneth quit; said he was done with New York."

"Huh, nice. Any idea who's gonna replace him?"

"Not yet. We'll see. How was your day, other than busy?"

Luke walked around the couch and sat next to his fiancée, holding her hand. "Interesting, I'd say. We made good progress.

I wish I could tell you more, but things came up that make this case a lot more complicated and..." He shrugged apologetically.

"Luke, honey, my mom works for the FBI, I'm used to not being told about work. It's totally fine. I'm happy to hear you made progress, and I hope that will help you in arresting the killer. Everything else is just details."

"You're pretty amazing," Luke told her and leaned in for another kiss.

Smiling against his lips, July answered him. "Oh, I know. So, do you want your surprise now, or have dinner first? I brought you something from the place mom and I went for lunch."

"Dinner can wait."

"Good answer." She deepened the kiss for a moment, then drew back to stand up. "Follow me."

Stepping into the bedroom behind July, Luke came to a halt. She had put up several more fairy lights and put some LED candles in colored glasses. Soft music was playing quietly, and massage oil was waiting on their nightstand.

"Wow, that's a wonderful surprise."

"I'm glad you like it so far. That's not all of it, though."

Taking a few steps to get closer to her, Luke wrapped his arms around July and drew her against him. "And what else is there?"

"Hm, it might spoil the mood a little to talk about it in too much detail now, but let's just say I'd like to explore more of what happened accidentally on the night of the blackout."

It took Luke a few seconds to remember what she meant, but then his eyes got huge. "Really?"

July nodded. "I can't promise anything, but yeah, I think I'd like to try. But first of all, we both should relax, I'd say."

"Hm, we should."

Lost in a deep kiss, they stumbled to the bed, half sitting

down, half falling on it. Luke carefully undid the buttons on July's blouse while she quickly tied her hair in a knot to keep it out of the way of the massage oil. Slowly unwrapping each other, they kissed every bit of newly revealed skin. July shuddered when Luke ran his fingertips down her ribs and up again before gently opening her bra. Luke moaned when she ran her nails down his chest, lightly scratching across his nipples.

With the rest of their clothes gone a little while later, July reached for the oil. Kneeling in front of Luke, she tilted the bottle and dribbled some onto her generous breasts. His hands reached for her, and he began to tenderly spread the oil across her body. Her head fell back, and for a moment Julia simply concentrated on Luke's fingers gliding smoothly over her skin and the light smell of vanilla coming from the now warmed oil. It felt indulgent, and she thought she could drown for hours in this sensation alone.

But finally she guided Luke onto his back and poured some oil on him as well. She took her time running her hands across his pecs, down his arms, covering him in oil. She followed his legs, then tenderly massaged his feet for a moment, before sliding her hands back up his shins, his thighs. She poured a bit more oil into her hands, but first bowed down to take Luke's already hard length into her mouth, swallowing him deep, then following her lips with her hands, spreading warm oil over him while she moved her head back up to smile at him. Her hands stayed where they were, stroking slowly up and down, Luke's skin feeling even silkier than usual under her fingers.

Loudly groaning, Luke pressed his head back into the pillows. Knowing she could tip him over the edge just like this, he shivered, then focused on forming a few words. "Wait, baby. Lay down on your stomach for me, please."

Following his request, July made herself comfortable and sighed happily when Luke dribbled some oil onto her back. His hands began to massage her, fingers digging gently into her back. He took his time, first easing the tension in her shoulders, then kneading the muscles along her spine. Sliding further down, he began with rubbing slow circles on her lower back and followed it by pressing a little harder, loosening a few knots there.

Luke could feel her relax completely, and he let his hands wander further down. Gliding over her buttocks, he could feel her muscles there as well, honed by the martial arts training she kept up with Scarlette. For any bad luck she might've had in the past when choosing a guy and her carefulness with relationships because of it, his woman was nothing but strong. And she was gorgeous. So gorgeous that even more blood rushed down and he felt himself twitch just from the look of her. When she moaned under his caress, he leaned forward and whispered into her ear, "Good so far?"

"Yeah," July moaned out even louder when the way Luke was straddling her and the angle he was leaning made his erection slide between her butt cheeks.

Smiling, Luke sat back up and shimmied a little further down her thighs. Bit by bit, he let his thumbs slide closer to her opening. When she sighed, he began to circle her slowly with one thumb, his other hand running further between her legs and a finger sliding into her velvet heat. He massaged her from the inside, while he kept gently rubbing her edge with his other hand.

When July unconsciously began pushing against his finger, Luke withdrew his other finger from inside her and reached for the lube, which she had put next to the massage oil on the night-stand. The oil was nice, but the lube was the better choice, at least for the first time. He carefully let some of it drop onto her and gave her butt cheek a quick kiss when she flinched a little.

"Sorry, I know it's cold. Now, let me know if you want me to stop, anytime, okay?"

"Okay."

Luke began caressing her again, his other hand unconsciously reaching between his own legs. He'd probably never know what he had done to deserve her, but aside from making him incredibly happy, she was the most beautiful, sexiest woman he had ever been with. And now she was asking him for something no other woman had ever given him. This was special, and he wanted it to be as amazing for her as it already was for him.

It didn't take long for July to move her hips back against his finger once again. And this time, he helped her, pushed so very gently against her entrance. She gasped when she felt his fingertip slip inside her for the first time. Luke didn't move his hand to give her time to get used to the feeling, and after a moment July nodded. "Go on."

He started with small movements, gently sliding inside, slowly drawing back. Over and over, all the time going just a little deeper. Beneath him, Julia hummed contently. When he thought she was relaxed enough, he asked her whether she was okay with a second finger.

July agreed with a nod. With Luke carefully pressing against her and slowly sliding another digit inside, July fleetingly thought she understood what Scarlette had told her about feeling a sting. Initially, it burned a little, but the feeling faded quickly. She let herself relax more and more and began to push harder against Luke's hand when she felt a small tingling creep up the nerves along her spine. "More, Luke, please."

He added a third finger to stretch her further, and with that one July hardly needed time to adjust. His breath hitched while July obviously enjoyed herself, moving herself up and down on his hand. Not long after, she slowed her hips and looked over her shoulder at her fiancé. "I think I'm ready."

"Are you sure?"

"Yeah."

"Do you want to stay like this, or do you want us to change positions?"

"I think like this is okay. Give me just a second," Julia said and dragged over a pillow to put it under her hips. "This should be good. So, uh, I bought condoms, if you want to, but I'd be okay without one, too. Just use some more lube."

"Hm, if it's okay with you, I wouldn't need one, either."

"Okay."

Luke took his time, kissing a slow path down July's spine while applying a generous amount of lube to them both, and finally knelt behind her again. Positioning himself, he gently pushed against her.

The pressure was different from what his fingers had felt like, and July clenched reflexively. Breathing heavily, she closed her eyes. "Okay, sorry, just give me a moment."

"July, baby, we can stop."

"No, I don't want to stop. Really. It's just a strange feeling." It was. But with all the strangeness, it also felt too good to resist going on with this. "Just... uh, maybe let me lead in the beginning."

"Whatever you want," Luke assured her and ran his hands up her outer thighs and to her back, soothing her with slow, gentle motions.

Making a conscious effort to relax, July nodded. "Okay."

Luke held himself still, only resting his tip against July's opening. She began to bear down on him oh so slowly, and he watched how her body gradually accepted him until he finally passed the first resistance. Both of them gasped. Luke felt like a vise was squeezing him, and July was cursing herself for a second, wondering why she had thought this was a good idea. But then Luke's hand circled her waist and ran down her stomach to end up between her legs, slowly, tenderly caressing her clitoris. "Are you okay?"

"Yeah, I just need a moment to adjust." There was definitely a sting now, her muscles protesting the unfamiliar stretch. But though the burn was a little unpleasant, it wasn't truly painful.

"Of course, baby."

Focusing on her breathing and Luke's fingers pleasuring her, July finally began to bear down a little more until her inner muscles relaxed as well. Inch by inch, she felt Luke sliding further into her and realized that she could make out so much more of him like this. The tightness of her body allowed her to feel every ridge and vein running along his shaft. And when her butt came to a gentle stop against his groin, July knew he was completely seated inside her. She had never felt so full before. It was a unique experience, and when she moved her hips just a tiny bit, her nerves fired and that primal part in her brain answered with a deep groan that sounded nearly like a growl.

Overwhelmed, Luke gripped her hip. "Oh god!"

"I know. Move, Luke," she muttered in a deep, husky voice that was far too enticing to not follow her order.

He was careful at first, sliding back and forth in slow, gentle strokes. When he felt her easily taking all of him, he moved a little faster. And faster still, when she looked over her shoulder again, her eyes burning with desire. She found his rhythm and pushed back against him. Feeling the lube getting sticky, Luke added some more. It made their motions even smoother, so he thrust into her faster and faster until they were both panting and desperate for their release. Reaching between her legs again, Luke hardly touched July, but it was enough to have her bury her head in the pillows and roar with her orgasm. She clenched so tightly around him that it was almost painful, and it pushed him to his own climax.

Feeling Luke pulsate inside her like this, feeling every wave of his orgasm, brought July another small peak herself, and she fell into the pillows, completely exhausted.

Luke eased himself out of her carefully, and ran his fingers through a few strands of her curls which had come loose. "Are you okay, July?"

"Uh-huh. Yep. All good. Bit braindead, but perfect. Probably a bit sore later."

Luke chuckled, but studied her with concerned eyes. "Are you sure you're good?"

It was an effort, but July turned her head to look her fiancé in the eyes. "Luke, honey, please believe me when I tell you: this was amazing. I loved it. Will I be a little sore after this? Yes. I've never done this before, so it's normal and nothing to worry about. But it was great. How was it for you?"

"Different, but great, too. It's something we need time for, and a chance to relax, but if you like it, I wouldn't mind doing it more often."

"Sounds good to me. We probably won't do it like this every time, but I'd also be happy to do this more often."

"Perfect. Do you want to take a shower with me? Aside from the lube, we're still covered in a lot of massage oil, too."

"Yeah, good idea."

After their shower, Luke sat down with July to eat his dinner. He let her show him a few things in the magazine and was relieved to find they both disliked the same things. It gave him hope that even with the usual stress of planning a wedding, they would manage without nearly killing each other like a few of his friends and their spouses. Done with the food, he sent a quick text asking Scarlette's grandmother for a tiramisu he could pick up soon for Rose, then excused himself to look after Cory's laptop again.

"Don't worry. I have a quick call with one of the guys I've been working with in Australia myself. He's taken over one of the customers I was managing while I was there taking care of dad, and he has a question about something. Shouldn't take too long. I'll be in bed and reading afterwards."

"Okay. Thanks, sweetie. I know this case is taking up a lot of my time."

"Luke, don't worry about that. It's all good. I knew what I was getting into when I started dating a cop," she said with a wink and left for her office.

In his own office, he found the program still running. Most of the password had been deciphered, but a few characters were still missing. He should have better luck in the morning. For now, he took the time to disconnect whatever he could, so nobody could hack into his systems. Feeling like he had done all he could for the day, he finally made his way to the bedroom, too and snuggled up against Julia. He fell asleep almost as soon as he laid his head down, and July switched off the lights so they could both get some sleep.

Chapter Twenty-Six

Leroy woke to the notification dot on his phone blinking and Michelle lying in his arms, smiling in his sleep. Doing his best not to wake his boyfriend, Leroy reached for his phone. Luke's text made him grin and hope for a successful day.

Luke:
Laptop is open. Found the calendar entry and an address for it. It's a rental storage facility in Brooklyn. I already contacted SA Collins to request a warrant to get access to the customer list (in case they monitor our requests).

Leroy:
Good work!
Let's talk details at the precinct.

Luke:
Sure thing, boss!

He would've wiggled out of bed and let Michelle sleep, but the vet's alarm went off right when Leroy was putting his phone down.

"Hmm, morning, *mon coeur*. I hope my alarm didn't wake you," Michelle purred in his warm, soft voice.

"No, don't worry. Seems like we both have to get ready for work."

"Yeah. Wanna share the shower with me?"

Rolling out of bed and dragging Michelle with him, Leroy beamed. "Would I ever say no to that?"

Unsurprisingly, their shower ended with both men standing on weak legs and grinning madly after Leroy had wrapped a hand around both of them and stroked them until they had come together with a shudder. Given that they had also taken each other more than once the night before, it seemed each was insatiable for the other. Neither Leroy nor Michelle gave a damn: things felt incredibly right between them, and they were determined to enjoy every minute they could spend together.

Over a quick breakfast, they talked about yesterday. When Leroy had come home from the morgue the day before, he had said he needed to be distracted for the night, and Michelle had gladly given him what he'd asked for. Today, his cop was in a better frame of mind, it seemed.

"So, how's the case going?"

"Ah... it's gotten a lot more complicated. Unfortunately, I can't tell you a lot anymore. A new element has come up that makes this case larger and forces Luke and me to keep even quieter than we might usually be at home, even with people like you and July who've been kind of involved."

"That sounds very cloak and dagger to me."

Chuckling, Leroy leaned over and gave Michelle a sweet kiss. "Yeah, that's exactly what I said, too. Anyway, I can at least tell you that we made progress, even if it's the kind of progress that complicates things. Also, Rose had a first look at the head and gave us a good lead for the murder weapon."

"That's good. She's nice, I like her. We were talking for a bit before I left the morgue."

"She likes you, too. She told me she'd see to it to get an exoskeleton so she could use her own leg to kick me in case I was stupid enough to let you go."

Michelle almost choked on his coffee when he started laughing. "I definitely have to invite her to my birthday party in January."

"She'll love that, sweetheart."

"I think so, too. Oh, you'll find a full post-mortem report for the cat in the case file, by the way."

"Awesome, thank you. Anything interesting you can already tell me?"

"When it comes to anything regarding the case, then I can tell you that, yes, very likely the cat was hit by a car. Her injuries are consistent with being hit and dragged along the underside of a car. Her claws were splintered and partially ripped off, her pelvis showed multiple fractures. I hate to say it, but I'm almost glad one of the bone fragments severely injured her right external iliac artery. She managed to crawl a little further, but she died relatively quickly of internal bleeding. She didn't have to suffer the pain for too long. You might also get lucky finding some fur or tissue on the car; she had multiple deep abrasions and a few areas without hair with skin irritation indicating the hair didn't just fall out prior to the accident but rather was ripped out around the time of her death. We started running the DNA, so you have results to compare any possible evidence against."

Leroy could see the pity for the poor cat in his boyfriend's eyes, and he could easily admit he felt the same. Reaching over, he took Michelle's hand. "Thank you so much. Let's try to find something a bit more positive to talk about over breakfast. Have you talked to your neighbor?"

"Oh, yeah, I managed a short call before you came home. Mr. Davidson is doing as well as he can under the circumstances. Mainly he's annoyed with himself, and a little scared that he might not be able to move back to his own place. And the meds he's taking make him a little tired. But I think his son hasn't told him about my apartment yet, like we discussed, so he doesn't worry about that on top of everything."

"That's good to hear."

"It is, yes. I'll keep in contact with him and his son, so we'll see."

"Yeah. Let me know if there's anything I can do to help. He sounds like a nice man."

"Thanks, love."

A glance at the clock hanging on the wall told them they had to leave soon, and Leroy stood up with a sigh. "Let's try to get a long weekend off together soon. I'd say we could both use a few days out of town in a nice B&B, doing nothing."

Wrapping his arms around Leroy for a moment, Michelle smiled at him. "Sounds great."

At the precinct, Leroy had hardly put down his bag next to his desk when his phone rang. Seeing the number, he felt a buzz run through his body. He just knew this would be important. Grabbing pen and paper, he answered the call.

"Hello, Captain Russel," he greeted the owner of the fishing company Cory had worked for. Given everything he had learned from the Feds recently, he knew he needed to be careful with what he was sharing, but he had asked about the coordinates before he had even known about the investigation and his gut told him to trust the man.

"Lieutenant Porter, hello. Sorry it took me a while to get back to you. We had a storm out here that kept us quite busy. But now we're almost back home."

"No problem. Thank you for calling me."

"Sure. So, about those coordinates. All I can tell you is that there's nothing exciting at those locations. It's all just water, all near or on our usual fishing routes."

"Nothing ever happened there? No other ships nearby? Maybe ones you might've seen repeatedly?"

"No. Nothing like that. I... Well, there was one day when Cory asked me if we had had a problem with the engine during the night. I think that was on a morning when we had been close to one of those coordinates the night before, one of our regular routes. I told you, sometimes he had trouble sleeping, or was putting in some work for college. I figured he had just zoned out and didn't hear the motor running. It's pretty monotone, most of us don't actively hear it anymore."

"Do you remember which coordinates they were?" Leroy asked.

"I'd have to check the list on my laptop. I can send you an email right after the call."

"That would be very helpful. Did you talk to anybody about Cory's question?"

"Not for some time. Things get busy on the boat, and from what I had seen, we were on time and on course the day Cory asked me."

Leroy tapped his pen against his notepad. "What about later? You said not for some time."

"Right. A while later, I was talking with one of the guys about the engine. Just checking in, and I remembered that Ariel had been on night watch the night Cory had asked about, so I asked him if the motor had given him any trouble recently."

The name immediately caught Leroy's attention. "Ariel?"

"Sorry, that's Noah Kennedy. We all call him Ariel."

"Interesting nickname."

"It fits. He has a huge mermaid tattoo on his chest that he loves to show every chance he gets."

"Okay, makes sense. Did you tell him why you asked?"

"Kinda. I told him one of the guys mentioned there might've been some engine trouble one night."

"Did you mention Cory by name or the exact night?"

"Not that I remember. It was just a quick question in passing. Why? Do you think Ariel has something to do with Cory's death? He's on the boat with us, I'd like to know if I need to keep an eye on him. We're headed home now, but we'll still be on the water for a bit, and while they're on the boat, those men are my responsibility."

Damn, sometimes Leroy hated it when people could connect the dots so well. He shouldn't be surprised: he had seen Russel's background earlier in the case.

"Right now, we're just gathering information on Cory, and who might've known he'd been up some nights. He might've talked to the guys over a late coffee or a drink. I assume it is quieter during the night, more time to share some personal stories. I just wanted to know if Mr. Kennedy might be one of the people who knew Cory was sometimes up at night."

There was a moment of heavy silence before the captain spoke again. "Lieutenant, I respect that you cannot say anything about a suspect in this case. But I am sure you have checked me and seen that I was Military Police for two years in the past. It was a thankless job, but it paid well enough so I could put aside enough to apply for a loan to found my company."

"I did indeed run a background check. You are very observant, Captain. Just like me. You didn't even begin to deny the possibility Noah Kennedy might be involved. Most people would feel compelled to say he wouldn't do something like that."

"Hm. You aren't wrong. Ariel is doing a solid job here, he is one of the guys doing the night shifts on a regular basis. He has never caused me any problems on the boat. But he had an accident a few years back. Left him with a severe limp after his leg had been shattered and healed badly. He can't do the heavy, physical labor anymore. Now he's our man for the sonar, and when he's working nights, he's also the one steering the ship. The accident left him with a mean streak when he gets drunk, too. At least that's what the guys told me. Initially, they had tried to cheer him up, but finally had stopped inviting him to go out with them. I think he started to feel kind of useless, less manly, when he had to change his job on the boat, and the guys said he was constantly cussing when he was out with them. It got so bad that they felt they had to constantly keep an eye on him so he wouldn't pick a fight with somebody. Not exactly a relaxed evening off for the crew, so they started to go without him."

Leroy diligently took notes about it all. "I see. And on board?"

"On board he's not showing that behavior. He can be somewhat gruff, but we're on a boat full of guys doing hard work all day, everyday. Things often need to happen fast, the tone is rough, that goes for all of us. But under it all, it's a good, loyal crew, and at least while on board, Ariel is part of that crew. Those men are my responsibility. If I have to protect them, I will, even if it means I have to protect them from somebody in their midst. Which is why I'd appreciate it if you told me about your opinion in any way you can. I can guarantee you, I learned enough not to show my hand to them."

Leroy took his time, evaluating everything he had just heard. "I believe you. As you know, I cannot tell you about a possible suspect. I can tell you that our investigation covers all angles, that includes your company and the men working for you. As the man in charge of your crew, I can tell you that being vigilant has never hurt anybody."

"Thank you."

"I'll be in contact."

"Of course. Goodbye, Lieutenant."

"Goodbye, Captain Russel."

Looking at his notes, Leroy decided Luke had the right idea that running the background check on Noah Kennedy on his own computer might run the risk of flagging the search for any possible mole. Instead, he hoped the FBI would have more resources to protect their systems. Reaching into his desk and grabbing a burner phone that he usually only used to call the most nervous of his informants who were worried that the whole precinct might listen in on his regular phone, he called Special Agent Collins to ask her to check Noah Kennedy.

Luke entered his office with a gentle knock the moment Leroy was hanging up. "Hey."

"Hey. I just got an interesting call from Captain Russel," Leroy began and updated his detective on everything.

"Okay, that really was an interesting call. Regular night shifts on board would've given Kennedy an easy opportunity to pick up something. Let's see what the customer list of the storage facility tells us. I'd be interested to know whether he rented something in his own name. We should still do a cross-check with the other crew members."

"We should and will," Leroy agreed. "And I'm just as interested in the customer list."

"Yeah. I hope Special Agent Collins won't feel like our secretary by the end of the day, but I didn't want to spook anybody."

"I think she'll understand where we're coming from."

"Yeah, that's what I'm hoping for. And that the FBI might get a warrant faster than we would."

Nodding, Leroy got up. "Good point. For now, let's get our 'suspect' out of holding and into an interview room. We should update her as well."

Several hours later, Leroy was glad that another bad weather front delayed the arrival of Captain Russel's boat.

Special Agent Collins had come through with a warrant, not just for the customer list, but also with a warrant allowing them to search Noah Kennedy's car and his apartment after her background check on him.

Currently, Luke was going through said apartment with a team, looking for any evidence tying Kennedy to the murder, while Leroy was observing a CSU technician looking at the underside of Kennedy's car. They had towed the car half an hour earlier from the garage where Russel was renting parking spots for all his employees for when they were out at sea. Leroy had called the captain back earlier to ask him about his arrival time and if he by any chance knew where Kennedy was parking his car. At the end of the call, Russel had offered to text when the boat was about an hour away, so Leroy and Luke would have time to meet them at the harbor and pick up Kennedy for questioning themselves.

The technician looked over at Leroy, dirt staining her face, gloves, and coveralls. "I'll have to dismantle some of this, take off the front bumper at the very least for now. There's no obvious blood or hair visible, but with the weather and the street conditions after the storm, I'm not surprised. And from what I've seen, the car has recently been cleaned as well."

"Interesting. Yes, please do what you have to. I know it's a long shot."

"Ah, come on Lieutenant, you know our team, we live for long shots and beating the odds of finding trace evidence here."

Leroy smiled at her. "I know, Deena. And it's always appreciated. Will you need a colleague to help with dismantling it?"

"Need? No, not necessarily. But it will be easier and faster. Riley should be almost done with his break. If you could grab him for me from the break room, that'd be great."

"Sure thing."

A short while later, Leroy watched a grin spread across their faces when both techs looked at each other. Carefully stepping over, Leroy followed the beam of their flashlights and saw a few tufts of fur the same color as the cat in the morgue and a tiny drop of blood.

"You guys are my heroes."

"Oh, we know. And from what you said earlier about Dr. Jenkins' findings during the post-mortem, I think we could be lucky and find more at the rear of the car. If Dr. Jenkins is right and the cat was dragged along beneath it, there could be more traces of her there. But we'll need to take off the tires for that, remove even more parts to look in detail."

"I understand. But this is already great. The lab has a DNA analysis running. Once the lab has results and you collect this, it can be tested against them."

"We'll get right to it."

With an incoming text from Captain Russel, Leroy left the CSU team to do their magic while he got into his car and called Luke.

"Hey. The boat is on its way in, they're about an hour out."

"Okay. I'll get to the harbor, too. The apartment was a bust for obvious things. Nothing here. No large, serrated knife, no bolt pistol, none of Cory's belongings. We found a roll of extra-large, heavy-duty trash bags, though."

"It would've been too much to ask to have the murder

weapon on a pedestal right there, I guess. Good thinking with the trash bags, though. CSU found some fur under the front bumper. Visually, I'd say it could belong to the cat Michelle found. There was a tiny speck of blood, too, and Deena hopes to find more. We should have enough for a comparison. We'll see. And they'll get more samples of the car's interior for testing, too."

"That sounds promising. Nice job. Now, let's pick up Kennedy. I'll see you at the harbor."

Standing at one of the piers, Luke and Leroy looked at some of the information SA Collins had sent them. If it held up, neither of them would be surprised she had gotten a warrant for the searches without a problem. She'd also let them know, if things turned out as expected, the arrest warrant would be ready within minutes. On top of all that, she had contacted the storage facility, had gotten a customer list, and was now on her way to search two storage units after a cross-check of the customers had yielded interesting results.

Now the two cops were waiting for Captain Russel's crew to leave the ship. They'd talk to Kennedy before he reached the garage, offering him a ride and hoping he wouldn't realize his car wasn't in its spot. Not that it mattered necessarily, but it could set an easier tone for the beginning of the interview, giving him the impression he was there just as a possible witness, not a suspect.

The captain hadn't exaggerated when it came to the limp. They had no problem spotting Noah Kennedy coming towards them along with several of his colleagues. Of course, they had studied his photo as well, but his gait alone would've given him away. And though he didn't look like he was lazy, he had lost some of the rough edges and the muscles attributed to hard, manual labor his colleagues were still sporting.

When the group was close to them, Luke took a step forward and held out his hand to Ariel with a friendly smile. "Hello. You're Noah Kennedy, right?"

Just like Leroy, Luke could switch attitudes in a heartbeat and never truly let his guard down while on the job, but he excelled at portraying the laid-back, amicable type if he wanted to.

Surprised, the man in front of him looked from the outstretched hand to Luke's face, to Leroy, and back. "Yeah. And you are?"

"I'm Detective Preston. This is my colleague, Lieutenant Porter. We'd like to ask you a few questions. You see, we're looking into Cory Gilbert's murder, and we found that you might be able to help us piece together his last evening before he was killed. Would you please come with us to the precinct?"

There was a second of hesitation, and Luke could see Kennedy trying to figure out the best way to react. "Oh. Yeah, sure. But, uh, I don't think you'd like to have me sitting with you in an office right now. A shower and a change of clothes would be good for all of us, trust me."

Agreeable, but evasive.

Luke could work with that. "We don't mind. We'd interview you here, too, unfortunately procedure dictates an 'official setting' for all steps of sensitive cases like this," Luke said with a sigh and an eye roll while making air quotes. Was it a lie? Sure. But seeming annoyed by the bureaucracy himself usually did the trick to convince people he didn't take the job too seriously. "So, why don't you just come to the precinct with us, we ask you the few questions we have, and we can all check the whole thing off?"

"Ah, yeah, okay. Let me know where it is, I'll just get my car."

"It's not that far from here. We can take you along, and I'll just drop you back here after. Trust me, you don't want to try finding a parking spot there at the moment. Our visitor lot was washed out by the storm and hasn't been cleared for public use again, so everybody is parking on the streets. It's absolute mayhem, even more than usual for New York."

"I don't want to burden you with bringing me back here and all."

"You wouldn't. I have another errand to run around here later. You can probably imagine how many things we have to take care of during a murder investigation. Being understaffed doesn't help, and we get stuck with doing everything on our own."

Luke could imagine Leroy was mentally grinning at him for bringing up the overworked civil servant angle, but what could he say, it worked most of the time – people felt instantly safer knowing the cop in front of them had no time to look too deep into them.

Seemingly out of options, Kennedy shrugged. "Yeah, I guess you got tons of stuff to do. If you really don't mind the smell or dropping me here later, sure, I can ride along with you."

"Great. Let's go. The faster we get this done, the faster you can get home. I bet those days out on sea are exhausting," Luke said to keep the small talk going, all the while leading Kennedy to Leroy's car. He'd get an earful for the smell later, but Leroy's car was a bit larger and gave them more room to maneuver in case Kennedy got any ideas, and putting him in the back of a cruiser would be too obvious. But he knew no matter what Leroy might say later, he agreed that neither of them should drive alone with a suspect in the car.

And when Kennedy fell silent during the car ride, Luke

could almost see the thoughts running through the man's head. So the detective decided to give him some time to come up with a story while he pretended to be going through notes on his phone. In reality, he was keeping a close eye on the fisherman in the backseat.

Luke knew some people would think it unwise to give the suspect more time to prepare answers to possible questions. But in his experience, those neat little answers and colorful stories all began crumbling down once he presented his suspect with hard evidence during the interview. Of course, there was the odd one or two percent of people who just kept going, stubbornly sticking to their version of events. But with these people, it usually didn't matter what you did during an interview, they'd never deviate from their story – or they'd just make up something completely different in a heartbeat. Those cases often ended without a confession. But Luke was thorough, so there was usually enough evidence for a conviction if a case went to court. The confession always was the cherry on top, though, he could admit that.

Chapter Twenty-Seven

Shit, shit, shit. This wasn't supposed to happen. There shouldn't be anything tying him to Cory's death.

Calm down. Don't act like you have anything to hide. They can't know. You got rid of his phone; nobody saw you. This is just some routine bullshit, and that guy apparently doesn't have a clue. If they knew about you, they'd arrest you, wouldn't they?

Talking himself down, Noah Kennedy did his best to keep up an easy conversation and stroll nonchalantly between the two cops towards their car – *easier said than done with this fucking leg,* he thought grimly – and got in with a quiet "Thank you" after the detective opened the door for him. He threw in the bag with his clothes, inwardly sighing with relief that in it were only clothes.

He could do this. He would tell them something about Cory complaining about a colleague at his other job or something. Maybe that would even be enough to get them off his back. After all, they didn't seem like they'd think too hard about things as long as they had a nice suspect in front of them. And he had done a good job creating one.

Should he ask for his phone call, for a lawyer, upon arrival?

No, that would seem conspicuous. He was just a guy shocked that his colleague had been killed, and of course he wanted to help the cops find the killer!

But no matter how much he tried to assure himself that he would be fine, his mind raced with possible questions the cops might have, with things they might have found. But no, he had been careful.

Wasn't it weird that they offered him a ride, though? It seemed odd. Then again, they probably just wanted to get this over with quickly, and taking him was faster than driving in separate cars. They had their own entrance from a garage and all, right?

To give himself some time to think, he leaned against the window and pretended to drift off. The detective guy had said it himself, days on the water were exhausting. No need to keep talking the whole drive to the precinct.

He woke with a jolt to gentle knocking, startled that he indeed had fallen asleep for a few minutes. Well, that meant he was calm enough, didn't it? That he had nothing to worry about. Yes. He'd go in there, talk with them, and just get home after.

Chapter Twenty-Eight

In the front seat, Luke began to grin when he heard his suspect snore surprisingly softly. It would make this even easier. Of course, Leroy was smart enough to take the route to the garage that didn't have them pass the – very much open and intact – visitor parking lot, and instead passed close to a diner which was full of people at this time of the day, all parking as close to it as possible. There wasn't a problem keeping up the ruse, but with Kennedy falling asleep for real, not the pretend nap Luke had seen for the first few minutes, it was smooth sailing all the way to the precinct.

Getting out of the car, Luke and Leroy shared a look across the roof, a small smirk showing on both their faces when they nodded toward each other. Rose had texted them with some more information after she had more time to work on the body parts, and Luke had used the drive to ask Special Agent Collins and Agent Ward to arrange something for the interview room.

Now he knocked against the backseat window, waking up his passenger. Kennedy seemed confused for a second, then put some effort into looking embarrassed while collecting his things and sheepishly opening the door. Any other time, Luke would refrain from forming his opinion without having interviewed somebody. But the man just wasn't as good an actor as he likely thought himself to be.

Together, they led him through the precinct. They took a small detour, giving him a little more time to stew. By the time they were at the interview room, a small sheen of sweat covered Kennedy's face despite the chilling outdoor weather and the AC keeping the building at a constant temperature.

The door to the room was already open, and Luke gestured invitingly. "After you, Mr. Kennedy. Be careful not to slip."

The man took a step toward the threshold, glancing at the plastic sheets on the outside of the doorframe and a piece of painter's carpet on the floor.

Luke cleared his throat. "Please excuse the chaos. We had some water damage indoors as well. Maintenance had to paint a few spots and covered things quickly for us when I let them know we'd need the room."

"That storm was a bitch, all right," Kennedy said, and with a nod stepped onto the carpet and into the interview room. Luke and Leroy followed carefully, and after closing the door the three of them settled around the table.

The trio spent the first few minutes with formalities like recording time and date, case number, and names of the people present. Luke hadn't lied completely: some parts of the job were tedious. But he knew there were reasons for it, and he took every part of an investigation seriously.

Finally, Luke put down the case file and looked at Noah Kennedy. "Mr. Kennedy, thank you again for coming in. Now, there's one last thing I have to do. I must mirandarize you. It's for your own protection, just so you know your rights about whatever we'll discuss here."

Kennedy was visibly uncomfortable, but nodded after a few seconds. "Ah, yes, of course."

Luke went ahead, and after getting confirmation that the man had understood his rights, he smiled at him. "As we mentioned, we have a few questions for you in connection to the murder of Cory Gilbert. You and Mr. Gilbert worked for the same company, is that right?"

Kennedy nodded. "Yeah. We've worked together for Jake for several years."

"That's Jake Russel?"

"Uh-huh. We work for his fishing company."

"All right. How did you and Cory get along?"

Kennedy shrugged. "Pretty good, I'd say. It's not like we were best buddies, but we didn't fight or somethin' like that."

With Luke asking the questions for now, Leroy was taking notes. He tilted his head just the slightest bit, but he knew Luke would ask the right questions.

His detective didn't disappoint. "So you weren't friends? I was under the impression a crew spending a lot of time together would be close."

Kennedy scratched the back of his neck. "Ah, yeah, Cory was a busy guy, you know? He had a girlfriend, was doing college courses and had another job, too. It's not like he had a lot of time to hang out with us."

"I see. But when you were on board together, you got along?"

"Sure. I mean, we weren't on every tour together, and it's not like we spent a lot of time together even if we were. After the accident that busted my leg, I switched to watching over the sonar, mostly keeping an eye on things at night, when the rest of the crew's sleeping. Some boats work nights, too, but Jake says we're doing well enough with only day shifts, and the job is dangerous enough during the day."

Luke nodded. "I can only imagine. Do you mind me asking, was the accident a work accident?"

His demeanor changing quickly, Kennedy nearly snarled, "Nah. If it had been, I'd have gotten more insurance money." He caught himself and added in a friendlier tone, "It was a motorcycle accident. I slipped on a wet road, and the bike landed on my leg."

"I'm sorry to hear that," Luke said, and he was. Still, it wasn't an excuse. But it was an interesting glimpse into Kennedy's character to see him react like this.

Kennedy grunted in acknowledgment.

"Well, let's get back to why we asked you to come here. Can you tell us when you last saw Cory?"

"Uh... last week, I think. We haven't been out on sea together for a bit, but last week, there was a team meeting. We have one every month, planning the schedule for the next month."

Luke nodded. "Nothing after that? No drinks or anything like that?"

Shaking his head, Kennedy took a second to answer. "No. Like I said, he was often busy. I think he was on his way to his other job at the Aquarium."

"Do you know how things were going there for him?" Luke wanted to know. It would be interesting to hear what the man had to say.

"Good, as far as I know." Then he seemed to remember something. "But, ah, I think there was this one chick he had some problems with. He mentioned her hitting on him even after he told her that he had a girlfriend."

"Really? Do you by any chance know the name of that woman?"

"Nah, sorry. Wait, wait, he said she was one of the showgirls."

"Showgirls?" Leroy kept his voice neutral. Luke was right:

the overworked, clueless cop angle worked well enough. So far, there was no need to change the tone.

"Oh, yeah. The Aquarium puts on this whole mermaid show. They say it's for the kids, but if you ask me, most of the people watching them are guys. But hey, whatever pays the bills, right?"

"Right," Luke said with a shrug. "Anything else Cory might have said?"

"No, I'm sorry, that's all I know. Wish I could tell ya more," Kennedy drawled and seemed pleased with his own answer. He likely didn't notice it himself, but there was no way Luke or Leroy could miss his speech continuously shifting the more confident or nervous he felt. They both made a mental note of it and shared a knowing glance.

Luke laid it on thick when he sighed. "Oh, no, it's all right. You've already given us a lot of insight. Lieutenant, I think you said you had a question or two, right?"

Leroy sat up a little straighter, inwardly grinning over Luke's performance. "I have, yes. Mr. Kennedy, you said Mr. Gilbert left right after the team meeting last week."

The man across from them nodded seriously. "Yeah, he did."

"Did you two make any plans to meet up this week?"

"No."

"And Mr. Gilbert wasn't supposed to help you recently?"

"What do you mean? Like outside of work?"

"Yes, exactly."

"No. There wasn't anything I needed help with."

Leroy tapped his pen on the notepad in front of him. "So the entry we found in his calendar wasn't referring to you?"

"How did you... Uh, what entry do ya mean?" Kennedy nervously bit his lip.

And Leroy made sure to take his time, pulling over the case

file still lying in front of Luke and leafing through it until he found the entry he knew more or less by heart anyway. With every passing second, he could see Kennedy fighting the internal battle between nervous sweating and showing composure.

"Ah, here it is. We got lucky, you know? He had a smart-watch in his locker at the Aquarium."

"A smartwatch?"

"Yes. It's amazingly helpful how much tech people have nowadays."

Kennedy cleared his throat. "Didn't know he had a smartwatch."

I bet you didn't, Leroy thought and suppressed a smirk. "Oh, yeah. Well, his colleagues at the Aquarium mentioned he usually only wore it when he came in from college or home, or when he left to go there. He apparently forgot it in his locker after his shift sometimes, since he didn't wear it while working at the Aquarium. He told them it could be damaged too easily. I guess he wouldn't wear it at sea, either, then."

"Ah, yeah, makes sense."

"Yes. But no matter the reason, we got lucky. And his watch had this entry when we switched it on. It said, 'Help Ariel.' Do you have any idea what he meant with that?"

Slowly, Kennedy shook his head. "No. But, ah, maybe that's the Aquarium chick? Could be she wore him down and he was meeting with her, couldn't it? And Ariel would fit, wouldn't it?"

Leroy nodded. "It would, yes. We thought the same and talked to all the women working there. They all told us there was exactly one woman nicknamed Ariel, and she had left the Aquarium quite some time ago. After that, no one else had gotten that nickname, because everybody thought it would be too confusing."

"Sure, yeah, could be. But, come on, none of them is called

Ariel when they swim around in their shiny little costumes? Don't tell me you believe that."

Leroy cocked his head. "You seem to know quite a bit about them."

Under the table, a foot began tapping on the linoleum. "Kinda, not really. But we're guys. Cory mentioned them, told us a bit one evening on the ship."

"Hm, I see. Do you have any tattoos, Mr. Kennedy?"

The tapping stopped abruptly, before it began once again, now accompanied by an uncomfortable shift in the chair. "Why?" Kennedy asked cautiously.

"Please answer the question."

"Yeah, I do."

"Would you tell us what kind of tattoos?"

"An anchor on the upper arm, a whale and a fishing boat on my thigh, covering some scars. Stuff like that."

Leroy drew up his eyebrows. "Now, Mr. Kennedy, for somebody who likes to show off his tattoos, I'm surprised you left out the large one on your chest. It's well done, by the way, the mermaid looks good."

"How... how did you...?" the man stammered.

"Oh, you know, as cops we might be quite busy, Detective Preston didn't lie about that, but we take our job very seriously. Your tattoo came up in a conversation, and aside from that, we also checked your social media accounts while waiting for your boat to arrive. You should consider switching to a private account, if you don't want people to see you half-naked showing off online. Do you want to know what else we learned?"

"Wha..." He couldn't properly finish the question with his breath hitching.

"We were told your nickname on the boat is Ariel. That's interesting, don't you think?"

Under the table, the tapping got faster. "Ah, don't know.

Guess lots of people have nicknames, pretty sure I'm not the only one with that one."

"You might not be," Leroy agreed, before continuing, "but for me, it is telling that you chose neither to mention that your nickname, coincidentally, is Ariel as well, nor tell us about your tattoo, the one that's your favorite to show from all we've learned so far."

"Man, can ya blame me? You're looking for somebody who murdered a guy," Kennedy babbled nervously.

"We are, yes. What was Cory supposed to help you with the night he was killed, Mr. Kennedy?"

"What? He wasn't supposed to help me with anything!"

Leroy folded his hands on the table, calmly looking at the other man. "So you want to tell me it's just a coincidence that Cory had plans to go to a storage facility that night to help this mysterious Ariel and then gets killed?"

"I have no idea what you're talking about!"

"Are you sure about that? We found the full calendar entry on his laptop, with the address to the storage facility as additional info."

"So what? I don't have any storage space anywhere," Kennedy nearly snarled, his confidence returning a little with the knowledge that there wouldn't be a unit in his name.

Luke and Leroy on the other hand smiled inwardly. SA Collins had been very thorough, and the information she had given them earlier regarding said rental storage, the reason why she had called in a search team, probably wasn't anything Kennedy expected them to dig up.

Just as calm as before, Leroy nodded. "Hm, you're right. We didn't find a unit in your name."

In his chair, Kennedy visibly relaxed.

"What we did find, however, was a storage unit in the name of your maternal great-aunt. Not an easy find: after all, she divorced your great-uncle and took her maiden name again. But for quite some time, she was a relative of yours by marriage. I'm just a little confused that she'd still need a storage unit, given that she died five years ago."

"How..."

"I'll admit, Detective Preston and I had help with the background check, or this would've taken a little longer. But you see, with so many archives being digitized, those family connections, name changes, divorces, they become so much easier to track. Just a search request, and a whole family history comes up."

If Kennedy had been nervous before, he seemed to slip closer to panic with every sentence he heard. "That's not... wha... I didn't know about any of that," he finally managed to say, trying to sound tough but failing miserably.

"Do you want to try that again? We were informed that you were mentioned in her will and were tasked to sell the last of her belongings in that storage unit."

"Nobody ever contacted me about that!"

"Are you sure? Because we got an email earlier with a copy of a document signed by you personally, accepting the responsibility to take care of the unit."

They both could see the color drain from Kennedy's face, but before the man could come up with a response, a knock at the door interrupted them.

Luke and Leroy traded places with a uniformed officer so somebody would have an eye on Kennedy while they talked to SA Collins and Agent Ward.

Once they were all settled in Observation, Agent Ward leaned against a small table. She had been released from holding after the FBI techs had put their heads together with the NYPD security techs and had fed a loop of footage of her in the holding cell into the system. It wasn't perfect, but anybody hacking the system and just looking at it for a quick check would think she was still being treated as a suspect.

Now she smiled at the two cops. "I like your pathologist. We scanned the print and sent it to her, and she got back to us almost instantly."

"No surprise there. She's awesome, and she probably had the pictures open for comparison."

"True. Anyway, she said she'd of course need to compare the physical prints against each other to make it official for her report. But even with just the scan and the picture, she's confident enough to say that they're a match."

Luke smiled wickedly. "Nice."

Nodding, Agent Ward continued. "Yes. Also, the lab got back to us about the fibers, the cat hair, and even the garbage bags."

Leroy cocked his head. "More good news, I hope."

"You're in luck. Yes. All preliminary, of course, but the lab techs said they were confident enough. The fibers optically match carpet fibers from Kennedy's car. They're running a chemical analysis to get as close as possible. Of course, those carpets are lining thousands of cars, but there are some differences between manufacturers nonetheless, so it can be used as supporting evidence."

She took a sip from the coffee mug she had brought along, then went on, "There were traces of blood in the car, too, but they will have to run more tests and check every single sample to determine whether there's human blood, too. One of the samples they had time to look at so far had nucleated erythrocytes, so it most likely is fish blood, which is no surprise given his job. For the garbage bags, it's the same as for the fibers. It's a mass product, so it's more supporting than pinning it on him a hundred percent, but still. The bags you found in the apartment, Detective, match what was found on the body," she said with a pleased smile.

Leroy grinned at the agents and his detective. "Oh, I like this. What about the cat hair?"

"They compared it under the microscope. Optically, a perfect match for coloring and structure, even up to a likely fungal infection that the vet noted down in his post-mortem report of the cat. An exact DNA match takes a little longer. But even though half the cops will hate us now, CIA and FBI put some pressure on the lab's director so our samples have priority and are already being processed."

"Oh, I bet he hated that. I, on the other hand, am very glad that you could arrange it. Usually, we'd have to wait a lot longer for them to even get started. And with your team as backup, everything, including the searches, is so much faster than we could usually do this."

To that, SA Collins nodded. "True. Though your people are doing a great job. Which brings me to my news. When I was with the team at the storage facility, we found some very interesting things."

Luke raised an eyebrow. "I can't wait to hear this. Please, do tell."

"Sure. In the unit belonging to Kennedy, we didn't find all that much. There was a larger empty area on the floor, but no weapon. We found some minute blood splatters, though. By far not enough for a person to be dismembered in there, even with plastic laid out. But after I talked with Dr. Miller, she confirmed the head wounds from the bolt pistol would've bled a little. It's apparently far less messy than a gunshot wound, and depending on how it's done, not necessarily deadly, but especially a penetrating bolt pistol like the one that was used in this case would leave a wound nonetheless. We took samples, but the DNA will take a little longer for this, too, of course."

"Still a good start," Luke said before continuing, "So that's Kennedy's unit, what about the other one? I assume that's where the 'interesting things' came up, then?"

Special Agent Collins nodded, gave up her professional posture for a second and held out her hand to Agent Ward for a quick fist bump. "You're right. In that unit, we found traces of blood as well. The amount and pattern are more consistent with what you'd expect for a room covered in protective sheets where somebody was dismembered. There's always some blood running under those sheets, let me tell you. We also found a carpet with tiny traces of blood as well. But to make all this even sweeter, we found another roll of the same garbage bags that you found in Kennedy's apartment, a captive bolt pistol, and a professional electrical bone saw with a serrated blade, like butchers use. And, because your ME is amazing, she already told us that the piece of metal found in the body matches a piece missing from the saw."

Grins spread on the cops' faces. "That's pretty great," Leroy said.

Agent Ward smiled at him. "It is. Even better, now that I'm back in the game, I had the chance to look at the surveillance footage of the night of the murder. The feed was disrupted at some point, so unfortunately, we don't have a clear image of Noah Kennedy and Cory Gilbert entering the storage facility together. But there's somebody rolling a cart with a rolled up carpet from one unit to the other. You can see that it's the units in question, and the man might've been wearing a hoodie, but he has a very distinct limp."

An anticipatory silence hung in the air for a moment, until Luke clapped his hands. "All right, all this together, especially with the video footage from the storage facility and the footprint calls for an arrest warrant in my opinion."

"I agree. I feel confident enough to charge him under these

circumstances, even with some of the evidence still running. I still would like to make two calls first, though," Leroy added.

Everybody nodded, and a short while later they prepared the paperwork for the arrest warrant before all four stepped into the interview room together.

Chapter Twenty-Nine

Upon seeing them, their suspect blanched. Even with the uniform stepping out, the room was crowded, and Kennedy looked like he couldn't get enough air into his lungs for a moment. His eyes were constantly drawn back to Agent Ward.

Luke took one of the chairs, Agent Ward the other, and Leroy and Special Agent Collins leaned against a wall. They had decided everybody should be present, but the main interrogators this round would be the cop who initially had taken Cory Gilbert's case and the agent who had been working with him.

"Is everything all right, Mr. Kennedy?" Luke asked, still in a friendly tone.

The man cleared his throat. "Uh, ah, yeah, yeah, 'course. Just didn't expect so many people to come back here."

"Yes, of course. Well, you see, as Lieutenant Porter mentioned earlier, we had a few helping hands in the background. This," Luke gestured at the woman standing next to his boss, "is Special Agent Collins. And this is Agent Ward."

"Hello, Mr. Kennedy," the agent sitting next to Luke said coolly.

"Hel... Hello," the man stammered. Any and all remaining confidence and brashness gone, he began picking at his fingernails on top of the tapping that had started again when the group had entered the room.

For effect, Agent Ward opened her case file again and gave the notes a cursory glance. "Mr. Kennedy, talking to our law enforcement colleagues here, a few more things came up that we'd like to talk to you about."

"Um, sure. What kinda things?"

Keeping him off-balance, Luke answered him this time. "To begin with, we need to know where you were the night Cory was killed."

"At home. Watching TV, there was a basketball game on," Kennedy answered immediately.

"Oh, you know that just like that?"

"I had a few days off after being on the boat for a longer stretch. I was looking forward to that game. Yes, I know that."

Luke nodded, then tilted his head. "It's interesting, though, that you know exactly which night we're talking about."

"I... What are you talking about? It was all over the news when they found his arm at the Aquarium!"

"That's true," Luke concurred. "But we never shared with the media that the arm came from somebody who'd just died the night before. And you said it yourself, you haven't seen Cory since the team meeting last week."

"I haven't!"

Luke interlaced his fingers on the tabletop and leaned forward a fraction of an inch. "Then how do you know Cory wasn't already killed shortly after the meeting, or any other day before his arm was found?"

Kennedy's eyes went huge for a second. "I assumed!

'Course I didn't know, just thought so. Who'd keep body parts lying around for days before getting rid of them?"

"Who indeed?" Luke drew up an eyebrow without further comment.

Into the ensuing silence, Agent Ward asked, "Mr. Kennedy, where were you the night of the blackout?"

The man glared at her. "At home, too. I had to pack my bag. We were supposed to leave the next day for a few days. I've been on the boat since the day after the blackout. They picked me up when I came back," he replied and pointed at Luke and Leroy. "Let me tell you, the boat was running better than the damn city. It was a bitch to get to the harbor that day."

"I can imagine. But since we're talking about traffic and transportation, have you lent your car to somebody recently?"

"No, why would I? I need that damn thing. With my leg, it's a bitch to carry stuff for days all the way from the subway station to the boat. The tourist boats are nice and close to the station, but us fishermen, we gotta hike."

"I see. So no lending your car."

"No."

"Good to know. Then you should be able to explain to us how it is possible we found evidence of a cat that was hit by a car near the dumpster where Mr. Gilbert's torso was found underneath your car."

Kennedy shook his head. "What are you talking about?"

"There was fur stuck underneath your front bumper, and blood traces as well."

"So what? I hit a cat. Do you know how many strays are running around near the harbor?"

"There are, yes. But I'm talking about a specific cat. A cat that was so severely wounded, that it had to have been hit by a car incredibly close to the dumpster since the poor creature barely even managed to crawl there."

"Now listen, Agent Ward, that wasn't me hitting that cat. Whatever hair you found, it must've been from a different one," Kennedy snarled.

"I doubt that very much. We have lab results that tell us the fur is a perfect match."

"Labs make mistakes all the damn time. What were you even looking at my car for? Do you even have a warrant for that?"

"We do, yes. And we were looking at your car because you're under suspicion for the murder of Cory Gilbert after you tried to frame me for said murder. The NYPD also found Cory's head in the building where I have an apartment." No need to tell him that it was only an apartment rented for her cover identity. Given his replies so far, he might just incriminate himself even further.

"What? No, there's no Ward in that build... shit, no, you're trying to trip me up."

Luke shook his head. "We're not. You're doing that all by yourself. Mr. Kennedy, there's substantial evidence tying you to Mr. Gilbert's murder. You can only benefit from coming clean now." He didn't come back to Kennedy's slip-up for now. It would be better to build up the case from the ground, starting with the evidence, and then go into the details of the how and why. Any potential jury would need to be able to follow their investigation and questioning easily.

"Bullshit. You have nothing on me! Why would I kill him? Whatever ya have is just a load of crap!"

"We'll come to the why later," Luke answered calmly. "But the 'load of crap' as you put it, is pretty damning. The carpet fibers of your car match traces of fiber found on Cory's body. And aside from your car, we also had a warrant to search your apartment."

"And I know exactly what ya found: nothing!"

"Yes and no. I agree with you that we didn't find a murder weapon or another body part."

"Told ya!"

"Hm. But we found garbage bags which match small pieces of plastic stuck to Mr. Gilbert's body."

Kennedy actually laughed at that. "Garbage bags? Are you crazy? Every fucking person in this city has garbage bags!"

"Believe me, that's not all. We searched the storage unit we were talking about earlier. The one you supposedly know nothing about."

"Still don't. No idea who signed anything about it."

Next to Luke, Agent Ward sighed. "Mr. Kennedy, be honest with us. We know it's your unit, we know you still use it on a regular basis. We talked to the manager, who confirmed this to us."

"He must be confusing me with somebody."

"Of course. Do you know what we found in that unit?"

"Nothing."

"Interesting that you can say that with such certainty, even though it isn't yours."

Kennedy slowly balled his fist, but released it, when he saw Luke observing him closely.

"Ya didn't find nothin' useful yet to pin this on me, did ya?" By now, he couldn't hide his agitation anymore, and his speech was layered with a thick accent, his words slurring together.

"We found plenty. In your storage unit, we found traces of blood, for one. Then there's the other unit we also had a warrant to search."

Kennedy's face froze mid-sneer. "What other unit are ya talking about?"

"The one belonging to a Hao Delan, known here as Dillon Hao, member of the Hao family living here in Chinatown."

His voice trembled, when Kennedy answered, "I... I don't know who that is."

"I find that hard to believe. After all, there is video footage of you entering the Hao family restaurant recently. We checked on that." There was no need to tell him which footage they had checked exactly.

"And? I entered a restaurant. No big deal. Doesn't mean I know any Dillon working there or whatever."

"In itself, it doesn't, no. The video footage from the storage facility showing you pushing a cart with a large, rolled up carpet from your storage unit into the one belonging to Hao, and carrying apparently heavy garbage bags out of there a while later suggests otherwise, though."

"Wha..."

"Yes, in case you're wondering, it's a cheap storage place, but even they've gone digital, and the footage from several nights ago hasn't been overwritten yet. We saw you. And in addition to all that, we also have video footage of you entering and exiting the Hao family's underground casino on multiple occasions."

They didn't show it, but every cop and agent in the room was pleased to present the man with this detail. There had been a separate, ongoing CIA investigation into the Hao family already, with surveillance covering their legal and less legal places of business. Running a facial recognition software had given them quick results, showing Kennedy as a regular guest. Knowing he wouldn't be allowed any further contact to let Hao know about it, they had decided to use the information to get him to confess.

"That's not possible."

"Oh, it very much is. On top of all that, we're currently reading out your car's data. Admittedly, it's not the newest car, but it has GPS data running constantly in the background. And since, again, as you stated, you didn't lend your car to anybody, we can pinpoint very accurately where you've been. Same goes for your phone, by the way. We're just waiting for your provider to send us the data to track your movement."

Kennedy wildly shook his head. "No, no. Uh, look, I forgot, but I think my car was broken into, somebody took it for a joyride or somethin'. My phone was in there. One mornin', my car wasn't in the same spot I left it the night before."

Luke took over again. "Interesting. And you failed to report this to the police?"

"I, man, look, I figured, the car is back, you'd probably never catch the guy anyway. And I was busy, had no time for sittin' in a police station and all that."

"But look what a mess this is. Now we have data and physical evidence linking your car – a car only you drive – to a murder. The whole joyride story isn't exactly convincing. Why would that person even bring back your car?"

"To frame somebody! See, it's all there, it's working, you think I killed Cory!"

Luke sighed heavily. "Mr. Kennedy, the car, the phone data, even the cat hair, they're all supporting our case, yes. But there's more evidence pointing directly at you."

"What evidence ya talking about? There can't be, I didn't do it."

"Then please explain to us, why Cory Gilbert was killed by a captive bolt pistol like the one you had access to?"

"I don't have access to anythin' like that."

"I can only advise you to tell the truth. The more you lie, the worse this will end for you."

"I'm not lyin'!"

"Mr. Kennedy, our team found a bolt gun in Hao Delan's storage unit."

"Then it's his! What's that to do with me? Drag that guy

here!" Kennedy was clearly trying to mask his panic under his aggressive tone, but he couldn't hide the cold sweat on his face.

"Ah, see, we know it's not yours, that's true. But we checked the serial number, and we called your boss. Mr. Russel confirmed to us, that yes, he had a bolt pistol on board for surprisingly large fish or incidents of severely injured seals, things like that, to incapacitate those animals in a humane way before they could injure his crew. He also gave us the serial number of that bolt pistol. It matches the one in Hao's unit. Mr. Russel also told us that although the bolt gun is secure in a safe on board, you all know the combination in case of an emergency. And after checking for us, he was sincerely surprised to see it was gone."

"Doesn't mean I took it."

"Not necessarily," Luke concurred. "Your fingerprints on it make it a lot more likely that you took it, though. Especially since the bolt gun hadn't been used in a long time according to Captain Russel, and had been thoroughly cleaned and checked only a few weeks ago by himself. If you didn't take it, your prints should not be on there."

Kennedy crossed his arms in front of him. "How do ya even know they're my prints, huh?" he asked defiantly.

"You have a file, Mr. Kennedy. Those bar brawls aren't doing you any good. You might not have been charged, but when you were drunk and spent the night in a cell last time to sober up, our colleagues took your prints. Maybe you forgot about that: it happens with the alcohol levels you showed that night."

"Damn it," Kennedy mumbled.

"So, as you can see, we were able to take prints from the bolt pistol and compare them to the ones in your file. They were a match."

"Whatever. Jake's prints are on there, too. Ya wanna drag him here, too? Say he killed Cory?"

They were waiting for Jake Russel to come in and give his prints to compare with the set that hadn't matched Kennedy's. The man had freely offered to come by, and at this point, Luke and Leroy had no reason to suspect him. But Luke wasn't in the habit of discussing other people in detail during an interview with a suspect. "Let's focus on you for the moment, Mr. Kennedy."

"I didn't do nothin'!"

"Then, again, please explain to us why we can place you at the scene of a body drop, can link a storage unit to you in which we found blood, and saw footage of you transporting a large carpet from your unit to Hao's unit – a unit with a bolt pistol and a bone saw in it – and also you bringing large plastic bags to your car later."

Luke hadn't mentioned the bone saw earlier on purpose. With this suspect, it had paid off so far to give out information in pieces; Kennedy was growing more nervous every time something new came up.

"I told ya about my car bein' stol'n. Not my fault ya don't believe me. And... yeah, okay, I know Dillon a bit. We talked, I told him I had some old rug from my family lyin' around, he collects stuff like that. So I brought the rug over to his unit. And he knows where I work; they do some butchering for their restaurant, their stun gun broke, the order of the new one got delayed, he asked if they could borrow one from the ship. I didn't think it was an issue to lend it to them for a short while until they got their new one, so I brought it over with me. Dillon had said he wanted to meet at the storage unit, but in case he couldn't make it, he gave me a key for the lock. He wasn't there, I was busy, I brought the stuff over, left the bolt gun there, too. Don't know about any bone saw, though. I saw the garbage bags, and thought I'd be helpful and took them with me on my way out." Kennedy took a deep breath; the words had spilled out of him as soon as he had deemed them plausible, and he hadn't taken a break to breath during the explanation.

"A good Samaritan, I see," Agent Ward commented with a raised eyebrow.

"Yeah. I'm a nice guy."

"A nice guy who's suspected of killing and dismembering his colleague and trying to frame me for it afterwards," she replied with a predatory smile.

"How often do I have to tell y'all I didn't kill nobody?! And I don't even know ya!"

"It's interesting though, that you knew earlier my name wasn't on the tenant list for the apartment building where we found Cory's head."

"I... you all confused me! And whatever, I didn't do it, you can't prove any of that. You can't even prove it was Jake's stun gun that killed Cory, or that bone saw."

"Oh, we can. The pathologist confirms that the muzzle of the bolt pistol fits perfectly to the wounds. Also, the DNA sample will confirm this. Same goes for the bone saw. A storage unit is no professional cleaning area, there was enough sample material left. You should've used a bigger bucket to submerge the saw better while cleaning it," Agent Ward told him, hoping he would give them even more ammunition to use against him.

He didn't disappoint her. "Submerge? I don't wanna get electrocuted, do I?"

"We never said it was an electrical bone saw, Mr. Kennedy."

"I... you must have."

"No, we didn't. It's time to come clean, you know that."

"I didn't do..."

Luke tapped his finger on the table a few times. "Let me stop you there. We have prints on the body linking you to it."

"You can't, I wore glo..." Kennedy stopped himself, then mumbled, "Fuck."

"Ah, yes, I'm sure you wore gloves. But you stepped on Cory Gilbert's body while you were cutting off his limbs and head. Your injury leaves you with a very distinct footprint. Our pathologist confirms that the pattern on the body matches your boot print."

"And how would ya even know that?"

"You stepped on painters' carpet with a print set of ink and paper underneath when you entered this room. You only put weight on certain parts of your foot. It leaves a unique pattern of footprints, which translates to equally unique boot prints – on paper and body parts." They hadn't been following procedure completely and perfectly in the way they had gotten the print, but they wouldn't have done it had they not been almost a hundred percent sure it would be a match. They weren't out to frame anybody, after all. And Luke knew once they charged Kennedy, if the DA decided they couldn't use the print like this – even though nobody had forced Kennedy to step onto the carpet – they could file the paperwork to get a new print. For now, the man didn't need to know this.

In the face of the mounting evidence, every last ounce of defiance finally left Kennedy and he began to shake. "You... I... fuck, fuck, fuck. I had to. I didn't have a choice."

"You had to what, Mr. Kennedy?" Luke asked seriously and quietly.

"I had to kill Cory. I'm sorry, but I had to."

Nodding, Luke looked from Kennedy to Agent Ward and saw the woman nodding, leaving it to the detective to officially make the arrest.

"All right. Before we discuss anything else, Noah Kennedy, you are under arrest for the murder of Cory Gilbert."

Chapter Thirty

Kennedy ran his fingers through his hair, pulling hard on some strands, but nodded. "Yeah, didn't expect anythin' else."

"Tell us what happened. Start at the beginning," Agent Ward requested.

"The beginning? That would be the fucking accident. When I slipped, my insurance denied me payments for a lot of my medical bills. They blamed me for the accident, said the tires were run down. I was on the way to have them replaced! Those bastards didn't give a damn, told me they wouldn't cover all the costs for my surgeries."

Kennedy lowered his hands and clenched them repeatedly. Agent Ward and the others could understand his frustration, but what he had made of the situation didn't leave a lot of room for them to be too empathetic.

"And then?"

"Look, I'm a decent poker player. I needed money, so I hopped from game to game. One night I ended up at the Hao family casino. It went well, so I went back there again, several times."

"But one day your lucky streak ended?" Luke asked.

"Yeah. I lost, big time. And I still had medical bills to pay."

"So you decided to work for them," Agent Ward concluded.

Kennedy shrugged and, strangely, his resignation seemed to calm him down. "'Decided' is one way to put it. Like I said, Hao knows where I work, that wasn't a lie. He gave me the 'generous option' to do what he told me to, and he wouldn't hurt me. Or I could try to leave, and they'd hold me down while he cut open my thigh to remove the remaining screws in my leg one by one, making me watch and fucking up my leg completely. What was I supposed to do, huh?"

"What did he ask you to do for him, Mr. Kennedy?" Agent Ward asked, ignoring the man's question.

"I can't tell you that. I blab to you and I'm dead."

"Let me be frank, *blabbing* to us is the only thing that might help you get out of this unharmed. If you don't cooperate with us, the DA, or my agency won't be inclined in the least to see to it that you'll be set up safely away from the part of the prison population who might want to get their hands on you."

"You don't understand. Those people..."

Agent Ward folded her hands on the table. "Yes, those people are ruthless. I am well aware. But I get the impression you don't understand the seriousness of the situation. You're not just facing murder charges here, Mr. Kennedy."

"What... what do you mean?"

Agent Ward drew up an eyebrow. "Association with organized crime, including weapon smuggling, and even charges regarding a possible terrorist threat."

"I... wha... you can't be serious," the man sputtered.

"I am very serious. You failed to ask which agency I work for. Given that you were supposed to frame me, I assume you know that I am CIA. We do not take it lightly when people smuggle weapons and possibly explosives into the country." The agent was aware of what she was giving away, but with his severely restricted contact in the future, the man would hardly be able to tell anybody, and her cover was blown anyway.

"Consider very carefully whether you think it's a good idea not to cooperate with the CIA," she added to stress her point.

He blanched. There wasn't an ounce of blood left in his face. "CIA... Terrorists... Oh god, oh fuck. No, no, no, I had no idea. I was told you were an undercover cop, and when you said 'agent,' I didn't think that meant CIA. I just did what they told me to do!"

"We need details, Mr. Kennedy," Luke said.

"Fuck. You gotta keep me safe. I'll talk, but you need to protect me. They'll come after me."

"They'd have to find a way to get to you. That won't be easy, I can guarantee you that," Agent Ward replied.

"I hope you're right." Kennedy dragged his hands over his face, then sighed desperately. "Okay, okay. Like I said earlier, they forced me to work for them. I was to pick up small crates from the water and deliver those to them. The crates were always just large enough for me to smuggle off the boat with my usual bag after a trip. It wasn't huge amounts all at once, but it was quite often."

"What was in those crates?"

"Guns. But no terrorist shit! I never saw anything like that! I wouldn't be part of something like that!"

"Did you check every crate?"

"Kinda. There were smaller boxes inside sometimes, which I wasn't supposed to open, so I didn't. I just checked the crate inside, and if it was dry, I packed what was inside in my bag, resealed the crate and threw it back into the water so nobody would see it and wonder where it came from. Then I'd just walk off the boat with my bag as usual and deliver everything to Hao."

"How did you know where the crates would be? Were they anchored out at sea somewhere?"

Kennedy shook his head. "No. Not flexible enough. We have our fishing routes, but they can change, bad weather, no or not enough catch on a given day, things like that."

"Then how?"

"Some kind of underwater drone or something. It's kinda like this miniature version of a submarine."

"An ROUV or an AUV?" Agent Ward asked.

"What now?" Kennedy seemed confused.

"A remotely operated underwater vehicle or an autonomous underwater vehicle," she explained.

"How should I know?"

"An ROUV most often comes with a long line, a long cable attached to it, though not always."

"No, that one doesn't have a cable."

"All right. You said something anchored wasn't flexible enough. How did you make contact to let them know where you could pick something up?" They could get into more details of what was used when they interviewed him in more detail about the weapons operation in a CIA-led interview, not Cory Gilbert's murder case; but they still needed to know more to understand what had pushed Kennedy to kill his colleague.

"I didn't, really. They gave me a GPS transponder. I switch it on once it gets dark and I take over on the bridge. The crate has one, too, and I get a notification on my phone when it gets close. The drone carries the box in some grabbers, and the crate has a loop for me to grab from above with a hook. Once I'm done, I throw the crate back into the sea, the drone fishes it out of the water and leaves with it. That's all I know. The whole thing usually only takes a few minutes, and since it's deep in the night, the crew don't realize when I have to switch off the engine or at least throttle the speed for a moment."

"Until Cory," Luke said, when Kennedy fell silent.

"Yeah, fuck, until Cory."

"Tell us what happened," Luke encouraged.

Noah Kennedy sighed heavily and grabbed his hair with both fists for a moment, leaving it in disarray after. His eyes showed sincere despair when he began to talk again. "Look, I know I can be a dick. I'm no fancy businessman or whatever. I drink too much when I'm in a bad mood, and I get rowdy. I know that. But I never wanted to kill him. I liked that guy!"

He ran his hands over his face, then let them fall onto the table. "I liked Cory, he was okay. I didn't lie, we weren't friends or anything, but we were friendly when we worked together. And I didn't even know he knew about anything until Jake asked about that one night the engine went off."

"Did he mention Cory by name?" Luke asked. From what Leroy had told him about the man, the detective knew the captain would blame himself, at least partially, whatever Kennedy would say. But if he hadn't mentioned Cory's name, he might not feel like he served him on a silver platter.

"No, he didn't. He just asked whether there had been any trouble lately, because somebody thought the engine had been off one night a while back. That's when I knew one of the guys might be on to me. After that, I hid a small camera to find who it was, or if there even was somebody looking deeper into it. Could've been just one night, right?"

"But you didn't get so lucky," Agent Ward concluded.

"No. I saw Cory coming up on deck, at first hiding while I was still there. Later, he began coming up a little later, once the boat started moving again. He always checked his phone, then left again. I couldn't really see what he was checking, but he never called anybody or typed like a longer message, so I thought he wasn't up on deck just for reception for a call or text to his girlfriend. I figured he was checking the coordinates we were at; it was the only thing that made sense with how quickly he vanished again."

"And then, what?" Agent Ward asked flatly.

"I tried to talk to Hao, tell him we couldn't do this anymore. But Dillon wouldn't hear any of it. He said I had to take care of it, but we needed to know what he was doing with those coordinates. Said he had a contact who could check if there was, like, already an investigation ongoin' or something."

Cocking her head, Agent Ward asked, "What contact?"

"Don't know. Not something he'd tell me. I'm their damn mule, not a big player. He just handed me a phone, nothing on it, and I can't do anything with it, really. Said he or somebody else would get in contact. They did a few days later, told me there was some kind of snooping going on, some file, but it was sealed before they had time to really look at it."

Agent Ward didn't let her gratitude show, but inwardly, she thanked her boss. With the other investigation into the Hao family not leading anywhere even after quite some time, her boss had already been suspecting a mole and had told her the case file for her work with Cory Gilbert would be for their eyes only until they had results. Even another agent couldn't just open it, and knowing her boss, he had also set up a system that would alert him to any hack.

"Anything else you might know?"

"No, I swear. Look, at that time, I didn't even know there was someone other than the police involved. Again, when I set things up to make it look like it was you, I thought you were a cop, not a freaking CIA agent."

"Yes, let's get back to that. Why did you decide to frame me? Why not just push Cory into the sea, for example?"

Kennedy stared at her like she had slapped him. "I said I liked him, didn't I? I never wanted to hurt him, let alone kill him. But when I told that to Hao, he said either I would do it, or he'd grab him and really make him pay for snooping around. That would've been painful, believe me. And the ocean isn't that much friendlier. It's either slowly freezing to death, being attacked by a shark that wants a taste, or you drown. None of those are ways I'd want to go. Least I could do was make it as painless as I could. And yeah, I know how crazy that sounds." He shook his head about his own argument. "Aside from that, you realize that this is a relatively small boat with a limited crew, right? There's always somebody close by. And Jake takes the safety of the crew very seriously. It's pretty much impossible to 'just push' anybody into the water without being seen during the day, if you manage to do it at all. And had I confronted Cory at night, he would've put up a fight. With my leg, I'd've been the one in the water in the end. But even if anybody would go over-board, during the day, somebody would realize it quickly and there'd be a search. And even if I had somehow managed it at night, the next morning Jake would've started the search. Plus, that would make me one of the main suspects right away, working the night shift and all."

He wasn't wrong, and for once, Luke and the rest of the group nodded in agreement.

"All right, I see your reasoning. But again, why me? How did you even find me if the file was sealed?"

"I didn't. Hao's contact did. Took some time but he said he checked all kinds of places Cory was regularly, like his college and the Aquarium. I think he mentioned hacking into some security feed or something. Honestly, I didn't even want to know, so I didn't try to remember the details. Said he saw Cory near the show pool, and you close by more than once. I have no idea how, but somehow he found out who you are and told me it would be a good idea to frame you, get you off the case."

Agent Ward nodded contemplatively. It wasn't too far-fetched that somebody was hoping to disrupt the investigation like this. And she knew Luke had found her the same way, though he had only found her cover identity. Face recognition would bring up her personnel file at the very least. And despite a sealed case file, most cover identities were visible to other agents within the CIA network even if no case was mentioned, so that in case an arrest was made, the arresting agents knew he had a colleague in front of them. No wonder a mole would have enough information on her to set her up to be framed.

"What else can you tell us about him?"

"Nothing. Never met him or anything."

"How did his voice sound? What kind of words did he choose?"

"No idea. I can't even tell you if it's definitely a guy, I just assumed. The voice was distorted, like he used some kind of app to disguise it, like some people do for prank calls, you know? And what kind of words? No clue what you want to hear. Didn't sound like a gangster from the ghetto, didn't sound like a snob, just normal. And with the app, I can't tell you if he has an accent or not. Look, we only actually talked like once or twice when I was told what to do, other times, I'd get a text."

"A text about what?" Luke asked while taking notes.

"Where to pick up some other phone, for example."

"What was the phone for?"

Kennedy shrugged. "Can't tell you the details, I was just supposed to pick it up, get it to the Aquarium and get it to the Lost & Found so it would stay at the Aquarium."

"Interesting," Luke noted, and in his mind, the picture of how the Aquarium's security footage had been overwritten became clearer. A device within the facility might have provided better access to the network than a hack from outside, a chance to constantly monitor it and find a weak spot. "How did you get it in there?"

"I pretended to interview for a cleaning job, ran along with the crew during the night, dropped the phone in the Lost & Found box. Afterwards, I just said I couldn't do it with my leg."

Surprisingly simple, yet effective, Luke had to admit. There was one thing he wondered, though. "Weren't you worried about the cameras?"

"Kinda, but I wore a ball cap, kept my head down. Easy enough when you're scrubbing floors. And the guy said he'd use it as a first test and delete the footage for that night, if everything worked as planned. If it didn't, we just weren't going to go with the Aquarium and would come up with a different plan. He said he'd be somewhere near the Aquarium the night I was going to bring Cory's arm and leg there. No meeting, but he said he'd know and tell me if it was safe to go in and to just use Cory's card so he wouldn't need to work on that system, too. Said he'd test the overwrite again earlier that day and drop something in the Security office while the guards were out of there and doing a round near the end of day shift; said he knew something to keep the night guard busy. Don't know what, though."

And that explains the porn magazine, Luke thought. If the mystery man in the background had watched the feed for a while before the night of Cory's murder, he'd have picked up on the lazy guard. And if he was indeed Intelligence, then it would've been easy enough to look him up and see that the night guard paid a lot of money for porn any given month, just like Leroy had found out and had told Luke about earlier in the case. It would've been a good last-minute test to see if the override would work when it counted, just sneaking in, dropping the magazine, and leaving again, no trace left.

"All right, that explains how you got in and out of the Aquarium. What about the actual murder?"

"What, for the security?"

"For all of it. How did you come up with the storage facility, how did you get Mr. Gilbert there? We need details of everything," Luke clarified.

"Ah, yeah, okay. After the team meeting, I asked Cory to help me. Told him I had a storage place and there was a large rug I couldn't handle on my own with my leg. He agreed and we picked the day. I told him to take the subway, that parking was always bad at the place, which is true. I said I'd just pick him up at the station; I knew I'd get a parking spot, there's a disability spot I can use 'cause of my leg."

Luke cocked his head. "What about Cory's phone?" He remembered that he had tracked the last pings of Cory's phone to towers near the river, and yes, shortly before that, it had been close to a subway station as well, so he would've had it on him for the ride.

"Don't know exactly. I was worried about that: after all, all those crime shows always say you guys can find where people have been. When I asked about it on one of the phone calls, Hao's guy told me to make sure to tell him which train Cory would be on, he'd take care of the rest."

"And you believed him?" Agent Ward asked flatly.

Kennedy scoffed. "It wasn't exactly a question of believing him. He doesn't seem to be the type to react well to people questioning him. And, honestly, he was planning a freaking murder with me, I kinda think he doesn't want to be caught, either."

"Fair enough. Did Mr. Gilbert say anything about something happening on the train ride? Did something happen after he got off and met with you?"

"Nah, nothing. It was the usual, crowded station, some teenagers mouthing off, bumping into people. Look, I don't know how he did it, I just got a text when Cory was getting into the car that his phone wouldn't be a problem anymore. Maybe he did some spy shit or whatever. You're the cops, you're the agents, I think it's your job to find that out."

And they would, Agent Ward was sure. The "spy shit" was likely just as easy as paying a teenager to do a little pickpocketing and throwing the phone into the river after. Simple, just like the cleaning charade, but simple often went a long way. In this case, however, the person would've needed to talk to the teenagers, and a glance at Detective Preston's notes told her he had the same thought, writing down the station and time to try to get his hands on the security footage later.

"That won't be a problem," she answered confidently. "We just want to offer you the chance to do some penance. The more helpful you are now, the more forgiving people might be towards you later when it's time for a trial and sentencing."

"I know, I know."

"Then keep walking us through what happened next," Luke brought them back on track.

"Yeah, all right. When we came to the storage place, I led Cory to my unit. I had a rug there, told him I couldn't get down low enough for long enough to roll it up and everything. He bent down, and I reached over to the right where he couldn't see. I had stashed the bolt pistol there earlier. I took it, went over thankin' him and tellin' him I'd try to help. He said it was okay, I wouldn't have to, and when I stood next to him, I set the bolt gun against the back of his head." Kennedy took a shuddering breath. "I don't think he even realized what was happenin'. I stunned him, and he just fell forward onto the rug. I wasn't really sure he was dead, so I shot him a second time, lower. I did a bit of readin' before and kinda hoped if I hit the right spot and got his brainstem, that he'd at least die quickly."

The man was pale once again, but none of the officers in the room pitied him, especially knowing what had happened next.

"What did you do then, Mr. Kennedy?"

"I rolled him up in the carpet and used a cart to bring him to Hao's unit."

"Why did you use his unit? Why the extra step?"

"Why? Because I hoped I could avoid sitting here. I thought nobody would ever know my connection to the Haos, so if anybody found that storage unit, nobody would know it was me."

"And Hao Delan just let you in there?"

"For this? No. And he's gonna kill me if he finds out. He initially had rented the unit as a dead drop, so I wouldn't show up at the restaurant or casino with a bag full of stuff all too often. One day I went there to deliver the content of a crate. We came back from the tour a day early 'cause of bad weather. Hao hadn't cleaned up the unit, yet, and I saw things lying around and an open trunk where they obviously came from."

"Things?" Agent Ward inquired.

"Knives, saws, tarp. Things like that. I never asked, never told him I saw anything. I don't know what he uses the unit for, and I don't *wanna* know. I just knew I'd be alone, the security video was supposed to be taken care of, so I brought Cory over there. I knew Hao would be busy the night I took Cory there and the day before. There was a big poker game going on over several days. So I had snuck in there earlier, covered everything up. I put on a coverall and then... then I..."

Kennedy's face took on a grayish-green tint before he stammered, "I cut him up. Oh god..."

Not wanting the man to puke, Leroy took a step to the door and asked the uniform stationed out there for a glass of water. After a sip, Kennedy looked briefly at them. "Thank you."

They gave the man a minute to compose himself, but Luke soon gestured to him. "Go on, Mr. Kennedy."

"Okay. I, ah, I cut Cory up using one of Hao's saws, so it couldn't be connected to me."

"Why did you cut him up at all?" Agent Ward asked.

"I didn't want to! But Hao's guy told me to. Said it would be more believable with framing you and all, no woman carrying a complete man's body around. And for the sharks, he thought they might eat the limbs more easily."

"All right. What did you do next?"

"I had those large garbage bags there, I put Cory in 'em. Stuffed Cory's clothes and all the tarp and stuff in there, too. I was bringin' everything out when I saw I had gotten a text from Hao's guy at some point, tellin' me he had to go to work on the Aquarium video, and the cameras at the storage place wouldn't be disrupted any longer. So I hurried getting outta there. I hoped he had been there long enough. I didn't even know me bringing Cory and the rug to Hao's unit was on tape until you told me."

Agent Ward nodded. "Okay. Then what?"

"I drove to the Aquarium. When I got there, I already had a text tellin' me the guard was busy, the video was taken care off, I could go in. That's what I did."

"How did you know you'd have Mr. Gilbert's card to get in?"

"I knew he would have his key card with him, cause he once told me he stopped by the Aquarium spontaneously sometimes and almost got locked in there one time when he had studied the tanks at night but wasn't actually on shift. Said since then he always had it on him."

Luke nodded. "All right. So, then what happened next?"

"I carried two bags in there. I found my way to the staff area for the tanks, and I threw in the leg and an arm. I thought those sharks would go crazy; I even had put a fish from the boat into each bag, thinking the smell would be more like what they're used to. But the smaller sharks didn't seem too interested. Guess they had been fed just before or somethin'. They hardly took a look at the arm I threw in, and then it got caught in the current from the pump and the sharks didn't go near it after that. For the leg, I thought the bigger sharks might be better. So I went over there."

Agent Ward studied the man in front of her. "Okay, so you stunned and killed your colleague, you cut him to pieces, and you fed parts of him to the sharks. Why not feed the rest of him to them, too?"

"Like I said, the smaller ones weren't even that interested in the arm. And I still had to make it look like it might've been you who did it. I remembered I had seen a mermaid costume during that cleaning interview. I snuck to the locker rooms and one was hanging there, I guess to dry or whatever. I picked at one of the scales, and when I got it off, I pushed it into the open cut of the leg before throwing it into the water. I thought, if the sharks didn't eat the leg either, then it would be found with the scale on it."

It wasn't an entirely stupid idea, she had to admit. And it had worked, even with a shark eating the leg. "And after you fed the leg to the sharks?"

"After that, I decided I wouldn't try to feed them more. They didn't seem like they would eat any more, and I didn't want to stick around longer than needed. I got out of there, got a call right away askin' me if I was done, so the guy was either somewhere there to see me get out or could see the real video, no idea. I told him what was goin' on, and he said I'd have to find a way to drop at least some of the body at your place or near it. I wasn't gonna do that right away, though. It was almost mornin' by the time I left the Aquarium. After all that stuff goin' on, I figured this might be bigger than just cops and I only wanted to be done with it. And I haven't heard from the guy since."

"So you waited for a good opportunity with the body pieces in your apartment?" Luke asked, his voice betraying nothing. Internally, he was furious on Cory's behalf and on his own for the careless attitude toward a life. Unfortunately, he wasn't even surprised anymore – over the years, he had seen and heard too much about the things people would do to each other to be surprised anymore. Outraged, angry, sick, yes. But not surprised.

"Well, I had heard about the storm in the forecast, and Jake had already postponed the next tour because of it, so I planned to use the chaos. I didn't know it would be that bad, but it made things easier. I burned the garbage bags with the tarp and all, got a lot of ice, and left the window in the bathroom open. I put the bags with Cory in them in the bathtub, and when the storm hit, I drove to the address the guy had told me before was yours," Kennedy explained, looking at Agent Ward.

"What did you do when you arrived?"

"I found your building. But I couldn't get in, nobody could buzz me in after the blackout. I found a basement window I could wiggle open a little, but I could only fit Cory's head through it. I did that. Then I saw a dumpster and put the torso in there. When I wanted to get the other leg and arm, I thought I heard somebody, so I got into my car and got outta there as soon as I could."

"Do you remember running over the cat?" Luke asked.

"No. Didn't even realize I hit anythin', but maybe it was the cat makin' some noise earlier, scarin' me, and when I drove off, I must've scared her, too, and hit her."

Luke didn't say anything to that, but agreed that it was a likely theory. But there were more important questions left to ask. "What did you do with the other arm and leg after that?"

"With the storm going on and everything being flooded, I threw them in the river. I thought they'd be carried out to sea."

"And then?"

"Then I drove home, waited out the blackout for the rest of the night. In the morning, I cleaned my car, then got to the harbor and left with the boat." Kennedy finished his confession with a heavy sigh. "Look, I fucked up. I majorly fucked up. There's no excuse, I know that. I'll do my best to help you now, though. Just try to keep me safe, please. Or kill me yourself, you're CIA, you make people disappear like that, don't ya? Just, whatever happens, please don't let Hao get his hands on me."

Agent ward tilted her head, staring into the man's eyes for a long, long moment. "Yes, you majorly fucked up, and it cost a good man his life. And yet, you might be a useful asset. I will talk to my boss, and we will decide what to do with you. You will be questioned again, after that we will evaluate just how useful you can be for us."

Both cops and both agents left the room after finishing the formalities for the record, and two of the uniforms Luke and Leroy trusted went back into the interview room to keep an eye on Kennedy.

They all settled in Leroy's office, each of them with a fresh coffee. It had gotten late, and all of them were looking forward to getting home, but they needed to discuss a few things.

Special Agent Collins tapped her finger against the mug in her hand. "All right, I would say Agent Ward and I will take Kennedy from here. You have a confession, and depending on how things go, if there's a trial, you'll be involved of course. No matter if there'll be one or just a guilty plea with a sentencing without trial, we'll make sure the murder will be taken into consideration, not only the smuggling. It's shitty, I know, this is your case, but unfortunately, it's connected to ours, and that one isn't closed, yet."

Leroy lightly kicked his desk. "Ah, I knew you'd say that." When the agent wanted to say something, he held up his hand. "No. It's all right, really. We knew the federal case would override our murder case in the end. But you helped us put together our case, get a confession. We can tell Cory's next of kin something. It won't bring him back, but it will help. We can close our case and, hopefully, you'll make progress with yours."

Luke nodded in agreement. "Leroy is right."

"Thank you for understanding, Lieutenant, Detective. Rachel, I suggest taking Kennedy into custody and bringing him to our FBI facility here right away. It's heavily secured and nobody knows of the FBI's involvement so far."

"Yes, I agree," Agent Ward said. "I'll let my boss know, and we can meet there, discuss the weapons operation, and work on pinpointing the mole. We'll need to go through agents having shifts allowing them to be near the storage facility at the very least, since Kennedy's story sounded like the person used a jammer and had to be at the location for that. But we'll get more details out of him on all that with the next interview and a different focus for it. I want to keep up the momentum on all this. From what Kennedy says, even without him being in the know, it doesn't seem like the mole knows about the larger Hao investigation, yet, or at least nothing detailed, and I want to keep it that way, and just catch that bastard quickly. There are too many open questions at the moment."

After a few more minutes of talking and thanking each other for the good cooperation, the agents left Leroy's office again and made their way back to the interview room to pick up Kennedy.

Leroy glanced at his watch and sighed. "You know what, paperwork can wait until tomorrow. Get home, I'll do the same. Write it up, close the case in the morning. And tomorrow evening, we'll grab a beer on the way out of here."

"Music to my ears, boss," Luke said with a tired smile and grabbed his leather jacket that he had thrown over the back of one of Leroy's visitor chairs.

Epilogue

Two weeks later, Halloween had taken over the city, and Halloween headquarters were without a doubt the restaurant belonging to Scarlette's grandmother and father and the streets around it.

Indoors, almost the whole place had been transformed from the cozy Italian restaurant to a haunted old tavern. Fake cobwebs were hanging everywhere, and lanterns with candles were giving off an eerie light. They had switched to electric lanterns years ago, since the restaurant became busier every year and nobody wanted the fire hazard of real candles, but with some fake soot smudges on the glass and the constantly more realistic-looking LED candles, nobody cared. Old wooden crates held empty, dust-covered bottles; benches and tables were covered in ragged sheets.

One corner of the restaurant had gotten a quick makeover with props to look more diner-like, and tables had been pushed to the walls to create a small dance floor. Unsurprisingly, Bea had commandeered July and Luke to keep people entertained with their *Pulp Fiction* dance moves until the parade started.

Outside, the street was filled with people looking at the

decorations set up along the whole street. Kids gazed at the prop of a witch riding her broom across the roof of one of the lower buildings; teenagers spotted the animated projections in some of the windows and squealed when a skeleton seemed to jump in their direction or blood ran down the façade of a building. Street lights had gotten covers of soft, thin fabric for the night to give them different colors.

The horror maze covered almost an entire intersection, but left open a path for the parade – and of course possible emergency vehicles, because even with all the fun, safety was important to all of them.

Yes, Scarlette's family organized it all, got all the permissions and props, but none of it would have been possible without all the neighbors helping out, or even just allowing them to set up a projector in their apartment or agreeing to endure a long night of laughter and screams.

Ty looked around the street in awe. "You weren't lying, Sparks. This is amazing. Are you cold, though?" He was wearing his Jack Skellington suit, but his wife was wearing a dress.

"Nah, all good, don't worry. You saw me get ready: the dress is loose enough for a second layer underneath, the stockings are warm, and the skin color on the arms isn't just make-up but another pair of tights. And should I get cold, I can always grab you for some body heat," Scarlette said with a grin and pressed a kiss to her husband's lips, which made a group of nearby kids giggle. Grinning at them, she took a handful of candy from a large sack next to her and took a few steps over to them. Conspiratorially, she put her finger to her lips. "Psst, don't tell anyone you already got some. These are for the parade later."

Strolling back to Ty, she spotted her truck coming down the street. Her brother-in-law, Josh, had asked to borrow it to get from Hope to New York for the Halloween party. He still hadn't told her what exactly he and his girlfriend would be wearing, but had at least let her know that their costumes would be fairly large, hence the need for a car with lots of space.

She directed them to a parking spot and followed the truck together with Ty. After greeting Josh and Bonny, she looked at the closed truck bed. "So, will you two finally tell me what you put together?"

Josh grinned at her. "Yep, Come here, sis," he said and unlocked the back. After opening the bed herself, Scarlette stared at the parts in front of her. "Holy shit! You two made those yourself?"

"Mostly Bonny, you know she's really good at crafts. I helped with the cables, so everything really works, at least rudimentarily. Can you already see what it'll be?"

Scarlette studied the costume parts in front of her with admiration. "Oh yeah, of course. You know I love *Aliens*. A Powerloader and a Xenomorph. This is epic, guys."

Josh chuckled and nudged his sister-in-law with his elbow. "Thanks. I knew you'd love it. We might be younger than you, but we do have a similar taste in movies." He wasn't wrong, he and Bonny were eighteen compared to Scarlette's thirty, but they all had grown close over the last year and had regular movie nights together.

"Yep, that's true. Now come on, let's get you suited up, the parade is supposed to start soon."

She led them inside, and given the size of the costumes, she chose the wine cellar to get them dressed. "You guys can manage the stairs back up?"

Bonny nodded. "Yeah. The legs of the Powerloader are stilts to slip into with a simple Velcro strap, I can just leave those up here and step into them when we're back upstairs again. Most of the tech is in the arms."

"Great."

Walking along a small bend, Scarlette bumped into Wolverine and Deadpool making out passionately. When she looked beyond the suits, she burst out laughing. "Oh my god, you guys are awesome," she said to Leroy, who was wearing the Wolverine costume and kept his hands around Michelle in his Deadpool outfit. She hadn't seen them before, because she had been busy with preparations and lending a hand at the maze earlier, and hadn't known they had finally arrived after Leroy's shift had been longer than he had initially planned.

"Thanks. The costumes were Michelle's idea, though, so I can't take credit," the cop said with a grin.

"Very nice. But as much as I love the costume idea, no making out near any food or drink."

"We weren't..." Leroy began sheepishly.

"You still have your hands on my vet's ass. No making out down here." She fished a key from one of the hidden pockets in her dress. "Use the upstairs emergency apartment like the rest of us," she said with a grin and tossed them the keys with a wink.

Leroy blinked in confusion for a second. "Why does your grandmother have an emergency apartment here?"

"In case it's a very late evening and someone from the staff can't get home easily," Scarlette managed to say, before Michelle cut in.

"Uh-huh, really interesting, boss, but we have to go. Come with me, *mon coeur*," he said to his boyfriend and tugged eagerly on Leroy's hand while stepping around Scarlette and the rest of the group.

Laughing, Scarlette called after them, "It's 2A. Have fun!"

Shaking his head with a grin, Ty stepped close to her. "Guess they'll miss the start of the parade."

"Likely, yes. But they weren't supposed to be on the float anyway, so it's no problem."

A moment later, they helped Bonny and Josh into the costumes, and once they were done, Scarlette clapped. "Wow, just wow. You look epic, both of you. You'll blow everybody's mind."

The parade was supposed to be ending soon – after all, it was just a tour around a few blocks. July and Michelle had offered to help out in the restaurant since they knew the ins and outs, while most of the Langella clan that usually lent a hand in the restaurant was on the float. Luke had stayed outside to hand out candy and was standing next to Leroy, grinning cheekily at his friend. "I assume you had a good reason for not being down here when the parade started."

"Shut up," Leroy replied with a smirk.

Luke gave candy to a few children, then focused on Leroy again. "Oh, SA Collins and Agent Ward contacted me today. They couldn't say a lot, naturally, but wanted to thank us again for the help with the murder investigation. They also let me know that, thanks to Kennedy being oh so helpful in hopes of a lighter sentence and being protected, they made progress, both in the internal investigation and the larger investigation into the Hao family, and that they'd make sure, once both are closed, it would be mentioned how much we supported the Feds."

"Ah, nice. And nice of them to keep us apprised and see to it that we'll be mentioned kindly. It's good to know some Feds in different agencies are working on better relations with local law enforcement and not just looking to shine light on themselves. I let the brass know, too, that the FBI and CIA representatives cooperated well with us. Should we ever need them again, we might get lucky and somebody might ask for one of them specifically."

"Good thinking."

The two men kept talking shop a little longer, then had drifted into talk about wedding plans when they both saw the float coming around a corner.

On it, Scarlette and Ty had gotten a smaller version of the curled mountain from *Nightmare before Christmas* towering over the heads of most other people on the float. Not all, though, since Bonny's Powerloader and Josh's Xenomorph costume were both huge. They had needed to rearrange the layout of the float a little to fit everybody as it was.

But judging by the cheering crowd of children and adults alike, it had been well worth it.

Scarlette and Ty were standing on their hilltop, waving to the left side of the street, while Bonny and Josh had gotten the right side of the float and were entertaining everybody with a playful fight between the alien and the mech suit operator.

But Scarlette turned around quickly when she suddenly heard Bonny shout, "Fuck, no!"

The yell was swallowed by the crowd and only the people on the float heard it, so Scarlette wasn't surprised that nobody on street level reacted at first. But she saw what was happening clearly enough.

On the sidewalk a few yards away from Luke and Leroy, who were waving at some kids, a disheveled-looking, stocky man had drawn a gun and was pointing it at Leroy, who stood with his back toward him, just like Luke at that moment.

Bonny seemed to recognize that shouting anything else would be futile with all the noise, and just reacted. She managed a few quick steps around Josh and leaned over the guard rails of the float with the long arms of her costume. She must've been practicing beforehand for the grappling with Josh, because her coordination was impeccable. She grabbed the man's arm with one of the huge clamps at the end and pushed him to the ground with the other. A muffled, heavy "oomph" carried up to them.

Scarlette, Ty, and Josh reacted equally fast and all yelled for the float to stop. For a few seconds, the float kept moving, so Bonny was almost dragged over the guardrails, but Josh held onto the back of her costume with one hand before guiding the tail of his costume around her waist with his other hand and steadying her with that as well.

Luckily, they were going very slowly, so when the cart stopped, Bonny managed to keep her balance even in the awkward position she was in, hanging half over the side of the float.

Scarlette checked on her for a second, but when she saw Bonny was all right, she jumped down and, after a quick assessment, helped keep the man on the ground with her knee in his kidney. Her costume was large and functional, but most parts were made of lightweight material, which didn't give Bonny a lot of leverage from the angle she was in.

Contrary to the yell, the turmoil wasn't lost on the crowd and Luke and Leroy ran over, initially thinking there had been an accident.

Scarlette looked up at them. "I hope you guys have cuffs with you. This guy had a gun."

From the cart, Bonny explained, "He did, and he was aiming at you, Leroy."

"What the..." But when he got a chance to see the man's face, Leroy wasn't surprised. "Fuck, Hawkins, have you completely lost your mind now!?"

Luke reached beneath his suit jacket and leaned his knee on Hawkins' back. He took the wrist Scarlette was holding and put on the cuff, then reached for the second wrist when Bonny opened the claw still holding it.

Meanwhile, Hawkins was hollering: "That fucking asshole and his little boyfriend cost me my job!"

Luke shook his head. "No, you managed to do that all by yourself. And now you're under arrest for the attempted murder of a police officer. And this time, you won't get out of holding while the investigation is ongoing."

Leroy had his foot on the gun that Bonny had managed to make Hawkins drop, and he was on his phone already, calling in uniforms to pick up the former cop.

Seeing the crowd edging closer and closer, Ty made his way down from the float as well and put on a show, distracting people and keeping them away from the scene. Others on the float helped Bonny down and Josh, seeing everything was under control, climbed the mountain and struck a victory pose as if he had won the fight and the others had fled. The cart slowly began moving again, drawing the crowd along, so that the crime scene was quickly forgotten.

By now, July and Michelle had noticed the commotion and were coming out of the restaurant to check what was going on. As soon as Michelle saw the man on the ground, he muttered, "*Merde.*"

The group formed a circle around Hawkins, shielding the bystanders from his curses.

"What the hell happened?" Michelle wanted to know, and July nodded in agreement.

"Yes, I'd like to know that, too."

Luke dragged Hawkins up to a standing position, flanking him together with Leroy, then explained the situation. "Leroy and I were talking, and Leroy had his back to the street for a moment. And Bonny, I guess from your vantage point with the extra height, you could easily see over the crowd."

The young woman nodded. "Yeah. I was grappling with Josh, and over his shoulder I could see a guy drawing his weapon. It felt wrong already, since I know Scarlette said the family usually doesn't allow anything with such realistic-looking weapons with such a crowd, and people go along with that. And then he aimed at Leroy, and I just reacted. A second later, I thought it might've just been a joke, but then I could still apologize. Seems like it wasn't."

Leroy shook his head. "No, sadly not. That's the ex-cop we talked about last week during dinner here."

They had all been sitting together, eating at the restaurant the week before to finalize Halloween plans and catch each other up, when Leroy and Michelle had told them about Hawkins and his behavior toward Michelle the night of the blackout, and that the man had been put on suspension after being released from Holding after the initial arrest Leroy had made. None of them thought he would do anything as stupid as this while Internal Affairs was running a detailed investigation. He hadn't. But then word had gotten to Leroy that Hawkins had indeed been fired for multiple violations of duty.

By that time, Michelle had picked up Leroy several times from work and had befriended some of the other detectives under Leroy's command. So it hadn't been a secret that Michelle and Leroy would attend the Halloween parade, and with people teasing their boss about possible costumes and all, probably most of the precinct had known where Leroy would be tonight. It wouldn't have been difficult for Hawkins to find out.

Michelle sighed. "I told you he should never have been released from Holding."

"And I agree, sweetheart. But that wasn't my decision. And while the violations of duty were clear, any possible criminal charges are still under investigation, so they didn't have a lot of grounds to keep him – and put him in danger. Cops don't exactly have a high standing as inmates."

"True. But shouldn't he at least have given back his gun?"

"He did. That's not a police-issued weapon. I'd say it's his personal one. Isn't it, Hawkins?"

"Fuck you, Porter."

"That's what I thought you'd say. Anyway, he won't get out this time," Leroy said and dragged Hawkins forward when he saw two uniforms arrive in a cruiser.

The interruption cut the evening short for the two cops, who decided to accompany Hawkins to the precinct and fill out the paperwork. They briefly thought about bringing Bonny and the rest along for witness statements, but then thought better of it. Halloween was always a crazy night at the precinct; there was no need to put them through that. It was pretty much a clear cut case and their statements could wait until the next day.

They left with the promise to come back later, since the party for the neighborhood might end earlier in the evening but the family always celebrated until late at night.

Knowing the night would turn out to be great even after all that, Luke gave Julia a kiss, then got into the cruiser next to Hawkins and Leroy dragged Michelle close for a kiss as well before climbing in the back, too.

Even with a cussing and sneering Hawkins between them, they both grinned at the others when the car drove away.

<h1 style="text-align:center">Author's Note</h1>

I've had a lot of fun writing this book – and it sometimes almost made me feel a little too much like a criminal myself.

Let me tell you why. When I came up with the ideas in this book, I first wrote down my story in a rough outline before delving deeper into research. I usually start out like this, because it helps me to not get lost into all the interesting things out there before I even get started with the writing of the actual book.

But coincidences are a funny thing, and just a couple of weeks after I brought the scene of sharks being fed with body parts to paper, I was listening to a true crime podcast talking about the "Shark Arm Case" from 1935 in Australia. It didn't happen exactly as it did in my book, but it's an interesting case, if you're a fan of true crime.

After that, I outlined the weapon deliveries with unmanned underwater vehicles, and when I looked deeper into what kind of vehicles would be useful, I found out that something similar has been done for drug trafficking in the past. And even captive bolt pistols have been used as murder weapons in very few cases.

So yes, if you read this book and thought some of it sounds familiar, I can only say that there's probably no crime that's really original anymore, either in fiction or in real life.

I just tried to come up with an entertaining case for our cops to solve.

For my readers interested in medicine or veterinary medicine, the contraption being used to operate on the shark might sound weird at first, but trust me, my veterinary colleagues all over the world are great at being medical MacGyvers; there are lots of interesting articles online detailing shark surgeries, many of which require special tanks or constructions to support sharks during operations because their cardiovascular system differs from that of mammals.

But to fit all of this into one book, I'm the first to admit I had to take some creative freedom when it comes to locations, commercial fishing, police procedure, and inter-agency cooperation, as well as as forensic and medical details and timelines.

On another note, while reading you might've stumbled over the term "queer" several times, either being used by a bi, gay, or straight character.

For a long time, it has been used as a slur and has understandably been avoided. But with the queer community doing their best to reclaim it, the negative meaning is beginning to fade slowly (depending on who uses it and how, of course). So far, it's often still a sore spot to have straight characters use the word, though.

Yes, words have power, but only the power we give them. For me, it was important to have a straight character use the word in a positive way just like the queer characters do. Acceptance and equal rights for everybody, no matter their race, sexual orientation, or religion should be a given nowadays. Unfortunately we don't live in that world yet. All I can do to get closer to that equality is to be a decent human being myself, and try to show through my writing that even straight characters can use former slurs and not mean them in a hurtful way, but give them a positive meaning and by this, support the queer community as well.

closer to that equality is to be a decent human being myself, and try to show through my writing that even straight characters can use former slurs and not mean them in a hurtful way, but give them a positive meaning and by this, support the queer community as well.

Acknowledgments

As always, I want to thank my wonderful husband Chris for all he does for me. Thank you for being there for everything and all of it, be it book-related or anything else. Your love and support always give me strength and help calm me down when I need it. And of course thank you for feeding me delicious food and coffee!

Thanks again to my amazing friends who gave me some of their precious time to discuss crime, medicine, and sex with me to make this book so much better. I sincerely appreciate all your help!

And of course, thanks again to my awesome editor and publisher Jessica A. Scott from Tuxtails Publishing. Your patience, support, and guidance make it a pleasure to write these books and see them published!

About the Author

Lyv Lamere grew up in Germany and still lives there with her husband, their cat, and her snake, even though they plan to relocate in the future.

Lyv successfully studied veterinary medicine and worked at a laboratory before following her other interest, which has her currently working as a contractor in the tech industry.

One day she found she had developed yet another passion – writing – and her first novel was completed sooner than expected.

Today she's still working at her "day job," but continues writing and hopes to bring a smile to people's faces with her stories.

To learn more about Lyv, visit
www.lyvlamere.com.

 instagram.com/lyvlamere

Also by Lyv Lamere

Couples & Crime Series:

Generational Payment

Pieces of a Murder

9 781957 211343